MY DARLING DAUGHTER

JP DELANEY

First published in Great Britain in 2022 by Quercus
Part of John Murray Group
This paperback edition published in 2025

1

Copyright © 2022 Shippen Productions Ltd.

The moral right of JP Delaney to be
identified as the author of this work has been
asserted in accordance with the Copyright,
Designs and Patents Act, 1988.

The Wikipedia extracts on page 52 are excerpted from
the Report of the APSAC Task Force on Attachment Therapy,
Reactive Attachment Disorder, and Attachment Problems, 2006.

All rights reserved. No part of this publication
may be reproduced or transmitted in any form
or by any means, electronic or mechanical,
including photocopy, recording, or any
information storage and retrieval system,
without permission in writing from the publisher.

This book is a work of fiction. Names, characters,
businesses, organizations, places and events are
either the product of the author's imagination
or used fictitiously. Any resemblance to
actual persons, living or dead, events or
locales is entirely coincidental.

A CIP catalogue record for this book is available
from the British Library

PB ISBN 978 1 52944 496 4
EBOOK ISBN 978 1 52942 330 3

Typeset in Swift by CC Book Production

Printed and bound in Great Britain by Clays Ltd, Elcograf S.p.A.

Papers used by Quercus are from well-managed forests and other responsible sources.

Quercus
Carmelite House
50 Victoria Embankment
London EC4Y 0DZ

John Murray Group
Part of Hodder & Stoughton Limited
An Hachette UK company

The authorised representative in the EEA is Hachette Ireland,
8 Castlecourt Centre, Dublin 15, D15 XTP3, Ireland (email: info@hbgi.ie)

Praise for JP Delaney

'Thrilling from beginning to end –
I couldn't turn the pages fast enough'
Claire Douglas

'Excellent . . . domestic noir in all its darkest shades'
Cara Hunter

'Absorbing and fast-paced'
Karin Slaughter

'JP Delaney is King of Thrillers'
Fiona Cummins

'Seriously, amazingly, awesomely brilliant'
CJ Tudor

'The kind of book that keeps you up at night'
My Weekly

'A twisty, electrifying read'
Woman's Own

'Original and brilliantly written'
The Sun

'Twisty, unexpected and utterly convincing'
Daily Mail

'Dazzling – a pitch-perfect thriller'
Lee Child

'Deeply addictive'
Daily Express

'Slick, sexy, suspenseful and smart'
Mail on Sunday

'Ingenious'
New York Times

'Outstanding'
Sunday Times

JP Delaney's first psychological thriller, *The Girl Before*, was an instant *Sunday Times* and *New York Times* bestseller and went on to sell over a million copies worldwide. His subsequent books *Believe Me*, *The Perfect Wife*, *Playing Nice* and *My Darling Daughter* were also top ten bestsellers, while *Playing Nice* was also a Richard and Judy Book Club selection. JP Delaney was heavily involved in the BBC adaptation of *The Girl Before*, as lead writer and co-executive producer, and was an executive producer on ITV's adaptation of *Playing Nice*.

Also by JP Delaney

The Girl Before
Believe Me
The Perfect Wife
Playing Nice
The New Wife

For Caradoc: agent, friend;
proof that these stories can have happy endings.

ONE

Gabe

It all starts with a message on social media.

In itself, that's not unusual – Susie gets at least a dozen of those every day; more, if she has a gig coming up or the band have just streamed a new track. She usually lets a few accumulate, then sits down and answers them in one go. *Hi – thanks for getting in touch! We love hearing what people think about our music . . .*

But this one's different. This is like someone's just ripped off her skin and exposed a fifteen-year-old wound.

> Hello Susie. My name is Anna Mulcahy, although the name I was born with was Sky Jukes. I am 15 years old. If you had a baby girl in St George's hospital on 6 March 2007 at about 5pm who was later adopted, could we perhaps meet? I believe you may be my birth mother.
> Best wishes
> Anna

Which in itself is devastating enough, but the kicker – the bit which causes her to run into my studio, ashen-faced and choked with tears, mutely holding out her iPad for me to see – is the final line:

ps: i am desperately unhappy

TWO

Gabe

She had Sky long before I met her, when she was twenty and just starting to get bookings as a backing singer. It was an unplanned pregnancy, the result of a casual relationship. In those days, most of the work for backing vocalists was on long tours, and a baby would have meant giving up the career she loved. That was before she knew she had fibroids, of course. Now, after five miscarriages and umpteen anxious waits between periods, she wishes she'd made a different choice.

Putting a baby up for adoption . . . People assume that, if you choose to do it, you can cope with the consequences. They don't realise that you make the decision long before the baby's born, when you're still trying to be rational, to make plans, to get things right. When you tell yourself you could be making a childless couple's life complete, as well as giving your child a better life. When things like careers – and, yes, the parties and fun any twenty-year-old enjoys – loom so much larger.

They don't realise that, when you actually do it, it can be like a death. A death you feel responsible for, because you played the biggest part in it. A death you grieve a little more every year, because your imagination torments you with the knowledge that your child is out there somewhere – that you might glimpse her in the supermarket one day as you pick up a tub of ice cream, or see her swinging her legs at the back of a bus. In some ways, it can be even worse than a child dying for real.

I know, because that happened to me. I lost Leah to childhood leukaemia when she was almost three. It was unspeakable and devastating, and it crushed my first marriage as surely as if someone had smashed a rock on it. But it was also final – there was no going back, nothing to debate; only a slow, agonising coming to terms with it. It was different for Susie. Giving up her baby meant she always had that cruellest of emotions, hope, even if it was mixed with despair. A part of her has always wondered: What's Sky doing today? Has she learnt her alphabet yet? Has she learnt to swim? Has she had her first kiss?

When people ask how we met, we sometimes joke that Susie was my groupie. At the time, I was . . . well, not exactly a household name, but the band I was in, Wandering Hand Trouble (I know – it was our label's suggestion; you'd never dream of calling a group that now), had made the transition from boy band to mum rock without too much difficulty. We were on the verge of amicably going our separate ways, keen to enjoy the money we'd made while we still could. *Going, Going, Gone* was our farewell tour, Susie one of the backing vocalists.

What we don't usually tell people was that one night I found her crying backstage and stopped to ask what was wrong. It turned out it was Sky's sixth birthday. She told me a little of her story, I told her about Leah, and we bonded. Not exactly rock and roll.

We do have some of the rock-and-roll trappings, though. Home is a beautiful farmhouse just outside London, with a couple of horses, half a dozen chickens and a rescue mutt called Sandy. We've made the interior light and modern, the walls lined with canvases by young British artists. There are six bedrooms – when we looked round, the sellers were keen to let us know what a great family home it was, and how many children did we have? Neither of us ever knows quite how to respond to that question, so the answer sometimes comes out more tersely than we mean it to. When I said, 'None,' they muttered something about the space being great for parties, too.

Outside, there's a small barn I've converted into a studio – for making demo tapes, not full-scale recordings; my day job now is writing songs for younger musicians. The chances are you've heard my work dozens of times without realising it wasn't penned by the winsome singer-songwriter performing it. It's a tragedy Susie and I don't have kids of our own, of course – it's particularly hard on her, since she'd make a brilliant mum and it's the thing she longs for more than anything. But there's still time, and, if there's a silver lining, it's that she's finally fronting her own band, a folk-rock ensemble that's just making the leap from pubs and clubs to being the support act at larger venues. There's no money in it, of course – there's no money in anything to do with music anymore – but she loves it, and I love that, when I go to watch, people hardly ever recognise me now; I'm just the supportive partner standing at the side of the stage. I wrote a ballad for them, 'Lullaby for Leah', that became a small hit on the streamers, and my heart is never so full of love as when I'm standing in the dark, watching her sing those words of mine, all the different sides of my life connecting in one ecstatic, emotion-laden instant.

So when she runs into the studio without even looking through the soundproof glass first to see if I'm in the middle of a take, I know instantly that something's happened – something big. It's with a feeling of dread that I start to scan the message. And although when I look up and meet her eyes I can see there's actually a mixture of emotions there – fear, yes, as well as shock and concern, but also overwhelming elation that this moment has finally come – my own feeling of dread doesn't lessen. Children or no children, we've achieved a fragile contentment, and I'm terrified it's all about to come crashing down.

THREE

Susie

Gabe's first question was, 'Are you sure? It's definitely her?'

I nodded – all I could manage.

'But . . . how does she know? All these details.' He read the message again. 'Your surname. Even the time of birth.'

'They have this . . . document.' I took a breath. 'It's called a Later Life letter. The social worker writes everything down – about me, the birth, the adoption process – so the child knows where they came from. It's given to them when they're old enough to understand.'

'But she isn't meant to get in touch with you, is she?'

I shook my head. 'The birth certificate's sealed until she's eighteen. But let's face it, I'm not exactly hard to find. Particularly if the social worker mentioned that I'm a singer.' Like any band, being active on Instagram, Facebook and Twitter is how we drum up publicity.

Gabe frowned. 'So presumably we're not meant to reply, either?'

'Well, I'm not going to ignore it.' I spoke more sharply than

I'd meant to. But Gabe, big-hearted though he is, has surprisingly law-abiding instincts for a musician. 'Apart from anything else, she needs my help.'

'Well . . . she's asked for your help. Which may not be quite the same thing.' He caught my look. 'She's a teenager, Suze. Being melodramatic is what they do. I know *I* was, at that age.'

'She's *contacted* me. Like you say – she's not meant to, so it must be something massive to have made her do that. Besides . . .' I stopped, too overcome for a moment to go on, then said quietly, 'I've waited fifteen years for this. There's no way I'm letting her slip through my hands now.'

It was a strange grief, because it got worse with time.

There was the initial devastation, of course – the feeling of having something you love torn from you. That ache gradually dulled, though it never entirely left. A therapist told me once that the pain of loss doesn't shrink, but sometimes we're able to let our lives expand around it, the way a tree can grow around a nail. I think that's what happened with me. As my career took off – not a glittering career, certainly not stardom, but, by the standards of the music business, solid and rewarding – my life started to feel fuller. And, I admit it, I was a wild child for a while, working hard and partying harder, and perhaps that was part of the coping mechanism too.

Then I met Gabe, and at pretty much the same time my biological clock kicked in. Or maybe it kicked in first, and without fully realising it I was starting to look around for the kind of man I could start a family with. Someone more steadfast and thoughtful than my previous partners – those clichéd rock-and-roll bad boys I'd been having fun with, until suddenly I wasn't.

A year after we got married, we decided I'd come off the pill. And that was when the pain started. It's often the way with fibroids, apparently – contraceptives mask the symptoms. Ironically, you start to feel discomfort during sex just when you're trying to have more sex to get pregnant.

By the time we went to a specialist, I'd already googled the symptoms, so I knew what to expect. Even so, hearing it spoken out loud made it real, in a way the internet hadn't. *Increased period pain. Reduced fertility. Possible increased risk of miscarriage.* So I opted for surgery, and was overjoyed when I got pregnant three months later. It felt like I'd beaten the odds.

My first miscarriage was quick and early – a pain in my lower back that sent me scuttling to the loo, where I found spotting in my underwear that for one confused moment I thought was a period. Agonising cramps. And then a dark-brown gush, a sludge like wet coffee grounds. It lasted a couple of hours, but the crying lasted on and off for days.

Each subsequent miscarriage came later and later in the pregnancy. Which was doubly cruel, because every time I'd think, Maybe I'm out of the woods. The second time, I was nine weeks. I rang the hospital, who told me to stay at home unless the bleeding became unmanageable. It was as if they were talking about a bloody nose. It took me ages to go out after that – I was avoiding anywhere I might see a mother with a baby. Even folding back the little seat on a supermarket trolley reduced me to a quivering wreck.

The third time, the sonographer broke the news at my twelve-week scan. *I'm so sorry. There's no heartbeat.* Seeing Gabe weeping uncontrollably was almost the worst thing about it. I was given meds to induce me, and after four hours of agonising cramps I passed the baby in our bathroom. It was the size and colour of a plum, but fully formed.

I used to mark my due date on my iPad calendar, but I stopped after that – it was too depressing to have to delete it, or, even worse, forget and have a reminder pop up on my screen months later. By the time I was getting D-and-Cs at sixteen weeks to cut out unpassed tissue, I dreaded getting pregnant as much as I longed for it. Though, as it turned out, a D-and-C isn't what they call it anymore. It's now an ERPC – Evacuation of Retained Products of Conception. If ever there was a crueller-sounding name for a procedure, I can't imagine it.

It was one particularly bleak Mother's Day, soon after my third miscarriage, that I started thinking about Sky again. Because, however difficult it was to get pregnant, however much of a failure I felt, I couldn't help reminding myself that I already was a mother. My child was out there somewhere. She was mine, or had been. And, somehow, all the pent-up love and expectation I'd been ready to attach to a new baby started to float towards her, to the adorable little face and light-as-air body I'd cuddled for such a short while before she went to her new parents. (In the UK, you can't formally agree to an adoption until the baby's at least six weeks old, although some people place them with a temporary carer before then.) I tried to imagine her in her school uniform. What kind of sports would she do? Would she have my strawberry-blond hair, and if so, would she wear it long and straight, the way I did when I was young? Would she be a rebel like me, or would that gene have passed her by? Would she be musical?

And sometimes, after one too many glasses of wine, I'd find myself on social media, obsessively trawling the web for any sign of her. It was all too easy to finish writing some glossily inviting post – *Wow! Can't believe our new single has had over five hundred plays already!* – and let my fingers drift upwards to the search box.

To begin with, whenever I thought I'd found her, I told Gabe. The first few times, he even shared my joy. It was only when he took my iPad, scanned the feed of the teenage girl who was making me so excited, and said nothing, that I realised he thought it was just wishful thinking. Which, of course, it always was. And I didn't even tell him about the really bad nights, the ones that still bring a hot flush of shame to my cheeks – the drunken messages on Instagram or Snapchat beginning, *Hello, you don't know me, but* . . .

I stopped those when one fourteen-year-old turned my private DM into a public post and added, *How creepy is this?*

I was looking for girls called Sky, of course. It didn't occur to me that her new parents might have called her something different, not least because preserving a child's original identity is considered incredibly important now and social workers always get would-be adopters to agree to keep the child's birth name. I'd read in my endless googling that some get round it by changing the middle name instead and using that, but it's certainly not common.

Discovering they'd changed it made me wonder what sort of people they were. The sort who think *Anna* is so much nicer than *Sky*, I supposed.

And that's what Gabe failed to understand at first, when I showed him her message. It wasn't just my elation at the fact we'd found each other. It was my fear – fear that I'd made a terrible mistake fifteen years ago. My life had a huge child-shaped hole in it that was only made bigger by knowing I'd given away the very thing I now craved. But at least I'd been able to tell myself that I'd done something good – that Sky was loved, that she had a stable, fulfilling family life.

But what if that wasn't true? What if she was with people who didn't truly appreciate her? Who – perhaps – didn't even really love her? I'd lurked on enough adoption forums to know that it happened, sometimes.

And that was why there was absolutely no doubt in my mind about replying. I had to find out if she was all right, even if it was technically breaking the rules. Even if – and this worried me far, far more than the legalities of it – all the secrets and evasions that my marriage had up to then comfortably accommodated could end up being swept away.

FOUR

Anna

Shit shit shit.

The moment I press *Send*, I look at the message and realise it's terrible. That PS – I sound like a stereotypical whinging teenager, just another self-obsessed snowflake who's upset because her parents won't let her watch *Love Island* or something. I should have been less needy, trusted that she'll want to meet me anyway.

Or will she? Maybe she hasn't given me a moment's thought in fifteen years. Maybe she's got her own happy family now, cute-looking kids half my age who she hasn't put on Insta or Facebook for privacy reasons. Maybe her response is going to be some curt, chilly put-down. *Thank you for your enquiry. Please do not contact me again.*

I *am* sure it's her, though. The stuff in the social worker's letter made her easy to find. And when I saw her band's feed, there was no doubt. *Wow. She looks just like me.* A much cooler version of me, if I'm honest – her strawberry-blond hair cut in a stylish short fringe, her teeth white and straight as she almost swallows the microphone reaching for a high note, her discreet diamond nose stud glinting in the stage lights. I look at the butterfly tattoo on her tanned, toned shoulder and think, My God, is that really my mum?

She couldn't be more different from the woman I've been calling Mum if she tried. She's about twenty years younger, for one thing. But it's her smile that takes my breath away. In almost every picture, she's beaming. Mum doesn't have to do anything to make an expression of sour disapproval settle on her face – it's there all the time, at least when I'm around.

Ever since I told her what's really been going on with the man I'm forced to call Dad.

Susie Jukes. I roll the name silently around my mouth. She's married now, but she hasn't taken his name. He looks even cooler than her – Gabe Thompson, short for Gabriel. If you google him, you get page after page of hits, fans gushing over how good-looking he is. Mostly from about twenty years ago, but still.

Will they want to talk to me?

Will they believe me?

Might they even love me?

Try not to get ahead of yourself. The fact you've made contact is massive enough.

Plus, she's really busy right now – they've got a big gig at the Roundhouse tomorrow. As support act, admittedly, but the last time they played in Camden it was at a pub called the Dublin Castle. I know all about her music. I've scrolled right back to the beginning of her feed, when Silverlink was formed, two years ago.

I'd love to show my support by clicking on the event – *371 people are interested* – but if I do, the monster will see it. That's right: he insists him and Mum are my friends on social media.

So we can keep you safe, Anna. So we can see when you start to indulge in risky behaviours.

Of course, that isn't the real reason. He doesn't want me posting about anything to do with home.

The way he handled the social worker's letter was typical. On the very first page she put, *The exact timing of when you'll get this is up to your parents, but I've written it assuming you're about twelve. Some parts you may find upsetting, so I recommend you show them once you've read it, so you can talk about it together . . .*

About twelve? So apparently it never crossed her mind he might wait another three years, then just walk into my room – he does at least knock now, but he barely waits for an answer – and toss the papers on to the bed as I was doing my homework.

I looked at it. 'What's this?'

'A letter. From the social worker you had at the time of your adoption.'

There was no envelope, just a thick sheaf of folded pages. 'I see you've read it.'

'I've checked it through, yes. To make sure there's nothing that might cause you harm.' His eyes were cold. 'In any case, there wasn't anything I didn't already know.'

'Why didn't you give it to me before?'

'It was never appropriate.' Which was another way of saying, *Because I wanted to exert maximum control.*

'Well?' he asked impatiently, when I didn't pick it up. 'Aren't you going to read it?'

'Yes,' I said. 'I am.'

I waited for him to leave. He waited for me to pick it up. Pointedly, I put my earbuds back in and picked up my homework.

He shrugged. 'In your own time, then.'

It was a crap last line, but it clearly mattered to him that he'd been the one to deliver it. Out of the corner of my eye I watched him go, careful to keep my expression blank until the door was completely closed. But already a surge of excitement was coursing through me.

Maybe I can use this to find her. Maybe she can help.

FIVE

Gabe

I suggest that Susie adopts the twenty-four-hour rule – write a reply, but don't actually send it until she's had a chance to sleep on it. This is too important to rush.

To my surprise, she agrees. She composes something and then, after we've talked about it, lets it sit in her drafts folder, unsent.

> Dear Anna,
> I think you are right and I may be your birth mother. I would love to meet you, assuming your parents are happy with that. There's so much to talk about but of course you mustn't feel any pressure from my side.
> Best wishes,
> Susie

Actually, there's quite a lot of my input in that. *Dear Anna* – because to call her Sky now, if it's a name she hasn't used in fifteen years, would simply come across as weird. *Assuming your parents are happy* – we debated whether to say *adoptive parents*, but, when you look at adoptee forums, the people on them generally say using that term is not only insulting, but flies in the face of the legal position, which is that the new family take on all parental rights as soon as the Adoption Order is made. As for checking they're OK with it, that just seems like the responsible thing to do, given her age. Susie only shrugged when I said so, though she did put it in. I suspect she thinks that, since she made her own decisions about what to tell her parents long before she was fifteen, Anna probably will as well.

The tone was my suggestion, too – underplaying the emotion. Too much too soon might scare her off. *Best wishes* instead of what Susie originally put, *With all my love*.

In the meantime, ravenous for more information, she scours the internet. She has Anna's name now, and of course she can simply click on the profile next to the message. But, oddly, that reveals very little – everything's set to *Private*, including *About* and *Location*, and the profile picture is just a greyed-out circle. Even the account name is only her initials, AM.

'Tell me this isn't all some horrible scam,' Susie says anxiously, showing me.

'Maybe this is what a teenager's Facebook looks like, these days. They're all on TikTok and Discord now, right?' We get attempted scams a lot – it comes with having a reasonably high profile – but this looks more like the Facebook account I set up for myself when the band was still active: a private, almost secret account for friends and family, completely separate from my public-facing page. 'Maybe she has another one as well.'

Susie types Anna's name into the search box. A moment later, she says, 'This might be her. Yes – it must be. Oh my God, Gabe – look.'

She turns the iPad towards me. The privacy settings are still blocking almost everything except the name, Anna Mulcahy, but you can see the profile picture. It shows a teenage girl waving a sparkler at some night-time party. She's wearing a beanie that hides the shape of her head, but there's no doubt. The strawberry-blond hair spilling down to her shoulders, the green eyes, the cheekbones – it's like looking at a coltish, half-formed version of my wife.

'She's beautiful, isn't she?' Susie says at last.

I nod. 'You gave her good genes.'

'All I did give her.' But she says it gently, the moment full of emotion.

'Why do you think she used a fake account?'

'I don't know,' Susie says slowly. 'But I think maybe she wanted to make absolutely sure no one else knew she was contacting me. Whatever this is about . . . she wants to keep it between us.'

Next morning, it takes her a while to gear herself up to press *Send*. 'Done,' she says at last. She stares at her iPad for a moment. 'Not that I'm expecting a reply any time soon. She'll have school, right?' She sounds like she's trying to convince herself.

After lunch, we load the car, then drive to the Roundhouse to set up. Susie's quiet on the way in. She's often like that before a performance, resting her voice, but today she seems different. Or perhaps it's just because I'm quiet too, thinking about Anna and what this contact might mean.

As we drive through Chalk Farm, Susie says suddenly, 'Gabe – pull over.'

I do, then look across at her. There are tears on her cheeks. 'What is it?' I ask, concerned.

She gestures at a couple strolling along the pavement. The man has a papoose strapped to his chest, the baby just old enough to be facing outwards. Its little knitted hat has become lopsided. The mother reaches out and adjusts it, and it looks up and gives her a smile of pure contentment.

'Sorry.' Susie's voice is choked. 'But it fucking *hurts* sometimes.'

'I know.' Which, I've learnt over the years, is all I can say. There's nothing that will make it better, nothing that will give her hope. I can only be there for her, someone to acknowledge what she's going through. What – if I'm honest – we're both going through. The first few times she told me she was losing our baby, I wept like a child myself. And the truth is, we're both tired of it. Grief is exhausting. Trying again is exhausting. Susie puts a brave face on things – she's a performer, after all – but, inside, I know she's only just coping.

After a moment I say, 'Suze . . . is there a chance that meeting Anna again could make this worse? You know – that seeing what you've missed out on might make the fertility issues even more painful?'

Fertility issues . . . Even between ourselves we use the careful euphemisms of medical professionals. Not *childlessness* or, God forbid, *infecundity*, as a thoughtless nurse once called it, as if we'd been smitten with barrenness by some vengeful deity.

'Yes,' Susie says quietly. 'I think it probably could. But we need to do it anyway. For her sake.'

I'm grateful, in that moment, she says 'we'.

We drive round to the back of the venue, passing the big vinyl banners at the front with her band's name, Silverlink, just below the headliner's, and get the gear set up. Gradually, the rest of the band turn up and they do a soundcheck. It won't be a lucrative evening – even at these mid-size venues, support acts only get a few hundred pounds, and the agent and promoter will take most of that – but it's an important one in terms of their profile, even though the place is still two-thirds empty when they eventually walk out to a thin smattering of applause.

It's two numbers in, during 'Red Rusty Mountain', that Susie falters mid-song. For a moment I think she's forgotten the lyrics – which is ridiculous; a pro like Susie never does that – then I see that she's staring into the audience, frozen. I'm at the side, waiting to hand her a guitar for the next song, so I can't see what she's looking at.

Then I move forward, and I do see.

Anna. The girl from Facebook is in the crowd, looking up at Susie. In person, she's even prettier than her profile picture – the fringe shorter, the hair pulled back with a scrunchie, just the way Susie used to wear it – and even more like a younger version of Susie, who's staring back at her, transfixed.

For a long moment, they hold each other's gaze, as if everything and everyone else has melted away. Then the bass drum kicks in, Susie somehow finds the next line, and the song continues as if nothing has happened.

Concerned, I keep my eyes on Susie for a second or two. When I turn to look at the crowd again, Anna's vanished.

SIX

Anna

Hi Susie,

I'm so so sorry I surprised you out of the blue like that at the gig. I wanted to see you in the flesh and I never thought you'd be able to see me too with all the bright lights! I went to the back as soon as I realised I might be a distraction.

I'm also sorry I couldn't stay for the whole thing or come and find you afterwards. The truth is, my parents didn't know I was there. They would never have given permission for me to go to a concert, let alone one with you in it, and if I'd stayed any longer they'd have found out where I was.

If you still want to meet I could do tomorrow at 3pm? There's a café called Bustos on Varley Parade in Colindale, North London. I'll only have half an hour though.

Anna x

SEVEN

Susie

I wasn't surprised to discover she lived in London – the original adoption had been handled by Barnet Social Services, where I was living at the time. Nor was I very surprised that she didn't mention asking her parents. It seemed pretty clear to me that they were the cause of the unhappiness she'd referred to.

At any rate, that was how I read it. Gabe was less certain. 'It was a school night,' he pointed out. 'Most parents wouldn't let their fifteen-year-old go to a gig in the middle of the week, especially on their own.'

'There's something odd about the way it's worded, though. You just said, "let their fifteen-year-old go" – that's normal, right? But she says, "permission". Like it's something she has to ask for formally. Doesn't that sound a bit *authoritarian* to you? And then there's that bit about them finding out where she was. How would they know?'

'I think you may be reading too much into it,' he said gently. 'So you *are* going to meet her?'

'Of course.' I looked at him, willing him to understand. 'When

I saw her in that crowd, Gabe – it was like an electric shock. A *connection*. As if we were plugging back into each other again after all this time. I couldn't undo that now, even if I wanted to.'

He nodded. 'OK. I get that.'

I picked up the iPad. But something made me hesitate. It was just too momentous. 'I'm terrified, though. What if I don't like her? What if she doesn't like *me*?'

He reached out and squeezed my shoulder. 'I think you have to trust your instincts. I think it's going to be fine.'

But he still looked worried.

EIGHT

Anna

I have exactly forty minutes when the monster thinks I'm in drama, not knowing it's been cancelled because they can't get a supply teacher. Or not caring, more likely, drama being *not a proper subject*. Somehow I know she'll be early, so I hurry, and sure enough, when I look through the café door I can see her, over at the back where it's quiet – just the table I'd have chosen.

And him. She's brought her husband. For a moment I freeze. What the hell does this have to do with him?

But then I realise it's a good thing. If I'm to get anything out of this, it's better they're united.

Besides, I remind myself as I go inside, my stomach full of butterflies, not all husbands are like the monster.

'Hi Susie,' I say nervously. 'And you must be Gabe.'

She jumps up. There's an awkward moment when we don't know whether to hug or kiss or shake hands. We kind of clasp our hands together and squeeze instead, but it's good, it feels like she's showing me how nervous she is, but also how much she wants us to get past the nerves and reach something more meaningful.

God, she's so beautiful.

Gabe and I shake hands more formally, but he's nice too, his eyes crinkling round the edges when he smiles hello. Bethany at school always says that's how you know a man's had plastic surgery, but that can't be right, he's so boyish-looking still. And sensitive enough to pick up on my surprise, as well.

'I hope you don't mind me being here,' he says. 'I can leave the two of you alone, if you'd prefer.'

'I asked him to come,' Susie adds. 'To be honest, I wasn't sure if I'd simply go to pieces. Still not sure I won't, actually.' She sounds dazed, but in a happy way, and it takes me a moment to realise, *That's because of me*. It's an amazing feeling.

So I say, no, it's great to meet him. And it's actually useful too, as it turns out, because he busies himself taking our orders – flat whites for them, tea for me – and going to the counter while Susie and I get over our nerves.

Glancing at him as he queues up for the drinks, I think how even the coolest boy at school would kill for those jeans and trainers.

She and I don't say much at first, just 'Wow' and 'We look so alike' and 'Where do you live?' But soon we're sharing details like who my grandparents are (her parents are divorced and remarried, but both of them live abroad – I get the impression she's not particularly close to them) and whether I have any half-siblings (no, though from the wistful way she says it I sense she's not ruling it out). She asks if I'm left-handed like she is. I'm not, but when we put our hands together they look eerily similar – same short fingers, same double-jointed thumb. Just then Gabe comes back with the drinks and she laughs happily and I realise we have the exact same laugh too, a kind of honking snort that Henry always says makes me sound like a pig. Now that I hear her, I can tell it's actually the opposite – it's the laugh of someone who's free and fun and exuberant.

We chat for a bit, then Gabe asks, 'Do your parents know you're here, Anna?' And I realise it was him who put that bit in the DM about *assuming your parents are happy*.

Perhaps if she'd come on her own I'd have told her everything. But that might have been a mistake. I have to assume that anything I tell them might get back to the monster. No one ever believes the adopted girl – I know that for a fact.

But I also need to say enough to make it clear to these nice, intelligent, open-minded people that he *is* a monster.

I look at my tea, which I realise I have no intention of drinking. There's too much riding on this.

'My parents are why I'm here,' I say at last. 'They're the reason I'm unhappy.'

NINE

Gabe

So it all comes spilling out, slowly at first but then faster and faster. Her family are religious – some strict Irish church. They say grace before every meal, and if Anna forgets and starts her food without waiting, it's taken away from her. They serve their biological son, Henry, second helpings before her, on the grounds that he's bigger and in the swimming team. Only last week, her father told her she was lucky to be there and not in a children's home.

'I'm not complaining about any of that stuff, though,' she says. 'I'm just giving you the context.'

She shows us her phone. On the screen is an hourglass symbol and the words, *Your device is resting until 20:00.*

'Parental spyware,' she says matter-of-factly. 'I can't get online until after eight o'clock. And they can track my location, read my messages and block any websites they don't want me on. I know twelve-year-olds who are made to have stuff like this on their phones, but at fifteen? Luckily I have a techie friend who showed me how to get round it. Oh, and if I run out of credit or battery, I have to go straight home or I'm grounded for a week.'

Susie gives me an agonised look. I know what she's thinking. *This isn't what I intended for her.*

Anna catches it too. 'You mustn't think I'm blaming you,' she says quickly. 'It's not being adopted that's the problem – I could have ended up with a fairy-tale family. I just got unlucky.'

Susie looks like she might be about to cry. 'On the plus side,' I say gently, 'you seem like a really well-adjusted, resilient young woman, Anna. You're a credit to someone.'

'Thanks,' she says, giving me a sideways look.

There's a long silence.

'Can I ask – what do you want out of this?' I say. 'It's wonderful to meet you, of course, but when you say your parents are the reason you're here – is there something in particular you want help with?'

'Well, the main thing is just to find out a bit more about who I am. And maybe even have a relationship with my birth mum.' She darts a quick look at Susie from under her fringe. 'If you want one, of course. It would be so great to have someone to talk to about things.'

'*Absolutely*,' Susie says. 'I'd love that.'

Anna hesitates. 'But there is something else too. Something specific.'

'What's that?' I ask.

'My school.' She looks at us seriously – those eyes, so similar to Susie's, clear and green, that it's all I can do not to automatically smile lovingly back at her. 'They've got me at this really strict academy, Northall.' She has the intonation many girls her age have, putting a slight question mark on the end of sentences, so it comes out as *Northall?* 'For sixth form, I really want to move somewhere I can do performing arts. My passion's music – particularly singing, but all music really. I haven't been allowed to do it there, and I really, really want to.'

Susie says nothing, just reaches across the table and puts her hand on Anna's. Music is so fundamental to her that not being allowed to pursue it would be unthinkable.

'When you say you haven't been allowed to . . .' I begin.

'Not as a school subject, not as private lessons, not even as a hobby,' she says flatly. 'It would be a distraction for me and practising would disturb Henry when he's trying to do his homework, apparently. I saved up and bought a guitar – I was going to teach myself how to play off YouTube videos – but they took it away.'

'OK,' I say, shocked. 'That really sucks – but I don't see how we can help.'

'You're both professional musicians, right? Maybe you could talk to them. At the very least, you're proof that music isn't just a distraction from accountancy or law or whatever the hell it is they want me to do.'

'Well . . .' I'm about to point out that, really, becoming a professional musician isn't so much a career choice these days as financial suicide, but Susie speaks before I have a chance.

'Of *course*,' she says. 'We'd be happy to do that for you, Anna. It would be our pleasure.'

Susie's quiet on the way home, as if she doesn't want to step back into the real world yet, savouring the memory of meeting Anna the way she sometimes savours the silence after a song.

I say nothing either, reluctant to interrupt her thoughts.

'So,' she says eventually. 'What did you think?'

'About Anna? She seems . . . great. Really lovely.'

And it's true – the fears I'd had about meeting some melodramatic emo who was going to accuse Susie of messing up her life had been way off the mark. Despite what she'd told us about her home life, Anna had seemed likeable, sensible and down to earth, with a self-deprecating sense of humour that made her account all the more believable.

And if *I* feel that way, I realise, Susie must feel it a thousandfold.

'I'm so glad you like her.' Susie's voice still has a far-away quality. 'And I'm so glad she reached out to us – that I can actually *do* something for her.'

I don't reply to that immediately. Anna might be charming, but the suggestion that we contact her parents and argue she should be allowed to study music seems to me a tricky one. 'If her parents agree . . . They may not be happy about two strangers sticking their oar in.'

'I'm hardly a stranger!'

'Of course not, but they may not see it that way.' We've reached our house and I park the car.

'But like she said, we can bring a different perspective,' Susie argues. 'It's no different from getting career advice from a mentor, is it? Maybe we could get her some work experience – in a studio, for example. They could hardly object to that, and we've got loads of contacts.'

As we go inside, she reaches for the iPad she left on the kitchen island. 'I'm going to look up that school of hers . . . Jeepers, can you imagine having someone watching every single thing you do online? They sound like a nightmare . . . Got it.'

I look over her shoulder. Northall Academy, the school's website informs us, is passionately ambitious for every pupil to reach their full potential.

More unusually, perhaps, it's rated Outstanding by Ofsted.

'Which, on its own, doesn't mean anything,' Susie says when I draw it to her attention. She herself went – by way of expulsions from several more conventional establishments – to Jordans, one of the most famously liberal schools in the country, where teachers were addressed by their first names, lessons were optional and the pupils literally wrote the rule book. She loved it, but it is, I've long suspected, the reason she fundamentally believes that every regulation or law, from a speed limit through to a customs declaration, is actually only a suggestion.

'I'll see what Mumsnet has to say about it,' she adds.

She scrolls through a few results, then stops, her eyes widening.

'What is it?' I ask.

'It's one of those zero-tolerance places. You know – a once-failing school turned around by a new head who insists everyone does things his way. There's a lot of talk about a new code of conduct he's introduced. Listen to this: *You do not slouch. By sitting up straight you demonstrate respect. You maintain eye contact with your teacher whenever they are talking. If you drop something, you do not pick it up until they give the signal. You never turn round, even if you hear a noise. Between lessons, you do not talk in the corridor unless a teacher addresses you. Then you smile and reply with an upbeat, "Hello, sir!" or "Morning, miss!" You do not walk around in groups of more than two . . .* It sounds *appalling*.'

'But Outstanding.'

'It's wrong for her,' Susie says firmly. 'Just like it would have been wrong for me. And what does it say about *them*, that they could send her somewhere like that?'

'That academic achievement is very important to them?'

She gives me a look and I realise I'm probably sounding insufficiently supportive. 'Look, I'm not disagreeing,' I say. 'I just think we need to be careful about how we handle this. It could seem like we're turning up out of the blue and criticising their parenting.'

'That's *exactly* what we're doing. Why let them off the hook?'

'Because they'll simply tell us to get lost, and then you won't have any kind of relationship with her. Go in a bit more tactfully and maybe they'll be grateful. No parent likes to hear their child's unhappy, after all – perhaps we can frame it in a way that reassures them we're not trying to usurp their authority, we're just concerned adults letting them know she contacted us and why.'

Susie frowns. 'Sneaking on her, you mean.'

'I just think that might be a more productive approach than if we turn up all guns blazing.'

She's silent a moment. 'You're probably right,' she admits. 'It's just that – after so long – the urge to protect her . . .'

'I understand,' I say gently.

She takes a deep breath. 'OK. Let's do this.'

She gets out the napkin Anna wrote her father's number on and taps out a text on her phone.

'*Sorry for contacting you out of the blue,*' she reads aloud, '*but this is Susie, Anna's birth mother. She recently got in touch about something that's worrying her and I wondered if we could meet to discuss it.*'

I nod. 'Sounds good.'

She's barely sent the message, though, the phone still in her hand, when it starts to ring.

'Jesus,' she says, looking at the screen. 'It's them – the number I just texted. That was quick.' She hesitates, then answers. 'Hello?'

I can tell it's a man's voice on the other end, but I can't make out the words. I can only hear Susie's side – 'That wasn't—' 'If you'll just wait a moment—' 'I think you're being—' – and her rising anger – 'No, you listen to me—'

Then, abruptly, it's over. She looks at me, shocked.

'That was Ian Mulcahy. He said we had no right to talk to her before she's eighteen and if we do it again, he'll go to the police. Then he hung up on me.'

'My God.' I'm shocked too. 'But I suppose . . . it must be quite hurtful for them. To discover she was trying to find you . . . That probably feels like some kind of rejection—'

'Will you *please* stop taking their side?' Then: 'Sorry. But it wasn't like that, honestly. He sounded *horrible*. Like an angry little sergeant major who's had his authority threatened. Who thinks bluster and shouting are the way to get me to back off.'

'I take it no one even mentioned schools.'

Susie shakes her head. 'But, you know . . .' she says slowly, 'I don't think this is really about schools, or studying music, or what software's on her phone. Not fundamentally. I think there might be something bigger going on here – something *worse*. Something Anna doesn't feel able to trust us with just yet.'

'What do you mean?'

'I don't know exactly. But he was so *defensive*. Like he was hiding something. What if it's the worst thing of all? What if—?' And here she breaks down before she can even put the thought into words, her head rolling into her hands. 'Oh God, Gabe – *what have I done?*'

TEN

Gabe

Dear Ian and Jenny

Now that the dust has settled and you've had a few days to reflect, perhaps you would reconsider meeting Susie and myself. Whilst we understand it came as a shock to learn that Anna had contacted us, there are some specific things she talked about that we found concerning and which we would still like to discuss with you.

Kind regards

Gabriel Thompson

ELEVEN

Gabe

I don't expect them to reply, to be honest. Wouldn't the simplest thing be to ignore it? But the answer, when it comes, is curt but clear. They'll meet us, though without Anna present.

'It's because he wants to know what we talked about,' Susie says immediately. 'He's worried she might have told us something.'

Or perhaps it's a sign the Mulcahys are actually more reasonable than Anna made them out to be, I think, but don't say out loud. Being strict doesn't make them unloving, after all. But Susie, whose own parents were laissez-faire bordering on lax, can't help but put herself in Anna's position, while to me, whose lower-middle-class Midlands upbringing was also pretty strict, things like insisting on a teenager's phone having credit and battery don't actually seem that unreasonable.

There's just a slight niggle at the back of my mind, too, that some of the other grievances she mentioned – her brother getting second helpings before her, for example – might have been lifted from the Harry Potter books. But I'd told Susie to follow her instincts, and her instincts are clearly ringing alarm bells.

We arrange to meet them in a Starbucks, a few streets away from the café Anna chose. When we arrive, we can tell straight away who they are – the middle-aged couple sitting tense and silent on one side of a table for four, two untouched teas in front of them. We go over and introduce ourselves, and Ian Mulcahy stands up to shake our hands – a gesture that's formal rather than friendly, but it means I can immediately see that Susie was right about one thing: he is indeed a very short man, while Jenny Mulcahy is thin and birdlike, wearing an expression of intense distrust on her face.

We've decided on a non-confrontational approach. 'We do understand that this meeting may not be very welcome for you,' Susie begins. 'But there were a couple of things Anna mentioned to us that we found worrying. I'm sure there *is* nothing to worry about, but we thought we should pass the information along. I know that's what we'd want, if we were in your shoes.'

Ian Mulcahy gives a tiny snort, as if the idea of us being in their shoes is faintly ridiculous.

Susie ploughs on. 'Specifically . . . I'm sure you can understand that, as musicians, music is incredibly important to us. I suppose I always hoped my daughter would take after me in that respect—'

'Don't use that word,' Ian Mulcahy cuts across her.

She looks at him, puzzled. 'What word?'

'She isn't your daughter. And you're not her mother.'

Susie flinches. 'Well – not legally, perhaps. But biologically . . . Musicality is often an inherited characteristic—'

'You know nothing about her,' Jenny Mulcahy says. They're almost the first words she's spoken. 'You have no *idea*. None at all.'

'My point is . . .' Susie struggles on. 'Refusing to let her have a guitar, for example. You might be denying her something that could be a real passion in later life.'

Ian Mulcahy snorts openly now. 'That's what she told you, is it? That we wouldn't let her have a guitar?'

Susie looks at me for support. I say, 'She told us she saved up for a guitar, but you thought it would disturb her brother's homework. She also said you wouldn't let her have music lessons.'

'What you need to understand about Anna,' Ian Mulcahy says, 'is that she lies.'

'*What?*' Susie says, outraged.

Ian nods. 'It's called confabulation and it's not uncommon in adopted children. Most grow out of it. Anna never did.'

Susie and I sit in shocked silence. It isn't just what Ian Mulcahy said, it's the matter-of-fact – even self-satisfied – way he said it.

He's pleased, I realise. Pleased he's found a way to burst our bubble, and indirectly blame Susie for it at the same time.

Susie says angrily, 'I think *you're* the one who's lying.'

Ian regards her steadily. 'We gave her a guitar two Christmases ago. She got frustrated when she realised that it actually takes months of practice before you can make a decent sound. So she kicked it to pieces. We told her she'd have to save up to pay for the repairs herself. Actions have to have consequences, right? She set fire to the pieces and burned them beyond repair. *That's* why she doesn't have a guitar. Not that it's any of your damn business.'

Again, there's a silence while we try to get our heads round this. Susie says defiantly, 'She told us about her school – all those ridiculous rules. And she showed us her phone.'

Ian frowns. 'What about her phone?'

'The spyware you put on it.'

'That's absurd – there's no spyware on her phone,' he blusters. 'As for her school, it's one of the most sought after in North London. We're extremely lucky to be in its catchment area.'

'But if her dream is to go to a performing-arts college—'

'Her *dream*?' Ian looks amused. 'If you were a parent, let alone the parent of a teenager, you'd know that at that age they have a different dream every day. Our job is to give them boundaries and consistency and an education that equips them for the real world, not try to be their best friend or encourage them to live in cloud cuckoo land.'

Susie's mouth falls open. 'Perhaps she needs to be believed, for a start. Encouraged. Not to mention *loved*.'

Jenny Mulcahy says furiously, 'Don't you *dare* talk to me about loving her.'

She speaks with such force that we both just look at her.

'I've shown my love for that girl every single day,' she adds. 'You have no idea what that means. How difficult it can be. And I'll go on doing it, at the very least until the day she turns eighteen.'

'I'm sorry,' Susie concedes. 'I didn't mean to imply that you don't love her. But it's precisely because you *do* love her that I'm sure you can appreciate my feelings, too. As her, her—'

'You don't *love* her,' Jenny Mulcahy says incredulously. 'How can you? You might love an idea of her. But she's literally someone you've met once in fifteen years, for coffee. And now here you are, telling us how to parent her, all on the basis of your extensive expertise and unique insights as the person whose womb she briefly inhabited.' She nods. 'It's a good thing you can't have kids, because you'd be terrible at it.'

'Now wait a minute,' I begin angrily. But Susie's ahead of me.

'I am *not* telling you how to deal with her. I'm simply . . . *advocating* for her. Because, yes, I do believe that I understand how she must feel about certain things.' She takes a breath. 'I wasn't always a well-behaved teenager, either.'

'We know,' Ian Mulcahy says crisply. 'We read the paperwork. Let's hope Anna doesn't follow the same trajectory.' He puts his empty cup on the table and stands up. Jenny immediately follows suit. 'Anna has been grounded for contacting you, but knowing the extent of her oppositional defiance, she may well do it again. If she does, I must politely ask you not to reply. I expect to be copied in on any communications you do have. And please know that there will be legal consequences if you ever try to see her again.' He turns, nods to Jenny to follow him, and leaves.

We watch them go, stunned.

'Well, that went pretty well,' Susie starts to say, before the tears overcome her.

TWELVE

Anna

I'm lying on my bed with my laptop, working, when there's a rap on my door. A moment later, he's inside, glaring down at me.

'If you're going to knock, could you at least wait for an answer?' I say coldly.

'I did. You probably didn't hear me the first time. That ridiculous music you insist on listening to.' We both know he's lying. He's never going to wait for me to give him permission to do anything.

'How long am I grounded for?'

'Until you've understood that what you did was wrong.'

I don't dignify that with a response.

'We met them, by the way,' he adds. '*Susie* and *Gabe*. This afternoon. We had a nice cup of tea together.'

I try to hide my shock. 'Good for you.'

'They've agreed not to communicate with you. But if they do, you're to tell us immediately. The rules around unauthorised contact are there for a reason. It could cause you psychological harm.'

Which is almost funny. 'Harm. Right. Like what?'

He considers me thoughtfully. 'The teenage years are all about finding your own identity. That's why it's only natural that you test your boundaries with your existing family. But, for the same reason, the boundaries have to stay consistent. For adopted children, whose identities may inherently be more confused, it's particularly important that they don't think they can pick and choose how they're parented.' The psychobabble rolls so smoothly off his tongue, I'm almost impressed. But, with a sinking feeling, I realise that any social worker or teacher who hears it will be impressed too. They'll think, *Well, he clearly knows what he's talking about*, and I'll be ignored yet again.

He nods, happy he's shut me up. 'You need to tidy this room before supper.'

When he's gone, I stick my earbuds back in – I'm listening to 'Lullaby for Leah'; I'm working my way through all Silverlink's songs – then turn my attention back to my laptop and the essay I'm writing, ironically enough, on modern slavery. I click on the corner to shrink the document down for a moment.

Just long enough to see again the message that came in a few minutes ago. The message that sent my pulse racing and made my heart burst with joy and relief.

I want you to know that we believe you. We will always believe you.
Much love, Susie.

It's working. And there's not a damn thing he can do about it.

THIRTEEN

Susie

It took about an hour for my tears to turn to anger. By the time we got home, I was actually shaking with fury.

'That odious little man. There's something very wrong in that family, I'm sure of it.'

'You know, I think you might be right,' Gabe said with a sigh.

'The way he talked about her – it was like he was *smearing* her. Setting things up so that, if she ever tells us something really big, we'll be primed not to believe her. And couching it in all that jargon, too – *oppositional defiance*, for God's sake. What the hell is that when it's at home?'

'I'll look it up.' Gabe got out his phone. 'Hmm . . . Effectively, it seems to be medical speak for not doing what you're told.'

'While you're at it, do a search for him, would you? Ian Mulcahy.'

He tapped in the name. 'Yup, got him . . . He's an educational psychologist. Works in-house for the local authority.'

'No wonder he knows all the lingo.'

Gabe said slowly, 'Look, this may be nothing ... but did you notice Jenny Mulcahy's bruise?'

I stared at him. '*What?*'

He nodded. 'When she reached for her tea, her sleeve rode up and I saw this bruise on her forearm. It wasn't big or anything ... But when she saw me looking at it, she quickly pulled her sleeve down. And she kept her hands in her lap after that.'

'You think he might be *violent*?'

'I think we have to be really, really careful not to jump to conclusions. But put it this way – I'm doing my best to stay objective and detached about all this, because I appreciate that you can't help but be emotionally involved. And that conversation ... Before we met them, there was a part of me that expected the four of us to have a laugh about how over the top teenagers can be, and then we'd come away reassured that they were fundamentally decent people doing their best to make her happy. But it wasn't like that at all, was it? He was basically saying, "Don't believe a word she says." Why would anyone go out of their way to say that about their daughter?'

'Because they don't want them to be believed about something specific,' I said immediately. 'Something lurking in the background that nobody talks about.'

Gabe looked troubled. 'Again – let's try not to get ahead of ourselves. But if we *are* talking about bullying or coercive control, or something even worse, what's our responsibility?'

'To tell Social Services?'

'Tell them what, though? Anna's not said anything that could trigger an investigation.'

I nodded. 'Which is why we need to make sure she knows she *can* tell us. I'm going to message her.'

'And copy him in, like he asked?'

'Screw that. This needs to be confidential. And she needs to know that, when it comes to choosing who to believe, we'll take her over him any day.'

It was only much later, when he'd opened a bottle of wine and was cooking, that Gabe said, 'How did Jenny Mulcahy know, by the way?'

'Know what?'

'That we've struggled to have children. That horrible thing she said, about how you'd make a terrible parent.' He glanced at me. 'Which obviously isn't true, incidentally.'

I thought back. 'I must have mentioned it to Anna.'

'I don't think you did. I'd have noticed.'

'Maybe it was while you were getting the coffees. Yes, that's right – she asked if we had children and I said something like, it hadn't worked out that way for us yet.'

'OK . . . But then Ian linked it back to you as a teenager. Something about hoping Anna wouldn't follow the same trajectory.'

'Perhaps he meant the so-called stigma of having a child out of wedlock. Anna said they were religious.'

Gabe came and refilled my glass, then topped up his own. 'Which is pretty insulting too, right? To adopt a child, but criticise the person who gave them that opportunity.'

I nodded, and took a sip without replying. Because it was

actually the other thing Ian Mulcahy said that was lurking at the back of my mind, terrifying me.

We read the paperwork.

Paperwork that, presumably, still existed. Paperwork that, if this all got nasty, could make my life very difficult indeed.

FOURTEEN

Gabe

For the next three weeks, things with the Mulcahys go quiet.

But that doesn't mean nothing's happening. I don't know who initiates it, but Susie and Anna start messaging. A couple of times a day at first, then more and more.

To begin with, Susie shows me. Then, as messages turn into longer conversations, she stops. After all, there's no point in showing me a WhatsApp that consists solely of two crying-face emojis and an exclamation mark when I don't know the context.

And sometimes, I can tell, the conversations become more serious. Like the time Susie's phone pings just as she's telling me a funny story about Jack, her drummer. She immediately breaks off and reaches for it. She does that a lot now, I've noticed – the phone's her priority, not the band. Or even me.

As she reads it, her face darkens.

'Anna?' I ask.

'Yes.' Quickly she taps out a response.

'What's up?'

To my surprise, she hesitates. 'I think I'd have to check with her before I tell you. She's starting to share some pretty private stuff. Not . . . specifics. Just how she feels about certain things. But I don't want her to think I'd tell people.'

I frown. 'I'm hardly *people*.'

'I know. And of course I'll tell you everything if she's happy for me to. But at the moment, I'm still earning her trust.'

'Sure,' I say. 'No problem.' But the truth is, I'm a little put out. Susie and I have never had secrets from each other.

Later, as we're going to bed, I ask her what Anna said. She looks at me blankly.

'You were going to ask her about showing me her texts,' I remind her.

'Oh. Yes. She said not yet, if that's OK.'

The following week, I have to go into Soho to have lunch with my agent. I notice in the morning that Susie seems a bit distracted, but I put it down to some problems she's been having with Marlon, her guitarist. I also notice that she's baking. That's nice, I think, I'll come home to cake, and I make a mental note not to let the agent talk me into dessert.

He does talk me into a second bottle of wine, though, and it's almost five by the time I get back. I walk into the kitchen – the smell of freshly baked cake drawing me in – and stop dead.

Anna's sitting at the island, nursing a bottle of beer. Susie sits opposite, a bottle in her hand as well. Both of them look wrung out. I'm clearly coming into the end of an intense conversation.

'What's this?' I say slowly.

Susie glances at Anna. 'Anna came round for a chat.'

It's clear from the way she says it that, whatever they've been talking about, it's been a lot more than just a chat.

'Over a beer?' If Ian and Jenny get to hear about this, I think, we're going to be in trouble.

'How was your lunch?' Susie says pointedly.

'Caspar—' I'm about to point out that my agent's well over eighteen, and entitled to drink all the alcohol he wants, but something in Susie's expression warns me off.

'Hi Gabe,' Anna says quietly. She glances at Susie and puts her bottle down. 'Look . . . I'll get out of your hair.'

'Wait,' Susie says quickly. 'I really think . . . if you were able to tell Gabe some of what you've just told me, it would make a huge difference. So we can discuss between the three of us what to do.'

There's a long silence. Anna takes a breath. 'OK. I'll try.'

She looks at the floor. 'Two years ago, I made an accusation of inappropriate contact against Ian Mulcahy.'

FIFTEEN

Gabe

Even through my shock, I notice the odd construction of that sentence. Not *I reported him* or *He hit me*, but *I made an accusation*.

As if she's only going to tell us what can be verified.

She takes another deep breath. 'When I was twelve, they decided I was "oppositional". Whatever that meant. Stroppy, I guess. And, yes, I probably was.'

'None of this is your fault,' Susie says.

Anna nods gratefully. 'They found this . . . therapy. The idea was that the . . . *behaviours* they didn't like were all because I'm adopted. That I must have what they called "attachment issues". I certainly didn't feel too attached to them at that point, so maybe there was something in it.

'They took me to this place in Enfield . . . The lead therapist was a big American guy who'd trained at some institute in Colorado. He got my parents to lay me across their laps – him, Mum, Ian – then they all tickled me as hard as they could.'

'Why would they do that?' I say, confused.

'To make me lose my temper. "Cathartic rage", the therapist

called it.' Anna pauses. 'Then, when I was exhausted with crying and fighting, I had to let them cuddle me. The moment I stopped being all lovey-dovey, it started again.'

I look at Susie, appalled. '*Seriously?*'

'It's called "coercive restraint",' she says numbly. 'Here, read this.'

I take the iPad she's holding out and look. She's got a Wikipedia page up. *Coercive restraint therapy,* I read, *also known as attachment or holding therapy, was developed in Evergreen, Colorado:*

> A central feature is the use of psychological, physical, or aggressive means to provoke the child to catharsis, ventilation of rage, or other sorts of acute emotional discharge. To do this, a variety of coercive techniques are used, including scheduled holding, binding, rib cage stimulation (e.g. tickling, pinching, knuckling), and/or licking. Children may be held down, may have several adults lie on top of them, or their faces may be held so they can be forced to engage in prolonged eye contact. Sessions may last from 3 to 5 hours.

Although written in a dispassionate, almost scientific tone, the article is quietly scathing, quoting from several authoritative-sounding reports.

> Children described as attachment-disordered are expected to comply with parental commands 'fast and snappy and right first time', and to always be 'fun to be around' for their parents. Deviation from this standard, such as not finishing chores or arguing, is interpreted as a sign of attachment disorder that must be forcibly eradicated. From this perspective, parenting a child with an attachment disorder is a battle, and winning the battle by defeating the child is paramount.

'*Jesus*,' I say disbelievingly. 'And this is what you complained about, presumably?'

Anna shakes her head. 'I hated it, of course. Those sessions – they made me feel like a zombie. For days afterwards, I kept having flashbacks and crying for no reason . . . But they'd already made it clear it was considered a legitimate way of treating behaviour like mine. No, my accusation . . .'

She pauses, as if gathering her courage.

'The tickling was meant to be done at home, as well as at the centre. They could restrain me all right when they were there, because they had the therapist helping them. But at home – well, you've seen my parents. Ian's not exactly muscled. When they put me across their laps and tickled me, I used to fight them – to thrash around. I couldn't help it. And that's when I realised . . .'

She hesitates, then says quietly, 'I think he got excited by it. Physically, I mean. I guess because of the way he was dominating me. The power he had.' She makes a face. '*Gross*. It makes me sick just to think about it.'

I'm almost lost for words. 'I'm so sorry, Anna. So, how . . . ? What did you do?'

'For ages, I kept quiet. But everything was . . . weird. Or maybe it just seemed like that, because the way I thought about *him* was different. Before, even when I hated him, I used to consider him my dad. But after that, I realised – he isn't, not really. I'm not his daughter. I'm just some random teenage girl he's got living under his roof. And that made me feel even more vulnerable.'

Beside me, Susie sniffs back tears.

'Anyway, Mum never did notice anything was wrong. At least, that's what she told them.'

'Told who?' I ask.

'Eventually, I spoke to someone. A teacher – Mrs Roke. She taught my drama class.'

'She took you seriously, I hope?'

Anna nods. 'That school's a prison camp, but they do at least have safeguarding procedures. The police got involved, then Social Services – the monster was hauled in for questioning.' She's silent a moment. 'That's what I call him now – the monster.'

'Then what?'

She shrugs hopelessly. 'My parents convinced them ... convinced them ...' She starts to cry, lines of clear liquid running down her cheeks. 'That I'm a liar. That I've always made things up. It was well documented, apparently. Stupid stuff, like saying my birth parents had a Bentley. Or that I'd won a prize at school when I hadn't. I don't know why ... But I grew out of it. At least, I thought I had. Unbeknownst to me, the monster had been keeping a log. Times and details of the ... the so-called ...'

'Confabulation,' Susie says quietly.

'Yes. That was the word he used. To make it sound more official.' Anna wipes tears away with her fingers. 'Which was really fucking ironic, because every single thing in that log was *confabulated* and I was telling the truth.'

'Jesus,' I say again. I glance at Susie. She's clearly already heard this, but she's crying too, the tears running down her cheeks in exactly the same way as Anna's. 'What happened after that?'

Anna shrugs. 'At least the therapy stopped. The monster agreed it probably wasn't *appropriate* to be holding down a teenage girl and tickling her until she almost wet herself, though he claimed he'd simply been following guidance from the therapist. But everything else . . . just went back to the way it had been before. Well, almost. He really hated me for calling him out – he was careful to make everything seem above board, but he was stricter than ever. There were rules for everything, with punishments for breaking them. Except they weren't called rules or punishments, they were *boundaries* and *consequences*. And I stopped complaining. Because, really, what would be the fucking point?'

'Is he ever violent?' I ask gently.

'To me?' Anna shakes her head. 'No, though I wouldn't like to make him lose his temper.'

'What about to your mum?'

'I'm not sure.' She sighs. 'Her part in this – it's really complicated. I feel like she genuinely supported the therapy at first, because she thought it would make me more like the sweet, loving little girl she imagined in her head. I think she found it hard that I was growing up and becoming more independent from her. And I freely admit, I went through a pretty bolshie phase.'

'We all do,' Susie reassures her. 'It doesn't make any of this all right.'

'I've thought about running away.' Anna looks anguished. 'Just take my things and leave. But where would I go? The women's refuges and so on say you have to be at least sixteen. And my parents go on about exams and qualifications . . . If I can just hang on for a couple of years, they won't be able to stop me. Legally, I can just walk out then.'

There's a long silence. For my part, I'm too shocked to say anything. When Susie speculated there might be something very wrong at the Mulcahy's, I never thought it could be this bad. I try to imagine what it must have been like to be forcibly held down like that. And then to be tickled, too, and made to lose your temper . . . and that was before you added in the horror of realising the effect it was having on one of your assailants.

'What do you want to do?' Susie asks her. 'I don't mean in the longer term, I mean right now.' She glances at the clock. 'It's pretty late.'

'Could I . . . maybe stay the night?' Anna says tentatively. 'I don't think I can face them again this evening.'

'Of course.' Susie looks at me. 'Will you let them know?'

'They won't be happy about it,' Anna adds fearfully.

'Leave that to me,' I say grimly.

I get my phone and go into the next room. When Ian Mulcahy answers, I say, 'This is Gabe Thompson. I'm calling you as a courtesy, to let you know Anna's safe. She's with us. She's going to stay the night.'

There's a long pause before he says, 'I thought I told you not to contact her.'

'She's been filling us in. About the coercive restraint and so on.' I let my words hang in the air for a moment. 'It's been quite difficult for her to talk about and she's understandably upset. It's best she stays with us until she's feeling less vulnerable.'

'What about school? She has double maths first thing in the morning, though I don't expect *you* to know that.'

'We'll make sure she gets to school when she's up to it,' I say impatiently. 'But clearly, that's not the immediate priority here.'

The line goes dead. I don't care. I've told him what he needs to know.

I go back into the kitchen and nod at Susie, who says, 'I'll cook us something. How about xitt kodi? We've got everything we need in the freezer.'

'I don't even know what that is,' Anna says, shaking her head.

'Oh – Goan fish curry. It's just that we try not to use that word – *curry*. It's ... well, it's controversial at the moment, in foodie circles. Colonialist language and so on.'

'You people are so *cool*,' Anna says, smiling through her tears. 'My parents don't even *eat* spicy food, let alone worry about what it's called.'

'We're not remotely cool, not really,' Susie says as she gets up. 'But we do try to do the right thing. Just like we'll try to do the right thing by you, Anna, if you'll let us.'

SIXTEEN

Susie

By the time we ate, Anna had recovered herself – chattering away cheerfully, quizzing Gabe and me about our life as musicians.

I gave her a few choice anecdotes, then indicated Gabe. 'Good luck getting any gossip out of him, though. On tour, he was famous for being tucked up every night by nine.'

'I had my moments,' Gabe protested. 'A couple of pints in the hotel bar.'

'And you must be the only boy-band singer in history who's barely been near an illicit substance. Not that I'm complaining.' I gestured at the interior of the kitchen. 'What other musicians put up their noses, Gabe spent on Farrow and Ball.'

'Are those real Banksys?' Anna asked.

I nodded. 'Gabe's pride and joy. Though what he's really proud of is that he spotted him early, before the show with the live elephant.'

'It's true,' Gabe said, smiling. 'On paper at least, I've made more money from those canvases than I did from the band's last single. Not that I'll ever sell them.'

'Can I have another beer?' Anna indicated the curry. 'I'm not used to this much chilli.'

I got up. 'I don't see why not. I should have thought to make it milder.'

'Speaking of illicit substances,' Gabe muttered as I passed.

I ignored him. Two beers was hardly a big deal, particularly with food. When I was Anna's age, I was drinking vodka and Coke when I went out, which was pretty much every night. And the important thing after she'd unburdened herself of something so huge was to build a relationship of trust with her.

Besides, the horrible discovery that I was right to be suspicious about the Mulcahys aside, it felt good to be there, the three of us, eating and talking, a chill-out beach-lounge compilation playing quietly in the background. Almost like we were a family.

After supper, she asked if she could watch Netflix, which they didn't have at home. She chose something terrible and girly because her friends were all talking about it, and I sat and watched it too, just for the pleasure of her company.

'Oh my God,' she said after a while. 'This is absolute rubbish, isn't it?'

I laughed. 'Even crap telly can be fun. Particularly if you watch it with someone who thinks the same way you do.'

Anna smiled. Then, abruptly, the smile vanished. 'I feel sick.'

'Really?' I said, concerned. 'Maybe it was the chillies—?'

She shook her head. 'Not that sort of sick. It's knowing I have to go back. Before, when I had no choice – I just had to get my head down and get on with it. But meeting you, Gabe, coming here . . . it's made me realise. Not all teenagers' lives are like mine.'

I squeezed her shoulder. 'We *will* do something to sort this out,

Anna. I don't know exactly what yet – I need to talk it through with Gabe; he's smart about stuff like this – but we'll think of something.'

'Thanks,' she said, her eyes shining. She leaned into me and I let my arm slide around her. I could smell her hair – so like mine used to be, it was almost uncanny. On the other side of her, our rescue, Sandy, climbed up on to the sofa too. Absent-mindedly, she reached out and stroked his ears.

For a long time, we sat like that, not speaking, and the crap telly programme suddenly seemed like the most beautiful thing in the world.

SEVENTEEN

Gabe

'So what are we going to do?' Susie asks as we get ready for bed.

'I don't know.' I sigh. 'The problem is, that allegation of hers has already been investigated and, effectively, dismissed. If she could give us something else – some proof that backs up her claim – we could take it to the police. But without that, I suspect we'd just get her into more trouble.'

'I don't want to ask her for proof,' Susie says firmly. 'For one thing, if there was any, she'd have told us, but for another, it might sound as if without it we don't believe her. And I want her to know that, in this house, she'll always be believed.'

'I get that. But I think it means our options are limited.'

'I'm going to suggest she has some sessions with Rowena.'

Rowena's the therapist who's been helping Susie deal with her miscarriages. I'd felt a bit excluded by those sessions, initially – I like to think Susie can talk to me about anything – but when I saw the change in her, I'd been impressed as well as grateful. Susie once told me that, sometimes, it's easier to talk about your feelings with someone you don't have feelings for, because you're not worried about being judged by them.' It was a sentiment Rowena had clearly put to her, but no less effective for that.

'That's a good idea. We'll pay, presumably.'

Susie nods. 'They make her allowance dependent on whether she's being polite. Every time she rolls her eyes at them, the amount gets halved.'

'Wow . . . Well, that's one thing we can do, then. But in terms of getting her away from there, I don't think there's much else. Do we think she's in any actual physical danger?'

'You mean, might he do it again?' Susie pauses and thinks. 'I'm not sure. From what she's told me, it was more like something that happened during the restraint sometimes that afterwards he was ashamed of. He's masked it by being cold and angry with her, but he's probably also angry with himself. I guess there's always a chance he could be provoked by something, though, and suddenly flip. And if he does, who knows where that could end up?' She shudders. 'I hate the thought of her being so vulnerable.'

'Look, why don't I speak to Marcus? He knows a lot about this area – he may have some ideas.' Marcus is a friend who fosters children for his local authority.

'Thanks. And, Gabe . . . if it's all right by you, I'm going to tell Anna she can come and stay the night any time she needs to. I'll give her some money, too. If the worst does happen, she needs to have an escape route.'

'Of course. You do realise, though – at some point, this may get us into trouble?'

Susie says slowly, 'Yes. And, to be honest, it would make me feel better if it did. Then at least we'd all be facing this together, instead of letting her try to deal with it on her own.'

EIGHTEEN

Gabe

But trouble, as it turns out, doesn't wait for some vague point in the future. Trouble turns up at twenty past seven next morning, in the shape of two police officers: a man in uniform and a woman in plain clothes.

'What's this about?' I say as I answer the door, although I've already guessed.

'Do you have a minor called Anna Mulcahy here?' the woman asks.

When I say we do, her eyes narrow.

Detective Constable Karen Eddo and Constable Jim Richards are calm, professional and utterly implacable. Anna's parents have reported her missing and named us as the people she's likely to be with. So they've come to collect her.

'She wasn't *missing*,' Susie points out. 'They knew exactly where she was. Gabe phoned them.'

'Did they give their consent?' Eddo asks.

'Well – no,' I admit. 'But she's here because she wanted to be. She's fifteen, for Christ's sake.'

'As far as the law's concerned, that makes her a runaway,' Richards says.

Anna comes into the kitchen, wearing an old Silverlink T-shirt Susie lent her to sleep in. She looks startled. 'What's going on?'

'You need to get dressed, Anna,' Eddo says. 'We're taking you home.'

Anna frowns. 'I've got school.'

'The law says we have to take you home.' Richards sounds peeved. I guess being a taxi service for teenage girls wasn't high on the list of things that drew him to the job.

'Great,' Anna mutters. She goes back upstairs and Eddo turns to us.

'You'll both need to come into the station to be served with a child abduction warning notice. What you have done so far does not constitute an offence, but once the CAWN is issued, any breaches of it will assist the CPS in determining whether you should be arrested and charged with child abduction.'

'*What?*' Susie says. '*Abduction?* That's *absurd*. We haven't abducted anyone.'

'There may also be grounds for charges under stalking and harassment legislation.'

'But . . .' Susie stares at her, too astonished for a moment to speak. 'But I'm her *mother*. Did they tell you that?'

'They told us you're her birth mother, yes. They also told us they've forbidden you from having any further contact with her until she's eighteen.'

'While they were at it, did they tell you they abused her?' Susie retorts.

The police officers glance at each other. 'Do you have any evidence to support that?' Eddo asks.

'There was an investigation,' I say. 'It'll all be on record.'

'So it was dealt with.'

'Well – yes. Badly. From a safeguarding point of view—'

'From a safeguarding point of view, she needs to be returned to her parents.'

'This is *insane*!' Susie bursts out.

'Someone will be in touch to arrange a time for you to be served with the CAWN,' Eddo says. Anna comes back into the kitchen, dressed now and with her book bag over her shoulder. Eddo turns to her. 'If you'd come with us, please, Anna.'

NINETEEN

Gabe

I meet Marcus in a pub in Ruislip, where he lives. We've been friends since the early days – in the noughties, when WHT started touring, his band, Bruvs, was one of our main rivals. But they split earlier than we did, partly because their sales never quite took off like ours. Marcus had two kids by then, and fostering two more was initially just a way for him and Jassie to keep the wolf from the door. But he discovered he actually liked it more than singing, and turned down a comeback tour to do it full-time. They've fostered eighteen children now, and every Christmas they have a legendary lunch to which every single one of them has a standing invitation. Christmas is one of the hardest times for young people who've been through the care system, he's told me: imagine being nineteen, with the state having officially washed its hands of you, and having no one to spend Christmas Day with.

We carry our beers to a quiet table and I tell him everything that's happened. 'So what I'm wondering,' I conclude, 'is what the hell we do next. Is there anyone we can report our concerns to? A social worker, say?'

Marcus rubs his head. 'Not really – she won't have had one of those for years. It's weird – we get well paid by our local authority to look after the kids we take, and if we run into problems there's an army of professionals we can call on for help. But when you adopt, you do it for free, and the state basically says you're on your own. There's a little bit of support for the first couple of years now, which is a big improvement on how things used to be. But it's quite common for it to be adolescence when the real problems appear, and then there's nothing.'

'When you say "problems",' I say slowly, 'are you implying there might be something in what her parents are claiming?'

'Well, obviously, I don't know either way. But I do know that issues with adopted children aren't all that unusual – around a quarter will have challenging behaviours of some kind. Of course, that means the vast majority of adoptions don't run into problems, and in most of those that do, they settle down eventually. But in a small number it can get worse, particularly if it's not dealt with properly to begin with.'

'Anna seems incredibly well adjusted to us. And charming.'

'That can actually be one of the indicators. Charming and over-quick to attach to strangers, cold and confrontational at home. It's not surprising, when you think about it – deep down, they're convinced they're going to lose their new parents too, so the only way they can control the situation is by pushing them away.' Marcus shrugs. 'It sounds to me as if, rightly or wrongly, someone's diagnosed Anna with reactive attachment disorder – what's sometimes called "adopted child syndrome". That would make sense of the holding therapy – not excuse it, because of course it's barbaric, but it would at least explain how they ended up thinking it might be the answer.'

'So that really is a thing? I couldn't believe it when Susie showed me that Wikipedia page.'

He makes a face. 'It's a thing, though I don't think you'd find more than a handful of professionals in this country who'd still go along with it – most would assume it would simply traumatise the child even further. But, yes, there used to be several centres with links to the US that claimed it could work miracles, with so-called studies that appeared to back them up. And if the parents were really desperate . . . I had a kid with reactive attachment disorder once. He was nine and totally uncontrollable – if I tried to make him do anything, it was like throwing a switch. He'd smash things without any fear of the consequences – almost as if he was willing me to lose my temper and hurt him. In the end I had to ask the local authority to take him away, for the safety of the other kids. If he'd been adopted, of course, I wouldn't have had that option. So I can see how someone who'd become frustrated with a child they perceived as refusing to love them back might explore that kind of therapy.'

That description might well fit Jenny Mulcahy, I realise. 'And the confabulation and so on? Might that be real too?'

Marcus nods. 'Unfortunately, her father's right – it's not unheard of among foster kids and adoptees. It doesn't actually mean they're lying. It's more like the brain's filling in any gaps with what it wants to be true, rather than pausing to work out what really is. But it would be easy for someone to blur the lines between that and lying, particularly an educational psychologist used to dealing with child-protection reports.'

'We believe her,' I say firmly. 'What she told us, about him getting aroused during the therapy – it happened, I'm sure of it.'

'Well, you've met her. I haven't.'

Marcus sounds troubled. I look at him. 'What?'

He hesitates. 'I've fostered girls who have been through all sorts of trauma. Sometimes they can't help but test you sexually – you know, try to get a reaction out of you. They can't stop themselves, and of course it all stems from the same fundamental inability to trust people. Look, I'm not saying it didn't happen the way she described, I'm just saying this is an incredibly complex area and determining what really took place isn't going to be easy.'

'Whatever happened, he should never have *let* it happen,' I say firmly. 'That's his responsibility as a father, surely.'

'Agreed.' Marcus takes a pull of his pint. 'But it makes your position complicated. Have you ever heard the term "ghost kingdoms"?'

I shake my head.

'It's used to describe the way some adopted kids construct fantasies of what their birth families might be like. For some, the fantasies become really powerful – almost like an alternative reality they can withdraw into.' He gestures at me. 'Just imagine what it must be like for Anna. Her birth mother's husband was in a boy band, for Christ's sake! A successful one, too.'

'We had our moments,' I say, grinning. 'Unlike some boy bands I could mention.'

'And Susie – I've seen her Insta, man. That house of yours . . . hashtag nofilter, hashtag livingthedream . . . She makes it look like you two spend half your time baking cakes with eggs from your own chickens and the other half doing club sets in Goa and Ibiza.'

'Our life isn't always plain sailing,' I protest. 'You know that.'

'Sure – but Susie doesn't post about the fibroids or the miscarriages on social media, right? From the outside, you're the ghost kingdom to end all ghost kingdoms. And the trouble with fantasies is that, at some point, they collide with reality and everything turns to shit. And that could be even more traumatising for Anna, ultimately – to find her perfect family at last, only to discover it doesn't solve her problems after all. Or, even worse, to start to live the dream, only to have it snatched away from her again, leaving her back where she was but feeling even more isolated.'

I'm silent a moment. 'So what should we do?'

'Honestly?'

I nod and he goes on, 'I don't think any of you will want to hear this, especially Susie. But now the Mulcahys have got the police involved, I don't think you have any choice. I think you have to walk away. And I think that'll actually be the best thing for all of you, in the end.'

CHILD ABDUCTION WARNING NOTICE – UNDER 16

I have been advised that the following young person has recently been in your company and/or that you have allowed them to be at your home address.

CHILD'S NAME: [Care needed where child's real name is not known to suspect] ANNA MULCAHY

I wish to make it clear on behalf of [insert name of person/s with parental responsibility] MR IAN MULCAHY, MRS JENNY MULCAHY that you have no permission or authority to communicate with this young person, either directly or indirectly, or to allow this young person to enter or stay in your home or other property, or to be in your company, at any time of day or night before they reach the age of 16 years.

YOU MUST NOT THEREFORE AT ANY TIME OF DAY OR NIGHT:
- *allow this young person to enter or stay in your house, flat, room, place of work or other property, whether you are there or not;*
- *allow this young person to enter or stay in any other property you are present in;*
- *allow this young person to enter or travel in any vehicle you own or are travelling in;*

- *meet with this young person or remain in their presence;*
- *telephone, text, email, write or communicate with this young person in any way, directly or indirectly through other people;*
- *provide this young person with any food, drink, gift or any other item.*

If this young person approaches or makes contact with you, you must immediately:
- *refuse to allow them to enter the property or vehicle you are in and ask them to leave, or, in appropriate circumstances, leave the premises or vehicle yourself;*
- *contact Social Services or the Police if they refuse to leave;*
- *break off any communication.*

If you do not comply and this young person is traced to your home / property / vehicle or is found in your presence, then you are liable to arrest and prosecution under Section 2 of the Child Abduction Act 1984, which carries a maximum sentence of 7 years imprisonment. You may also be liable for other criminal offences arising out of your contact with this young person.

Any suggestion that you are offering this young person necessary shelter or hospitality will be no defence. The Parents wish to make it clear that no such services from you are required and are indeed unwelcome.

Officer Issuing Warning [Collar Number & Name]: 847653 EDDO
Station: COLINDALE

I have read and explained this warning to the person/s named below.

TWENTY

Susie

'I can't do it,' I said dispiritedly, looking through the CAWN for the twentieth time. 'I just can't.'

'Unfortunately, I don't think we have a choice,' Gabe said quietly. 'According to Marcus, the courts take these things pretty seriously. They were introduced after the child-grooming scandals, but now they're used to stop any kind of unauthorised contact. The assumption is that the parents are always right and the other party should back off.'

'I gave her up once. I'm not doing it a second time.'

Gabe hesitated. 'And the other things Marcus talked about? The possible attachment issues and so on?'

I shrugged. 'I don't think that changes anything, does it? Not fundamentally. Even if the Mulcahys had good reasons for dragging her to that awful therapy, it doesn't excuse it or justify what happened. The only thing it changes is my degree of responsibility.'

Gabe looked puzzled. 'What do you mean?'

'If Anna does have issues as a result of having been adopted, they're *my* fault, aren't they? I'm the one who gave her up, so I'm the one who needs to help her find a solution. And I know it's unfair to ask you to come with me on that journey, Gabe, because she's not your flesh and blood. But I *am* asking. And, yes, I know it means we might get into trouble with the police, but realistically, the courts move so slowly that maybe, by the time anything actually gets done about it, she'll be sixteen and everything will change again – that's correct, isn't it?'

He nodded. 'Marcus said that, although sixteen-year-olds are technically still minors, in practice the system says they're old enough to make their own decisions.'

'Well, then. In less than a year, the Mulcahys can go screw themselves. What do you say?'

He was silent for a few moments. Then he said, 'I'm with you. For her sake, partly, because no fifteen-year-old should have to put up with what she's been through. But mainly because of you, Suze. When we got married, I promised we'd be in this together. And I meant it.'

Our wedding was in Ibiza, at a villa overlooking Cala Jondal. Just forty or so close friends, and a magical night of music and dancing on the beach. But the best thing of all was the song Gabe had secretly composed, which he sang for me that evening for the first time – a song that would probably be a hit if he ever released it, but which we decided was too personal ever to make money from.

> *We're in this together*
> *For the rest of our days*
> *In this forever*

> *In a thousand different ways*
> *Susie, oh Susie*
> *You're the best of my life . . .*
> *In this together*
> *Husband and wife.*

So when he said, *In this together*, it was more than a statement. It was a commitment. A promise.

Having sex with fibroids . . . People don't usually talk about that side of it, but it can be pretty tough. The usual advice is to 'seek alternative means of intimacy', and Gabe, bless him, has generally been fine about that. But after I was trying to get pregnant, that wasn't really an option. So we had to find workarounds – the first time our gynaecologist brought up the subject of 'penis buffers', I thought Gabe was going to have a fit. But, with plenty of good humour, lubricant and adaptability on both sides, we've managed to figure out some ways to make it work.

What there was no getting away from, though, was the schedule. My periods were pretty regular for someone with fibroids, so at least I knew when we should be aiming for, but it meant date night got extended into date-night-followed-by-another-date-night-followed-by-another-date-night, with not much room for flexibility. Romance didn't really come into it.

I wasn't particularly in the mood that evening, but one of the strange silver linings of having a schedule was that sometimes everything just . . . I almost said *came together*, which would be a terrible pun, but it's true. Sometimes my feelings just swept up unexpectedly out of nowhere, like a big wave on Cala Jondal, and everything worked. That night was one of those rare times when pleasure banished pain completely and the sheer force of my love for Gabe left me clutching at his shoulders and shaking.

Afterwards, he looked at me and kissed my forehead.

'Love you,' he whispered tenderly.

It felt like we could face anything, when we were so united.

TWENTY-ONE

Gabe

We drift off, still holding each other. I'm deeply asleep, the way I sometimes am after making love, so when the doorbell goes, I have no idea at first whether it's morning or night.

Struggling awake, I look at my phone. Just after one. 'Who the hell can that be?' I wonder aloud.

I pull on some pyjamas and go downstairs. Sandy has started barking without actually bothering to get out of his dog bed, though he gets up when I unlock the front door.

It's Anna. She has a small backpack slung over her shoulder.

'I'm sorry,' she says quickly. 'I'm really sorry, Gabe. But Susie said I could come if I needed to. And I couldn't think of anywhere else.'

Susie has put on a dressing gown and is coming down the stairs behind me. 'Of course you can come here, Anna,' she says, concerned. 'You can come any time. What's happened?'

He walked into her room while she was undressing.

'I mean, he knocks,' she says tearfully. 'One tap. But he doesn't wait for an answer. And I was listening to music – one of your songs, actually.' She nods at me. 'I had my AirPods in, so I didn't hear him. I was standing there half naked when I realised . . . I think I screamed.'

'Did he apologise?' Susie asks.

Anna shakes her head. '*He* got angry with *me*. Said he was fed up with my play-acting – like I was making a fuss about nothing. And then Mum came in and said he should leave, and he started shouting at her as well. Eventually, he bundled her out and I got dressed. I couldn't bear to stay there after that, so I grabbed some things and got the last Tube.'

'Anna – you need to put a lock on your door,' Susie says. 'On the inside, so you're safe. What's going on in your house is not OK.'

'I don't think he'll like that.'

'I don't see how he can object. Not after this.'

'Do you think it was intentional?' I ask.

She thinks for a moment. 'I don't think he was hoping to catch me like that, if that's what you mean. I feel like it's more about frightening me. Making it clear he's got the power and I haven't.'

'This isn't right,' Susie says, shaking her head.

Anna looks at us. 'You do believe me, don't you?' she says anxiously.

'Of course,' we say together.

As Susie and I sort out some bedding for her, we have a muttered conversation.

'You know that, if we tell the Mulcahys she's here, they'll be straight on to the police?' I say.

Susie nods. 'But if we don't . . . we'll be breaching the CAWN.'

'We're breaching it anyway, just by having her in the house.'

'Well, I'm not turning her away. I can't.'

'We can't let them think she's just wandering the streets, though. What about that app on her phone? Won't that tell them where she is?'

'She keeps it turned off when she's not using it.'

'Well, then – maybe she could quickly text them that she's safe, without telling them where, then turn it off again?'

Susie nods. 'I think it's all we can do.'

Even so, we're hardly surprised when, next morning, a police car turns up. It's DC Karen Eddo again, with a different uniformed officer this time.

'Is Anna Mulcahy here?' she asks wearily when I open the door.

'No.' *I'm lying to the police*, an astonished voice in my head says. How on earth can it have come to this?

DC Eddo looks at me steadily. 'I'm sure I don't need to remind you what the CAWN says, Mr Thompson, given that you were only issued with it a few days ago. You should also be aware that giving false information to the police is an offence under Section 5 of the Criminal Law Act 1967, punishable by up to six months imprisonment.'

'Even so,' I say firmly, 'she isn't here.'

'If you say so.' Eddo glances up at the house, then nods to the male officer. They go back to their car. I close the door and lean against it, adrenalin coursing through me.

'Well done,' Susie says quietly.

I exhale. 'Where is she?'

'In the top bedroom. I told her to stay out of sight until they've gone.'

Through the kitchen window, we watch as the police car executes a neat three-point turn and drives away. But I suspect it won't be long before they're back.

TWENTY-TWO

Anna

After the police go, we have an amazing breakfast, with fresh eggs from Gabe and Susie's own chickens that have been baked in the Aga with chorizo and tomatoes. It's a Spanish recipe – they have a friend with a house in Ibiza that they go to every year.

Then they have to go into London for a big music-industry conference, where Silverlink's doing a showcase.

'It's when you put on a small private gig for people in the business,' Susie explains. 'There'll be a few A&R people there, and Gabe's going to introduce us to some contacts from his old label. I'd much rather stay here with you, but if I pull out now, I'll be letting down the whole band.'

'Of course you should go.' Something occurs to me. 'Could I maybe stay for a bit, though? I've got an essay to hand in today and all my homework's on Google Docs – if I log into a computer, I can just get on with it.'

'I don't see why not.' Susie looks at Gabe for confirmation. She does that, I've noticed. Although on the face of it she's this strong, independent woman, she needs him to OK her decisions.

'Sure,' he says. 'You can use the computer in my study. Just close the front door behind you when you leave.'

'Though, if you're still here towards lunchtime, would you mind letting Sandy out for a pee?' Susie adds.

'Of course. I could take him for a walk, if you want.'

'That would be lovely.' She and I smile at each other. I can tell we're both thinking the same thing: *We get on so well. Wouldn't it be nice if every day was like this?*

When they're gone, I take a moment to enjoy the quiet. This house – it's so vast, so stylish, with gorgeous photo-worthy vistas everywhere you look. Even the kitchen appliances are amazing. The kettle is this special cast-iron one that only works with an Aga. There's an electronic coffee machine that grinds beans at the touch of a button, and the toaster looks like something a professional chef would have.

They both love to cook – exotic stuff from their travels. Not like the baked potatoes and sausage casseroles we have at home.

Imagine living here, I think. Imagine this being your life.

I go upstairs to get my things. The door to the master bedroom is open, so I have a quick peek inside as I pass. There's a big four-poster bed with a beautiful Indian cover. And loudspeakers on floor stands – they listen to music all the time, on a system where the song follows you from room to room. Bands and singers I haven't even heard of, but who all sound incredible.

On the bedside table is a bottle of lube – just casually placed there, like it's as ordinary as the bottles of upmarket handwash and body lotion I can see in the en-suite bathroom. They're so relaxed about physical affection – more like they're my generation than my parents'. You can tell how much they love each other.

Suddenly feeling guilty at peering into their private space, I go on downstairs to the small room Gabe uses as a study. There are a couple of acoustic guitars on stands, one of them a twelve-string, and an old farmhouse-style table with a gleaming Mac on it, one of the big ones with all the electronics built neatly into the screen. That's the one he said I could use.

I settle down to work, but I'm not really working. It's as if I'm looking at myself from the other side of a camera, sitting at my perfect desk in my perfect house, like it's a scene in a movie.

Then I think about what's coming – detention for missing half a day of school, probably a truancy fine as well, going back to the monster's lair, having to face up to whatever punishment or *consequence* he decides to dish out for running away – and I start to cry.

TWENTY-THREE

Susie

The showcase went well. Normally something like that would leave me so buzzed, I'd be the first to suggest we all pile into the nearest pub, but I was distracted by the silence of my phone. It was all I could do not to text Anna to find out how things had gone with her parents after she got back, but I didn't want to come across as an overanxious mother hen.

When we got home, though, I was surprised to hear music. For a moment, I thought she must have forgotten to turn it off when she left, but then I smelled food as well.

We went through to the kitchen. There was a pot of what looked like mince bubbling on the Aga, and the counter was littered with empty tomato tins and a tube of garlic puree. Anna, her back to us, was cooking.

'What's this?' Gabe asked.

She had the music on pretty loud, so it was a moment before she heard him. She whirled round, a big smile on her face. And it was probably because of the music that she didn't pick up on the faint note of annoyance, or possibly just tiredness, I could detect in his voice.

'I've cooked us all supper. Spaghetti bolognese.' Proudly, she indicated a packet of Costcutter spaghetti next to the Aga. 'I'll put this on now. It'll be ready in ten minutes.'

Gabe, who makes fresh pasta from scratch using a hand crank, said nothing.

'That's so kind, Anna,' I said quickly. 'We're both exhausted, so not having to cook is a real treat.'

She beamed. 'That's what I thought. And I took Sandy out for a walk, like you asked.'

'Where did you get the ingredients, Anna?' Gabe said slowly.

'Oh – in Chesham. That row of shops near the Tube?'

'Did anyone see you?'

'Well . . .' She thought. 'No one in particular. No police, if that's what you mean.'

'Yes, that is what I mean.' He turned to me. 'It's one thing to offer her a night's refuge. But if she wanders round the local shops, sooner or later she's going to be seen. And then the police will turn up again – with a warrant, this time.'

'We're all fugitives from justice here, right?' Anna said cheerfully. 'United we stand.'

Gabe took a deep breath. 'The thing is, Anna . . . we really can't afford to get into trouble with the police. Not for an offence involving a child.'

She looked puzzled. 'Why not?'

Gabe went to the fridge and pulled out a bottle of wine. Then he went over to the Sonos and turned the music down.

'Well, for one thing,' he said, 'it would completely screw us if we ever want to adopt.'

She looked at him, shocked. 'You're thinking of *adopting*?' Her voice shook a little.

He shrugged. 'Not "thinking", exactly. We're still hoping to start a family naturally. But, as you know, there have been some issues around that, so we wouldn't want to rule anything out. And a conviction for an offence involving a child would mean no adoption agency would even consider taking us on their register. It's a blanket rule for them.' He looked at me. 'I'm sorry – I didn't think of this yesterday when we were talking about it. It's only just occurred to me.'

'But . . .' Anna said, frowning. I willed her not to say anything.

'I know it must be hard for you,' Gabe added sincerely. 'Us talking about adoption, I mean. But the circumstances were very different, back then. Susie and I hadn't even met when she gave you up.'

Anna frowned again.

'I have fibroids,' I said quickly. 'Benign tumours in the uterus. I had surgery to remove them, but they grew back. It's actually unclear how they affect fertility, so I might just have been unlucky, but . . . I've had five miscarriages.'

'I'm so sorry, Susie.' Anna looked at Gabe. 'I understand. I'll leave first thing in the morning.'

The hurt and rejection in her eyes almost broke my heart. It was all I could do not to enfold her in a hug and tell her we didn't mean it.

'Thanks,' he said.

'Let's get the pasta on, shall we?' I suggested breezily. 'I can't wait to taste it.'

Supper was a slightly subdued affair after that. When we'd finished, Anna asked if she could hear some of the songs from the showcase, so Gabe fetched a guitar and I sang a few verses.

'Oh my God – you're *incredible* together,' she said, looking from one of us to the other. Gabe just shrugged modestly.

She asked if he could show her some of the chords and he helped her make a C, a D, an E minor and a G – enough to play a simple progression. Then he fetched another guitar and accompanied her, going at her speed, making it sound good for her.

He was trying to make up for telling her she couldn't stay, I realised. That was kind of him.

I went into the kitchen and loaded the dishwasher. While I was finding a chew for Sandy, to stop him licking the dirty plates as I put them in, Anna appeared.

'Hey,' she said. 'I'm so sorry about your miscarriages, Susie.'

'Thanks.'

She hesitated. 'When Gabe said you might adopt one day . . . There was all that stuff I read in the social worker's letter. Mightn't that be a problem?'

So she knows about that. I carried on with what I was doing. 'It might be, yes.'

I sensed her scanning my face. 'Does Gabe know?'

'Some of it,' I lied. 'Not all the details. Anna, look . . . I've no right to ask you this, because it's to do with him and me. But would you mind not mentioning any of that to him just yet? It's still very painful for me and I'd rather not get into it again right now.'

Her eyes widened. 'Of course. Of *course* I won't say anything. It'll be between us.' She nodded eagerly, pleased I was entrusting her with something so personal.

TWENTY-FOUR

Susie

I was in the bathroom, taking off my make-up, when Gabe came in. He perched on the side of the bath.

'I hope I wasn't too hard on her earlier. I was just a bit surprised to find her still here. I know she meant well.'

I smiled at him in the mirror. 'It was fine. And thanks for showing her those chords.'

'Yes . . .' He looked troubled. 'That's what I wanted to talk to you about, actually. When I was showing her – well, you saw how I did it. I got behind her and moved her fingers into the right position.'

I nodded. 'Sure.'

'And then, later, when you were clearing up, I taught her a couple more. But, as I was showing her how to make an A, she kind of . . . pressed herself against me.'

I frowned. 'In what way?'

'It was tiny. It could almost have been accidental. But I don't think it was. There was just this . . . slightly unnecessary contact between her back and my chest. And I can't help putting it together with me telling her earlier that she can't stay.'

'Jesus,' I said, perturbed. I exhaled. 'I read that can happen sometimes, though – when girls have been in abusive situations, I mean. Subconsciously, they think that's the only way to interact with men. If anything, it's just more proof that we need to get her away from there.'

'Marcus did say something along the same lines,' he admitted. 'But as for getting her away from them ... I just don't see how we can. Today's proved we can't simply hide her away. And what about going to school? I know she hates it there, but we can't really condone her bunking off.'

'Perhaps we should speak to a lawyer. See if we've got any wiggle room with that CAWN thing.'

He nodded and got to his feet. 'I'll see if the firm who did our conveyancing has anyone.'

'And – Gabe?'

He turned.

'What you said earlier, about keeping the possibility of adoption open ...' I took a deep breath. 'I'm not actually sure I could do that. Adopt, I mean.'

'Oh.' He was quiet for a moment. 'But you've always said—'

'I know. But things are different now I've met Anna again. If we adopted, I think a part of me would always be looping on the birth mother – wondering if she was suffering the way I had. It would feel all wrong, somehow.'

'OK,' he said slowly. 'Does that mean you'd be happy to be arrested for breaking the CAWN?'

'I don't know ... In principle, yes, if it helps Anna. But not if the police are simply going to take her away again anyway. Let's get some legal advice and take it from there.'

He nodded. 'Sure. Date night?'

'Date night,' I confirmed brightly. The schedule was the schedule, even though both of us were knackered.

Gabe went into the bedroom. I turned back to the mirror to finish taking off my make-up. I met my own eyes in my reflection and felt slightly sick at just how easy it was to lie to him.

TWENTY-FIVE

Gabe

Next morning, Anna heads – a little reluctantly – off to school, Susie goes to band rehearsal and I hole up in my studio, noodling over a few ideas. As so often when I'm writing, time does something strange, and it's with some surprise that I look up, see Susie waving through the panel in the door, and realise it's lunchtime.

I play her what I've got so far and she nods. 'It's beautiful.'

'It might be another one for Silverlink. I haven't written you anything for a while.'

'That would be great.' She seems distracted. 'Gabe ... I may have thought of a way to get Anna away from the Mulcahys. I should warn you, though – it would be a pretty big deal.'

'What is it?'

'We could send her to my old school – Jordans. As a boarder.'

'Woah – that *is* big.' I'm struggling to get my head round this. 'You mean, we'd pay the fees?'

'Yes. It's not cheap, but they have an amazing performing-arts programme and the whole ethos there is the complete opposite of that sweatshop they've got her at. And the beauty of it is, all the inspections and so on rate it as Outstanding in every respect, including academically. The Mulcahys could hardly object to her being given an incredible opportunity like that.' Susie crosses to the computer I do my composing on. 'Come and see.'

The pictures on the school's website show farm buildings, potteries, an Arts-and-Crafts library and a stunning theatre in a converted barn, all populated by girls in flowing long skirts and handsome boys in jeans and polo shirts. It looks, I have to agree, pretty idyllic.

I read some of the accompanying text.

> *Jordans was founded in 1910 as an alternative to other public schools of its time. Where most imposed rigid standards of obedience and conformity, Jordans fostered independent thinking, idealism and self-belief...*

There's a tab marked *Timetable*. I click on it.

> *Lessons start at 9.45 a.m. Teenagers' circadian rhythms differ from adults', with the last phase of sleep being the most important for consolidation of learning. We prefer to wait until our students' brains are at their most receptive, rather than force them to fit in with an adult-centred schedule...*

'Wow,' I mutter. I click on *Activities*.

> *There are three activity slots during the day. Students are expected to self-organise these into sessions supporting 'head, hand and heart'.*

'Bash', held twice weekly, is the equivalent of assembly in a more traditional school. At the end of Bash, each student shakes the hand of every member of staff and addresses them by their first name, fostering a sense of community that reflects our motto, 'Kinder together'.

'OK,' I say, sitting back. 'It seems great. Frankly, I'd quite like to go there myself. How much does it cost?'

'The fees are on the next page.'

I click again, and my jaw drops. The fees are £38,900 a year. I do a quick calculation. It will cost around £120,000 of pre-taxed income to send Anna there for sixth form.

'What about holidays?' I ask. 'She'd have to go home then.'

'They have loads of foreign kids. Even in my day, some stayed for half terms and so on.'

For which there would undoubtedly be an extra charge.

'Suze . . .' I say helplessly. 'I mean – we're well off, but we still have a mortgage, and this would be more than we've ever spent on anything.'

'We could sell this place,' she says quietly. 'We don't actually need six bedrooms, do we? And the holidays in Goa and so on . . . I'd far rather know Anna's safe.'

'Right.'

I suppose I've never really thought through all the implications of this reunion between Susie and Anna. Initially, I'd thought they might make friends, perhaps even have some kind of relationship. I'd been prepared for that, though I'd still have worried about the effect it might have on Susie emotionally. It had never occurred to me that she could end up reshaping her whole life around it.

And mine as well.

I look round my little studio, every piece of equipment hand-picked by me and purpose-built into the space. True, it cost almost as much as two years at Jordans, but it's how I make my living.

But, of course, Susie went to that school herself – unlike me, who went to the local secondary. A school like that doesn't seem like something reserved for a tiny, privileged elite to her. It seems completely normal.

She looks at me. I know what she's thinking: *Two nights ago, you promised we were in this together.*

'Look, let me think about it,' I say. 'Maybe there's another way. Maybe I could sell the Banksys.'

'Thank you,' she says, and I realise I'd been hoping she'd say, *No, that's too much.*

TWENTY-SIX

Gabe

That afternoon, I get hold of a family-law solicitor. He confirms what we've been suspecting – we have absolutely no rights over Anna whatsoever, and zero chance of acquiring any. We can ask Social Services to open a safeguarding investigation, but they'd have to conclude she's at risk of significant harm before they'd remove her – and, even if they did, it would only be to put her in emergency foster care or a children's home for adolescents. 'And outcomes for teenagers in those places are generally not good,' the solicitor warns. 'She may be better off riding things out where she is. As for the CAWN, I certainly wouldn't advise any client of mine to breach one without a very good reason.'

I go to tell Susie the depressing news. Silently, she turns her phone towards me. On the screen is a message from Anna.

Home now. All kicked off. Pretty shit actually

And I can't help but see the reply Susie sent back, moments later.

So so sorry. Thinking of you. We're always here if you need us Xx

About seven that evening, the doorbell rings.

We look at each other. Susie says quietly, 'That might be her.'

I go to the front door. But it isn't Anna, this time. It's Ian Mulcahy.

'I'm giving you one last chance,' he says furiously. 'One last chance not to be arrested for child abduction.'

I fold my arms. 'I don't know what you're talking about.'

He laughs. 'Don't be ridiculous. Do you think Anna could resist crowing about it? I know she was here the last two nights. I know you've been giving her booze. And I know you left her on her own while you went off to some rock concert.' He pulls a piece of paper from his pocket and waves it at me. 'I've been given a truancy fine by her school – they have a zero-tolerance policy for non-attendance. So I just wanted you to know – what she's going through now is all your fault.'

'What do you mean, "What she's going through"?' I say slowly.

He looks almost gleeful. 'Actions have consequences, right? Including yours. You know, in a way it's not her I blame – she's only a teenager, she's had her head turned by all *this*.' He gestures up at our house. 'But I can't punish you, so she'll just have to suffer for the three of you, until you all come to your senses.'

It's all I can do not to throttle him. 'What are you talking about? What kind of suffering?'

'She put a bolt on the inside of her bedroom door. Your wife's suggestion, I understand. Well, I'm not having that, not in my house. So I've put one on the outside too. It'll stay bolted until it's time for school on Monday.'

'You can't do that,' I say, outraged.

'I think you'll find I can. It's called justified deprivation of liberty and it can be done when those with parental responsibility consider it necessary. She's a runaway, remember?'

Behind me, Susie has come to the door and is listening too. I make a sudden decision. 'Ian . . . surely you must see this isn't working. Sooner or later, one of us is going to do something we'll regret. We think Anna should go to a boarding school. Jordans, for example – it's where Susie went. We'll pay, of course. We think, when you've had a chance to consider it, you'll realise it's a good idea – one that'll protect you, as well as giving her an incredible educational opportunity. It's the only way we can think of to get everyone out of this mess safely.'

'*Jordans?*' he echoes incredulously. 'The happy-clappy place in Devon where they call the teachers Bob?'

'It's got a very good liberal-arts curriculum—'

'She goes to an excellent school already, thank you very much. I'd put money on its results being better than *Jordans'*.'

'That depends on how you define "results", doesn't it?' Susie says from behind my shoulder. 'Jordans doesn't turn out little robots.'

'And Northall doesn't turn out drug-addicted whores,' Ian retorts.

Behind me, Susie gasps.

'*What?*' I say, furious.

He gestures at Susie. 'Ask your *wife*.'

I can't help myself. I step forward and punch him.

*

He presses charges.

It turns out he was recording the whole thing on his phone. We only discover that later, though. After the ambulance and the police car and the trip – for me – to the police station.

Luckily, I don't lie about anything. My account of our altercation matches his, so I get away with a police caution for assault.

I tell the police about the locked bedroom door, of course. The sergeant who interviews me only shrugs and says Ian Mulcahy's right: there's no specific law against him doing that, although it might be judged a fire risk by the council. He clearly thinks I'm trying to deflect the blame. On the recording, I didn't deny giving Anna beer, or leaving her alone at our house when she should have been in school.

Our breaches of the CAWN will be sent to the Crown Prosecution Service to review, he tells me.

It's late when I get home. I feel exhausted – not just because of the unaccustomed feeling of being treated like a criminal, but because, even after all this, we still have no solution. The Mulcahys clearly aren't going to let us send Anna to a boarding school. And Susie . . . I can't see her giving up. Of the many wonderful qualities that make me love her, her fearlessness and passion for justice are right up there. Once she sets her mind to something, she's unstoppable.

Although, as I'm starting to realise, this isn't only about justice. This is about something buried right in Susie's core that I never really understood before. Sure, we've talked about it, but I never grasped how deep the wound from giving up Anna really went.

Or what she'll do to heal it.

I go into the kitchen. She's got wine open, waiting for me.

'My hero,' she says softly.

'I'm an idiot,' I say shortly. 'I shouldn't have got angry. Now I've put us in the wrong and made things even worse.'

'You're still my hero.' But there's something strangely distant about her, and when she produces some food she's been keeping warm and I ask why she isn't eating too, she says she isn't hungry. I suspect that a part of her wishes she was twenty miles away, in a locked room, comforting a frightened teenager.

TWENTY-SEVEN

Gabe

Next morning, I go to the studio and try to lose myself in work. The song I'm working on is almost finished now, but it needs to be shaped around the lyrics, which means writing some.

You write about whatever's in your heart – you can't help it. So I write about Anna and Susie.

To anyone else, it would just be a song about unrequited love. But if you listened closely, you might realise that the lyrics aren't about someone who doesn't love you back. They're about someone who, through no fault of their own, is out of reach.

But, because I'm an eternal optimist, I give my lovers hope. Those are the songs I like best – the ones where sadness is balanced with the possibility of joy.

> *Some day*
> *The bells will start ringing for you.*
> *Some day*
> *The world will start singing for you.*
> *Some day in the future,*
> *You will find your past . . .*

I lay down a rough demo, then go back to the house to have lunch, checking the letter box on the way. There's a large envelope addressed to me. I take it inside, sling a vegetable pot into the microwave, and open it while I'm waiting for my lunch to ding.

Inside are three or four official-looking documents. At first, I think they must be something to do with my caution.

But they aren't.

I start to read, and my whole world falls apart.

TWENTY-EIGHT

Helen

Dear Sky,

You won't remember me, as you were very young when we met. My name is Helen, and I was your social worker when you were little – there is a photo of me in your life-story book. A social worker is someone who helps parents look after their children and, if they cannot do that, finds new parents for them.

I am writing this letter so you can understand a bit about your past, the reasons why you were adopted and how you came to live with your mum and dad. I'm writing it when you are little, but I've tried to think of the questions you may have when you are older. The exact timing of when you'll get this is up to your parents, but I've written it assuming you're about twelve. Some parts you may find upsetting, so I recommend you show them once you've read it, so you can talk about it together.

I knew Susie, and you, from when you were about seven months old and Susie was in trouble with the courts. From the start, I discussed with Susie our concerns for your care ...

TWENTY-NINE

Susie

I got back from rehearsal about two, my mood heavy. It was increasingly looking as though the situation with Anna was unresolvable. But it wasn't only that. This was bringing to the surface things I hadn't had to think about for years.

As I let myself in, I called, 'I'm home,' in case Gabe was in his study and wanted to join me.

He wasn't in his study. He was in the kitchen, waiting for me, his expression bleak. For a moment, I thought it must be something to do with the police again, but then I saw the documents strewn across the table and my mind went numb.

The paperwork.

'You lied.' Gabe's voice was flat, as if he could barely speak. 'You lied the very first time we spoke about this. You've been lying ever since. You never gave a newborn baby up for adoption. You had a seven-month-old removed by Social Services.' He gestured at the papers. 'It's all there. What you were charged with. The cautions and convictions. Drugs. Child neglect. *Prostitution*.'

'I . . . I . . .' I'd spent so long thinking about that moment, rehearsing what I'd say if it ever came out. But now the time had finally come, it was nothing like I'd imagined and I couldn't find any words, let alone the right ones. 'I was ashamed. I'm not excusing it but surely you can understand this wasn't something I volunteered to just anyone—'

Gabe flinched and I realised that had come out all wrong.

'Wait,' I said desperately. 'That night – when you found me crying – I told you the only version I could bear to tell. And then you told me about Leah, and I realised what you'd been through was actually a thousand times worse. What could I say? That I'd just told you a pack of lies? Perhaps I should have done. But the connection between us was so immediate – so *comforting*. I didn't want to take the risk of destroying it . . . And then there was never a moment when I *did* want to risk it. I was falling in love with you so quickly, and I couldn't bear to be the one to kick that to pieces.'

'You *married* me.' He looked baffled as well as hurt. 'Surely you can see that, before you spoke those vows, you had an obligation to tell me that you had a criminal record.'

He was right, of course, and it was self-disgust, not self-pity, that made me start to cry. 'I didn't want to face up to it. Being with you – it was like a fairy tale, Gabe. It still is. It felt like I'd been able to wipe the slate clean and start a new life. A ghost kingdom, I suppose. I'm sorry. I'm so sorry.'

'And that's the real reason you weren't prepared to think about adoption.' He gestured at the papers. 'You can't adopt. It would show up on a DBS check, wouldn't it?'

I nodded, unable to speak.

'So – another lie. And Anna knows. It's all in the letter the social worker left for her. Did you ask her not to say anything?'

I took a deep breath. 'Yes.'

He reeled as if I'd hit him.

'Gabe,' I said. 'Please . . . I love you.'

He looked at me, and I recoiled from the desolation and heartbreak in his eyes.

He didn't say it back.

I was twenty. I'm not excusing it. I'm just saying what happened.

I was hanging around musicians and getting the occasional gig as a backing singer. But backing singers are two a penny and – in those days, anyway – part of the unspoken deal was that you brought plenty of fun to the party. And I brought a *lot* of fun. Often in the form of condoms and cocaine.

It was a condom splitting unnoticed that resulted in my pregnancy – also unnoticed, until it was way too late.

Luckily, I hadn't been partying quite so much in the months before I found out. And then I stopped completely until Sky was born. It was only afterwards, trying to deal with the pressure of sleepless nights and session-filled days, that my coke use crept up again.

One day, I dropped in on my dealer – a pretty routine thing for me. I was picking up eight grams, because most of the band I was working with at the time had heard where I was going and wanted some too. I had Sky with me, but she was asleep.

It turned out the price had gone up since my last visit, and I didn't have the extra cash on me. But the dealer said he'd let me have it if we went to bed.

It wasn't like we'd never done that before. For a very brief period, before I came to my senses and realised what a lowlife he was, we'd actually been together. And I was desperate to walk out with that coke.

I didn't want Sky waking up and seeing us, so I put her in the next room. Stupid, I know. She was six months old. Even if she *had* woken up, she couldn't possibly have understood. But I was ashamed.

I didn't even hear the police burst in downstairs. It wasn't me they were after, of course. They'd simply been waiting to get the dealer in the middle of a transaction. The fact it was a big one was just a bonus.

Eight grams ... The duty solicitor explained to me how that looked like way too much for personal use. That it looked like possession with intent to supply, in fact.

Maximum sentence for supplying class-A drugs: life imprisonment.

He advised me not to tell them I was collecting it for friends – that would still count as supply. Better to say I had a really big coke problem and it was all for me.

By then, I was desperate to see Sky again – the police had taken her away in a separate car after the raid. When they asked if I'd cooperate by giving evidence against the dealer, I said of course, if it meant I'd get her back.

They said they couldn't make promises, but it would all help.

But first they issued me with a caution for soliciting, based on the fact I'd exchanged sex for drugs. My lawyer objected, but there's no right of appeal with prostitute cautions and no criminal offence needs to have been committed. If a single police officer decides to slap you with one, they can.

Looking back, it was all part of their strategy to pressurise me, so I wouldn't try to wriggle out of giving evidence.

But then I was told the emergency foster carer they'd taken Sky to had found a bruise on her. She was just starting to crawl, but they said it couldn't be from that. I felt sick – I'd only left her alone for ten minutes.

Next day, I had an interview with a social worker. She wanted to know who'd been hurting my baby. When I said no one, she looked at me with utter contempt. I realised later I should have made something up – that I'd dropped a bottle of formula on her or something. Saying I didn't know made it look like I didn't care – or, even worse, that I had something to hide.

First, there was an Emergency Protection Order, then an Interim Care Order, then a Section 37 report and, finally, a hearing in the family courts. By then, I'd pleaded guilty to possession, for which I got a suspended sentence, and accepted a caution for child neglect. I'd also got clean. The fear of losing Sky was more than enough to make me do that, but of course I had to prove it to the court. I took regular blood and hair tests. There was an agonising mix-up when a test done after a gig where a stylist had used alcohol-based hair spray came back positive, and by the time I got it redone it had already been entered into evidence.

Even so, my solicitor thought we had a very good chance.

But that year, 2007, was the year when everything changed in the social care system. A seventeen-month-old known as Baby P died after suffering months of appalling injuries, during which time he'd repeatedly been seen by Haringey Social Services. There was, quite rightly, a massive outcry. Perhaps less fairly, social workers were blamed for not removing babies soon enough.

Suddenly, the pendulum swung the other way, and the whole system started erring on the side of caution.

It still hasn't fully swung back. In the years following Baby P, there were more forced adoptions in the UK than the rest of Europe put together. There still are. But that's another story.

When a local authority goes to court for a Placement Order, they throw everything at it – they don't want to lose. The fact I'd said I had a massive cocaine habit was used as evidence that I'd almost certainly relapse one day, even if I was currently clean. Sky was 'at risk of future harm'. It's like locking up a burglar for life because you can't be sure he'll never reoffend.

At my hearing, the judge accepted all the social workers' recommendations. I was told Sky was being placed on a fast-track, foster-to-adopt scheme. I wasn't even allowed to say goodbye to her.

Even after years of therapy – yes, it wasn't only the miscarriages Rowena helped me with – I still find it almost impossible to describe my feelings about that. The grief. The shame. The sense of total, overwhelming failure. I'd lost my little girl as surely as if she'd died in a car accident, and I didn't even have a body to bury.

Of course, none of that excuses why I didn't tell Gabe as soon as we started getting serious. But – my God, the stigma. Telling someone that you are one of those appalling, uncaring, drug-addled mothers whose babies were actually taken away from them and given to someone else to parent – how do you even begin to do that?

Right from the start, I wanted a family with this man – wanted it more than anything. As part of that conversation, how do you bring up the fact that you have a caution for child neglect?

Rowena said something once, when I was talking to her about it. She said, 'Sometimes it's easier to talk about your feelings with someone you don't have feelings for, because you don't risk being judged by them. But sometimes it's a risk we have to take. You fear telling Gabe the truth will destroy his love for you. But you should also fear what not telling him might do to *your* feelings for him.'

It was such a wise statement that I relayed it to Gabe – well, some of it, anyway. It was my way of sharing without actually telling, I guess.

And the trouble with not telling was that I got comfortable with it, like a favourite jumper with a hole in it that you barely notice anymore. Every day when I didn't say something and was happy was another reason not to say something the next. I told myself that – to Rowena's point – it wasn't undermining my feelings for Gabe. Quite the reverse: it made him even more precious to me, because I knew how fragile our relationship was. Why hurt him by speaking up?

The lies we tell ourselves, so we can go on lying to others.

Though, as it happened – and I'm still not excusing it – if I *had* told him, I'd have been in contempt of court. As part of the judgement, I was banned from discussing the case with anyone but my solicitor for eighteen years. To protect the privacy of the child, they claimed, though a cynic might point out that it also protected the social workers from scrutiny.

No, there are no possible excuses for what I did, or the fact I didn't tell him. But how could anyone know all that about their partner and not wonder how damaged she really was, underneath?

I even had a secret box Gabe didn't know about: a small battered shoebox containing bodysuits and dungarees for a seven-month-old, along with a tiny sheaf of photos. There was a time when the clothes still smelled of her, but however quickly I put the lid back on, that eventually faded.

After I finished confessing, I went to get it, to show him. So there would be no more secrets between us. And, I suppose, because I wanted him to understand how much it had hurt.

But of course, he was in no state to hear any of that, let alone sympathetically. It would have been bad enough to tell him the truth on any day, but it could at least have been a day of my choosing. Instead, I had to do it on the day he discovered that his wife had been living a lie, and hadn't even planned to tell him.

THIRTY

Gabe

'What do you want to do?' Susie asks numbly when she's finished telling me.

'I don't know.' My whole body feels heavy, like I'm wading through sludge.

'Are you going to move out?'

'Right now,' I say, 'I don't have the energy to even think about that. I just want to sleep. But I'll move into another bedroom.' The advantage of having six bedrooms. We don't even have to be on the same floor.

'Of course,' she says quietly. She indicates the papers, still strewn across the table. 'This was Ian Mulcahy, wasn't it? Payback for thumping him. And to drive a wedge between us. So we won't go on fighting for Anna.'

I manage a shrug. 'So?'

'It won't work, will it?' she asks fearfully. 'I mean – I should have told you years ago, and, however that plays out between us, I take full responsibility. But none of this is Anna's fault. You won't let it affect how you feel about *her*, will you?'

I stare at her. I can't believe what I'm hearing. My wife – the wife I thought had no secrets from me – has just been forced to confess she's been keeping something this massive from me all the time I've known her. And yet her first thought, her overriding concern, is for Anna.

'You're obsessed,' I say disbelievingly. 'Utterly *obsessed*. Don't you see?' I gesture at the papers. 'This is like when Leah died. It's irrevocable. The Mulcahys have won and, in the process, they've probably destroyed our marriage. I just hope you think it's been worth it.'

THIRTY-ONE

Susie

The next twenty-four hours were utterly miserable. A week before, I'd thought I had almost everything I wanted: a promising career, a beautiful house, a wonderful husband – even a long-lost daughter.

But now that daughter was trapped in her bedroom, cut off from all contact with us, and my marriage was probably over. Everything else – the house, the band, the lifestyle – had been built on sand.

I spent Sunday crying. I tried not to let Gabe hear – I didn't want him to think I was wallowing in self-pity, not when it was all my fault and he was the one who'd been hurt. But when I remembered how glibly I'd told myself that being forced to reveal the truth about my past would be a price worth paying for getting Anna back in my life, I felt sick.

I couldn't bear to sleep in our bedroom on my own, so I moved into a different one as well. Gabe and I only crossed over occasionally in the kitchen, when we were getting food. We didn't speak. It wasn't that he was sulking, or even angry – it was more like he was reeling, as if this news had completely coshed him and left him concussed.

At least he hadn't moved out.

It was Sunday afternoon before I could bring myself to pick up the documents still lying on the kitchen table. Some I recognised – the Care Order, the judge's written ruling, all those horrible, damning reports. And then there was the Later Life letter, as well.

Dear Sky . . .

I hadn't been shown that at the time, so I started reading it. I skipped the stuff about me – it was too painful. I wanted to know about Anna – the period just after the Placement Order, when she went to the Mulcahys.

I had to read it twice before I could take in what was written there. Horrified, I almost shouted for Gabe, then remembered I couldn't, not with the way things were between us. I had to process this on my own.

I stared at the pages in my hand until the type went glassy and dissolved through my tears.

THIRTY-TWO

Helen

You had been placed with Jill and Mike, a foster family who were looking to adopt, so I was very hopeful they would turn out to be your new parents. The care system was very busy at that time and they also applied to adopt another baby they were looking after, a little girl about the same age as you. Unfortunately, as they worked through the adoption process and saw just how much work it would be to have two small children the same age, they decided it would be unfeasible and that, regrettably, they would have to choose just one of you. I don't know how they decided which it would be, but, as you will have realised, they chose the other child. You were two years old by then.

However, we were very fortunate that a lovely family called the Mulcahys had recently applied to join the adoption register. They already had one child, a four-year-old called Henry, but for medical reasons had been unable to have another. They were flexible about who they took, but we could all see that the fit with you would be a good one, both because they were hoping for a little girl to complete their family, and because they had experience of dealing with the needs of a child your age. We arranged for them to come and meet you at Jill and Mike's house, and I am pleased to be able to tell you that it was love at first sight! Your mum has told me how she first saw you through the wavy glass of Jill and Mike's front door as you ran to let them in, and how her heart filled with happiness when you excitedly shouted, 'Hello!' You played with her and the toys she had brought almost immediately, and at the end of that first session you took Jenny's hand as she was leaving and tried to go home with her that very same day. Of course, it was not quite that simple, but we were able to complete the process in record time, and you moved in with them six weeks after your third birthday . . .

THIRTY-THREE

Susie

I let the papers fall to the table. Dimly, I heard Gabe coming into the kitchen. He went towards the fridge, then stopped. I could sense him watching me, but I didn't look up. I didn't deserve any sympathy from him, not after what I'd done.

But he gave it, anyway. This man I'd lied to, and betrayed by my omissions, and generally treated like shit, was so fucking bighearted he actually came over and put his hand on my shoulder.

'What is it?' he said quietly.

I pointed to the letter. 'She was *three*. She was rejected by her first family and she didn't go to the Mulcahys until she was *three*, for Christ's sake.'

'Jesus. And you didn't know?'

I shook my head. There was a roll of kitchen towel on the table and I pulled some off to dry my eyes. 'That poor girl. I fucked her up even more than I realised.'

Gabe sighed. 'Look ... I'm hurt right now, and my pride's wounded, and on top of that I feel like an idiot because I never even suspected what you told me yesterday. But upstairs, just now ... I was asking myself what *I* would have done, in your shoes. And I can understand how, if you've done something you're ashamed of, it would be really, really hard to tell the person you love, particularly if you aren't sure yet how much they love you back.'

He sounded so serious that I glanced up at him. 'You mean – there are things like that with you? Things you haven't told me?'

He hesitated. 'I wasn't always tucked up by nine on tour. There was a period, after Donna and I split up, when I was pretty indiscriminate.'

I waved the confession away. In our business, that went with the territory, and, if we were going to compare one-night stands, I'd probably had far more than him.

'The point is,' he went on, 'I don't want to lose you. Not over this. It's going to take a while to get back to where we were ... if we ever do. I don't think we can know for sure yet. But if it's all right by you, I'd like to go and talk it through with Rowena – she seems good, and presumably she knows the whole context?'

I nodded. 'For what it's worth, she always made it clear she thought I should tell you. It's not her fault I chickened out.'

'Good ... Well, look, that's where I am, anyway. Maybe I'll feel differently as time goes by, but I'm going to try to make this work.'

More tears came to my eyes. But these were different from all the other tears I'd cried that day. I was crying out of relief, and love, and astonishment at how generous and compassionate this man was. 'I don't deserve you.'

'Well, you're stuck with me. Can't get rid of me that easily.'

I got up to hug him. And him putting his strong arms around me and squeezing me had never felt so good.

THIRTY-FOUR

Gabe

That conversation clears the air, but, even so, for the rest of the day, we tiptoe around each other. In the morning, I hear Susie quietly cancelling rehearsal. Making herself available, I guess, in case I want to talk again.

But I can't talk, not yet. I still feel like I'm sleepwalking.

Making music's impossible, so I listen to some old favourites instead. Songs I haven't put on for twenty years. Songs from before I knew Susie, though I don't know if that's significant.

But gradually I feel the gluey, leaden feeling lightening. The shock and sense of betrayal are still there, but I'm no longer just going through the motions.

I call Rowena to book an appointment. She doesn't ask what it's about, but neither does she sound surprised.

Later, I cook something – kway teow soup, one of our comfort meals. Without saying anything, Susie comes over and starts making the fishcakes alongside me. And that feels like a good step forward too, the two of us in sync, even if not quite in harmony.

In this together.

As I blanch the noodles, I hear the rattle of a diesel engine. I look up. A black cab is turning into our drive.

'Are you expecting anyone?' I ask.

Susie shakes her head, mystified. 'Not me.'

The taxi draws up and Anna gets out. Reaching back inside, she pulls out a large wheeled suitcase.

I go to the front door, closely followed by Susie. 'Anna? What's happened?'

She looks up. 'Oh, hi Gabe. I'm so sorry – I need thirty pounds for the cab. But the good news is, I don't have to go back.'

She's got a piece of paper.

TO WHOM IT MAY CONCERN
This is to confirm that I give permission for Anna Mulcahy to associate, stay with, and otherwise be the responsibility of Susie Jukes and Gabe Thompson. Neither my wife nor I wish to have anything further to do with her.

(Signed)

Ian M. Mulcahy

'But – how did you get this?' Susie asks, astonished.

Anna hesitates. 'Please don't be cross with me.'

'Of course we won't be.'

'Well . . . You know you told me to get a lock for my bedroom door?'

Susie nods. 'And we know he put one on the outside, too, and wouldn't let you out. We've been worried sick about you.'

'I was stuck in there all weekend. I was getting really desperate . . . so I catfished Henry. I pretended to be a girl he fancies at school and said I'd send him nudes if he sent me some dick pics.'

'But Anna . . .' Susie says, perplexed, 'why would you do that?'

'Some of the pictures showed his face as well. First, I emailed one to my school account, so he couldn't just get hold of it and delete it. Then I forwarded it to the monster and said I'd be sending it to the police unless he signed something letting me go. His beloved Henry, abusing his adopted younger sibling. *That* wouldn't have looked good.'

'Anna – that's . . .' I want to say *horrible*, but I'm trying not to sound judgemental.

'I was *desperate*,' she says. 'I hadn't eaten for two days. Anyway, it worked. The monster just *folded*. Like all his bullying was pointless now.'

I make a decision. 'Wait here.'

I go into my study and find my phone.

'What do you want?' Ian Mulcahy says when he answers.

'I've got Anna here. She says you don't want her back. Is that for real?'

He gives a hollow laugh. 'Too right it is. She's crossed a line now.'

'So you're rescinding the CAWN?'

'You're welcome to her.' The line goes dead.

I go back to the kitchen. Anna and Susie are locked in an embrace – their strawberry-blond hair so similar in shade, their pale skin so close in tone, it's almost impossible to tell where one ends and the other begins.

As I come in, they pull apart and look at me expectantly.

'I spoke to Ian,' I tell them. 'He said it's for real.'

We sit round the table and have the soup and fishcakes. Anna eats ravenously.

Susie says, 'Anna, there's something you should know . . . Gabe and I have talked about the Later Life letter. He knows the whole story now.'

Just for a moment, Anna looks surprised. Then she says, 'That's so great, that you guys have talked. I'm really pleased for you.'

Susie reaches for my hand. 'I hated having secrets from him. And I hated asking you not to tell him. That was wrong of me.' With her other hand, she reaches out and takes Anna's hand too, so the three of us are joined.

'I didn't mind.' Anna takes a breath. 'But, look . . . full disclosure. I told *you* a lie, too. A small one, but . . . it's been bugging me.'

'What was the lie, Anna?' I ask.

'That first time we met . . . I told you they put parental spyware on my phone? It was true – but it was actually a few years ago. It was still there in the iTunes account, though, so I could simply download it again.'

'Why did you do that?' I say, frowning.

'I wanted to convince you – to make you realise what they were like. But I didn't want to tell you all the big stuff straight away. In case you didn't believe me. It was basically true – they *had* made me have it, before. Everything else, though – all the stuff about having to go home if I ran out of battery or credit – was genuine.'

Susie squeezes her hand. 'Don't worry, Anna. We completely understand. Thank you for explaining.'

Without actually discussing it, we both go back to our own bedroom that night.

'How are you feeling?' Susie asks as we lie in bed. 'About the whole Anna thing, I mean.'

'Pretty shocked. That stuff about Henry . . .'

'I know.'

'It's just quite . . . *calculating*, isn't it? What she did with the phone app, as well. And I don't know much about it, but could she have broken the law? Effectively, she honeytrapped her brother, then blackmailed her father.'

'But he wasn't going to let her go any other way, was he? Let's face it, she's been more successful in sorting this out than we have. She's shown resourcefulness and initiative in getting herself out of an impossible situation.'

I'm silent for a while. 'We've never actually talked about this – what would happen if she ever became a free agent. Where she'd live.'

Susie turns on her side so she can scrutinise my face. 'We haven't, no. Are you all right with her being here?'

'I . . . don't know. Coming on top of everything else . . . It's just so sudden.'

'She'll be at school a lot of the time. We'll still have some privacy.'

'I guess.'

'And this *is* what we wanted, isn't it? To share our lives with someone. To become a family.'

'I never saw it happening quite like this.'

'Of course not . . . But people do make unconventional families work. Look at Ali and David.' Ali and David are friends who, between them, have five children from three previous marriages. 'Compared with that, this is tiny.'

She's right, of course. But somehow it doesn't feel tiny. 'I suppose I just don't want to get it wrong.'

'You won't. You're too good a person for that. But, Gabe . . . if you do find it difficult, we'll come up with some other solution. I owe you that, at least.'

She says it so sadly that I know it would break her heart. I squeeze her shoulder. 'Let's try to make it work. And if we can't . . . there's always Jordans, right?'

THIRTY-FIVE

Sky

The idea started forming the day they left me alone in the house. The day of the showcase. *Imagine living here. Imagine this being your life.*

Susie wanted that too, I could tell. That time we were watching Netflix, when she said she'd talk to Gabe about sorting something out – that was definitely what she was hinting at. And Gabe mostly seems cool with having me around.

But then the monster got that child abduction warning in place, so we were basically screwed. Because, I quickly realised, the only person who could cancel that was the monster himself.

The solution didn't come to me until after he locked me in my room. For a while there I thought I'd made a terrible mistake, telling him how Susie and Gabe treated me like an adult. The beer. The curry. The whole go-to-bed-when-you-feel-like-it vibe.

The monster hated that, of course.

'You've read the social worker's letter. You know what she was.'

'I know she fought to keep me.'

'The state decided she was an unfit parent then. So it's hardly surprising she's an irresponsible adult now.'

'And what kind of kid did you think the state was going to hand *you*?' I retorted. 'Someone who was going to be eternally grateful to you for being her saviour?'

'We didn't go into it blind,' he said curtly. 'We knew you'd be harder to parent than a normal child.'

A *normal child*. Thanks, monster.

He nodded, satisfied he'd managed to shut me up. 'I need hardly tell you that you're grounded. Go to your room.'

'With pleasure.'

The bolt and a screwdriver were in my bag – I'd got them from a hardware shop on the way home. It was just an ordinary bathroom bolt, so he could probably have kicked it in if he'd wanted, but that's not his style. He likes to be more subtle than that.

As I soon discovered.

A little later, there was a rap on the door, followed by the door handle turning. He pushed hard, then rattled it.

'For God's sake, Anna ... What is this?'

'I've put a bolt on the door.'

Silence. Then, a few minutes later, the sound of an electric drill, and something being fixed to the outside. Six long bursts of the drill. Six screws.

'Good *idea*, Anna,' the monster said calmly. 'A *bolt*. I can't imagine why I didn't think of that before. That'll stay there now for as long as you're in this house.'

And that's when I knew I had to get out of there. No more messing around. But how?

*

It took me all weekend to come up with the plan. My bedroom had a tiny en-suite bathroom, so at least I didn't have that problem, but the only food to hand was some chocolate I found in a drawer.

I tried shouting. I tried screaming. I tried banging on the door with a hardback. Nothing.

Until, in desperation, I thought of the Henry idea and sent the monster my ultimatum. Minutes later, quite suddenly, I heard the bolt being pulled back.

'There. I've signed it.' He handed me the paper I'd drafted.

I took it, not quite believing it. But when I looked, there was his signature. He'd even added an extra line: *Neither my wife nor I wish to have anything further to do with her.*

'So I can go?'

He nodded. 'You've got twenty minutes to be out of this house. If you're still here after that, I'll lock you in again.'

I looked around. 'I'll need some bags. And I'd better text Susie.'

'I'll find you a suitcase. And I wouldn't text them, if I were you. If you give them time to think about it, they might say no.'

He was right, I realised. It was an odd, unfamiliar feeling – to be standing discussing anything with him so calmly, let alone something like this.

Almost as if we were co-conspirators.

But I didn't have time to think about that. Instead, I found myself saying something I never thought I'd say to him.

'Thanks.'

He only nodded. 'Good luck, Anna. I hope this turns out the way you think it will. Though I have to say, I doubt it.'

'Why wouldn't it?'

He didn't reply to that. Which was even stranger. He always has to have the last word.

When I was packed, I paused by the front door. He was standing there, watching me.

'Bye, then,' I said.

He didn't reply.

I stepped outside, and wondered if it was the last time I'd ever do that.

And then . . . when I did show up at Susie and Gabe's, there was this really weird atmosphere. Instead of it being a momentous celebration, they were muted and quiet. I thought maybe Susie didn't want me after all, or perhaps Gabe was trying to persuade her to kick me out. I was feeling somewhat hurt and rejected, though I tried hard not to show it. But it turned out it wasn't that. Gabe had found out about Susie's convictions.

'I'm actually glad your father sent him those documents,' she tells me later, when we're alone together in the kitchen. 'It's been a tough few days, but it's better this way – so the three of us can start afresh, with no secrets.'

Start afresh. I like the sound of that.

She smiles at me, and I feel almost dizzy with delight. *Everything's going to be different here.*

THIRTY-SIX

Susie

I was happy.

It was such an unfamiliar feeling that it took me a week or so to work out what it was. And when I did, a part of me felt guilty about it. Of the three members of our household, two were having urgent sessions with Rowena to work through complex, difficult traumas, both of which, in different ways, I was responsible for.

As for me – well, it was extraordinary how accurate Rowena had been about the effect coming clean with Gabe would have. It was as if, for seven years, someone had been squeezing my heart in their fist, and then suddenly they weren't.

And Sky . . . Having her live with us was indescribable. (Yes – she asked to be called Sky again, and of course we were happy to oblige. It was a fresh start in every sense.) Quite apart from anything else, after so long with just the two of us, having a loud, messy teenager in the house was a shock. Her room looked like the aftermath of some terrible disaster. But she told us that just having a bedroom she could treat the way any normal teenager would was a really big thing for her, so I also looked at the mess and smiled, because I knew the freedom we were giving her was all part of the healing process.

To begin with, she was on her best behaviour the whole time – jumping up to clear the plates, stacking the dishwasher, offering to fold laundry. As if her presence was in some way conditional on her being useful. The first time she got up from the table and unthinkingly left a dirty bowl behind because she was late for school, I gave a silent cheer.

'School' wasn't Northall by then. She'd started going to Hilcham, a private day school in Amersham. Not quite a specialist performing-arts school, but almost. And, while it might not be as liberal or as quirky as Jordans, it was definitely a place that fostered individuality. I could sense, the moment I stepped through the doors, how the students were less pressured, less anxious than in the other schools we looked at.

She didn't talk much about her life at the Mulcahys. I wasn't too worried about that – she'd talk when she was ready. Besides, she had Rowena to help her work through things. Just occasionally, though, she'd mention something. Like, 'Do I have to tell you my marks every day?' Because, at the Mulcahys, anything less than an A was taken to mean she wasn't doing her homework well enough. They'd take away her earbuds and ban background music until her grades improved.

'I'd rather you set your own standards, actually,' I told her in response to that one. 'You already know what you're capable of, so I'm sure you'll feel disappointed if you don't achieve it.'

Another time, we were talking about birthdays – Gabe and I both had big ones coming up – and she casually mentioned that the Mulcahys didn't celebrate hers.

'I just got a card with twenty pounds in it. But even when I was little, it wasn't the birthday that was the big deal – it was the Special Day.'

'What's a Special Day?' Gabe asked.

'The anniversary of me getting adopted. That's when the cake and candles came out. There was this whole ritual of them telling me how lucky I was. I hated the Special Day, of course. It was the day I was forced to remember that I'd lost my real family.'

I put my hand on hers. 'You've found us now.'

She smiled back. 'Yup. Still can't quite believe it.'

As we were talking, Sandy came over and nuzzled us, eager for his share of attention.

'What was he like when you got him?' she asked.

'Well, he'd been badly treated by his previous owners and, for the first three months, he took it out on us. He peed on the furniture, chewed things and howled for no reason. But the shelter told us that, if we just gave him unconditional love, he'd get over it eventually. As you've seen, he's still not the most obedient dog and he tends to run away if you let him off the lead when there are other dogs around. But he's learnt to come and put his head in our laps when he wants affection.'

Sky stroked his ears. 'Hey – that's like me, isn't it? I'm your second rescue mutt. So you'll just have to forgive me if I pee on the furniture.'

'Date night?' Gabe asked euphemistically that evening, as I took off my make-up.

'That's what the schedule says.' I wiped my forehead with cleanser. Then: 'Gabe . . . ?'

'Yes?'

'How would you feel if . . . we paused the schedule for a while?'

He came to stand next to me. 'You mean . . . stop trying?'

'Just for a bit. To see how it feels. And to give ourselves a break.'

He gazed at me in the mirror. 'That's pretty big. Do you want to talk to Rowena about it?'

There was a time when I'd have run anything like that past Rowena first, but I found myself saying, 'Not really. If you're sure you're OK with it too, I mean.'

He didn't reply for a moment. Then he said, 'Yes, I'm OK with it. Let's pause things for a bit.'

THIRTY-SEVEN

Sky

And, just like that, my life has become beautiful.

My new bedroom has big sash windows that look out on to fields and woodland. If I wake up early enough, I can see deer nibbling at the grass. There's an en-suite bathroom with a free-standing oval bath and a separate rain shower. Above the double bed, and almost as wide, is some funky framed art by a street artist called Annatomix.

'We thought it was appropriate,' Susie said when she showed me the room. 'She's a redhead like us, and a single mother. I think her work's great. But you can choose something different if you don't like it.'

'No, I love it.'

I think of what the monster would say. *Street art? That's just a fancy name for vandalism. Who in their right mind would pay good money to put graffiti on the wall?*

I have a new school. And that's amazing too. When the three of us went to look round, you could see everyone trying to play it cool, but even the head, Mr Pelling, was fawning over Gabe and Susie as he showed us the facilities – *This is where we put on concerts, probably not quite as big an auditorium as you're used to, Mr Thompson, ha ha ha!* By the time we got to the classrooms someone had clearly circulated a WhatsApp, because everyone was openly staring. The fact that Gabe was dressed so casually, in G-Stars and Vans Old Skools, just made him seem even more stylish. Susie was wearing a dramatic green mohair shawl that showed off her red hair and although they acted like they weren't even aware of the effect they were having, they both exuded rock-star confidence.

When I started there, all the girls wanted to be my best friend. I spent a couple of days sussing them out, then went for the coolest, Annabel Rogers. Of course, everyone wanted to know why I was switching in the middle of a year, so I've been telling them the truth, or something very close to it – how I was adopted for a while, but Susie and Gabe spent years and years and a small fortune on private detectives trying to track me down. 'Like a fairy story,' someone said enviously, and I had to agree.

That's when I changed my name. A new, better version of myself. I was so not an Anna, I realise now. I was born to be Sky and that's who I'm going to become. Anna's in the past now, along with everything she did.

After I've been with them a few weeks, I tentatively ask Susie if I can get a piercing.

She looks up from her iPad and considers. 'I don't see why not. What kind were you thinking of?'

'Maybe a nostril stud? Like yours?'

'What a lovely idea.' She looks genuinely pleased. 'I'd better come with you, though – they may not do a fifteen-year-old without a parent there.'

A parent. It's the first time she's used that word with me. I have to pinch myself to make sure this isn't all some ridiculous dream. Or is it karma? All those years of shit at the monster's house, balanced out by what's happening now.

We go to a tattooist in Amersham. He asks whether I'd prefer a needle or the gun and I have absolutely no idea which is better. I'm about to go for the gun, but Susie says, 'I had mine done with a gun, but afterwards I wished I'd chosen a needle. They're sharper and you can't sterilise a gun.'

I try to imagine having that conversation in my old life and I can't – it's like my head will explode.

Choosing the needle feels a lot scarier than a gun, though. By the time he starts to sterilise the inside of my nose with wipes and cotton buds, I'm shaking so much I think I might faint. But Susie holds my hand and, when he gets the needle out of its sealed packet, murmurs at me to look at her, not him. Then she distracts me by giving my hand a squeeze.

'All done,' the tattooist says. 'Clean it twice a day with saline solution until it heals.'

I've chosen a stud with a small fake diamond on the end, because it looks a bit like Susie's. It's not an exact match, though – hers is from Tiffany, a gift from Gabe, with a small but really high-quality diamond on it.

'Wait,' Susie says, as the tattooist is clearing up his equipment. 'Do you have another one like hers?'

So he finds another stud like mine and she takes hers out and puts the new one in instead. Then she puts her face next to mine in the mirror, our cheeks almost touching, so we can see the effect.

That's Sky, I think. Sky and her mum, Susie.

And they might only be cheap fakes, but it feels like they're a million dollars.

THIRTY-EIGHT

Gabe

It's about five weeks after Sky's arrival that the idea of a party first gets mooted. The band have a double reason for celebration: following their showcase, my old label has offered to sign them, kicking off with an album of their new material. Then there's Susie's thirty-fifth birthday coming up, and my fortieth, and of course the fact we now have Sky living with us. Susie barely needs an excuse to have a party anyway, and it turns out Sky's the same. They throw themselves into planning it.

Sky didn't bring any party clothes, but one of our unused bedrooms is full of Susie's old stage outfits. They spend a day in there, trying things on – though when I ask what they've chosen, I'm told I'll have to wait and see.

On the evening of the party, I'm making sangria in the kitchen when I hear them come in behind me.

'Well? What do you think?' Susie asks.

I turn. She and Sky are wearing identical gold dresses, scooped low on the chest and high on the thigh, made of tiny overlapping strips that shimmer with every movement. I recognise them from a tour Susie did with a famous rapper, back in 2010. Sky's a little too skinny for hers, and Susie perhaps the reverse, and Susie's strawberry-blond hair is cut shorter than Sky's, but the overall effect is that I'm looking, not just at two backing singers, but at two backing singers who might almost be twins. The identical nostril studs only reinforce it.

'Wow,' I say.

Susie laughs. 'We might break into a little do-wop-wop every now and again.' She shimmies her hands in one of her old dance moves. Sky tugs awkwardly at her hemline, less confident than her mother.

The doorbell goes. 'That'll be Annabel,' Sky says. 'I'll get it.'

We've told Sky she can invite a friend from school. Annabel, it turns out, is almost as pretty as she is, with elaborate braids threaded into her blond hair.

'This is Susie and Gabe, my . . . Oh my God, what do I call you guys?' Sky asks as she introduces us.

'Gabe is fine,' I say, shaking the hand Annabel offers. 'Just don't call me Mr Thompson. That's my dad.'

Annabel giggles, a little nervous.

The idea is that the girls are going to take round the canapés we've made, as a good way to introduce Sky to our friends without any social pressure. We've agreed they can have a maximum of two bottles of beer each. As for drugs, our friends are aware we don't touch them, but Susie's had a quiet word with a few people anyway, to let them know any consumption is completely off limits now.

As the party progresses, I realise we needn't have worried about whether Sky would fit in. The fact that she's wearing an identical dress to Susie's, and their physical similarity, is an instant conversation starter. And, just like Susie, she lights up with the party atmosphere. More than once, I glance across and see her surrounded by people, taking demure sips from her bottle of beer but clearly loving all the attention.

People seem to like her, too, just as they've always liked Susie. As I pass Jack, Silverlink's drummer, he grabs me and says excitedly, 'I was just telling Sky she should be our backing vocalist. How cool would that be? Mother and daughter in the same line-up.' I pat him on the shoulder and move on.

I'm not really a party animal, so it's something of a relief when I realise it's gone midnight and people are starting to leave. It's only then, as the crowd thins, that I see Sky again, swaying to the music. She still has a beer bottle in her hand and, from the way she's moving, she's clearly drunk.

I go and find Susie. 'I think Sky might have had more than two beers.'

Susie looks over. 'Oh, shit. We'd better get her to bed.'

As we help Sky upstairs, we pass Annabel coming down with a young man I vaguely recognise as the son of Susie's publicist. I glare at them, but say nothing.

We get Sky into her bedroom. 'Oh, wow, I love you guys so much,' she murmurs woozily. As we help her on to the bed, she leans forward and, as effortlessly as a cat regurgitating milk, vomits a stream of liquid over the duvet. The sour reek of spirits fills the air.

The beer bottles don't contain beer, it turns out. Both girls have been surreptitiously topping them up from a bottle of vodka they've hidden.

'My drink of choice at her age too,' Susie notes.

She doesn't seem as perturbed by all this as I am. 'Should we take her to A & E?'

Susie shakes her head. 'She's got rid of most of it, and she's conscious and talking.'

That's certainly true – once she'd been sick, Sky recovered remarkably quickly, bursting into tears at the trouble she'd put us to. While Susie helped her into the shower, I changed her bedding. Then we took turns to stay with her, to check she was actually sobering up rather than getting more intoxicated, and Susie made her drink some water before she let her sleep.

'Suze . . .' I say. 'I know this is what you did at her age, and I know your parents believed in letting you make your own mistakes. But are we really just going to let her do whatever she wants?'

'We're not letting her do whatever she wants. We're trusting her to do the right thing. It's completely different.'

'So you don't think there should be . . . consequences?'

Susie flinches. 'Jesus, Gabe. You sound like *him*.'

'But don't all teenagers need some kind of structure? Rules?'

'Why? I didn't.'

I don't respond to that, and she sighs. 'It wasn't lack of structure that got me into coke, if that's what you're thinking. That came much later. And, before you say anything, it wasn't going to a progressive school, either. No one else from my year went off the rails like I did.'

'I guess the question isn't only what you did at her age,' I say at last. 'It's what you want for her.'

'What I *want* is for her to know she's accepted. That we'll take care of her while she heals. Christ, Gabe, you make it sound like she's the first fifteen-year-old to get drunk at a party. When, actually, it's a perfectly normal teenage rite of passage and we're lucky that she felt safe enough to do it here, with us to help her when she'd had too much, instead of in some sleazy public park. So no, we're not going to ground her, or ban her from seeing Annabel, or anything like that. We'll talk to her about the fact she hid vodka in the beer bottles, because that was unnecessary, as well as deceitful and dangerous. But we are not going to berate her or even tell her we forgive her, because this is her home now and there's nothing to forgive.'

THIRTY-NINE

Susie

The morning after the party, Sky slept in. When she did emerge, sometime after eleven, she wandered into the kitchen. 'God, I'm starving,' she announced. 'Are there any of those spring rolls left?'

'How are you feeling?' I asked.

She looked shamefaced. 'Fine. No, I mean awful ... That is, I'm OK in myself, but I'm so sorry for all the trouble I caused.'

'Well, if we'd known you were drinking vodka, we'd have kept a closer eye on you,' I said carefully. 'It's easy to misjudge spirits when you're not used to them.'

'Sure. Annabel said ... But, of course, I'll tell you next time. If there is a next time, I mean.'

Gabe came in. He'd been clearing up since first thing – he likes to restore order as soon as possible after a party, unlike me, who prefers to nurse my hangover over a Bloody Mary and a gossipy post-mortem.

He gave Sky a glance. 'How are you today, Sky?'

'Feeling like an idiot. But otherwise fine. Thanks for looking after me.'

Gabe nodded and turned to me. 'You won't believe this, but I've had some money nicked.'

'*What?*'

He gestured in the direction of his study. 'I had seventy-five quid on my desk and it's gone.'

I was stunned. 'Maybe someone took it for a taxi.'

'Without asking us? Who would do a thing like that?'

'That's *horrible*.' As it sank in that one of our guests had stolen from us, I felt violated. 'Are you sure no one else came into the house? We left the front door unlocked, after all, so people could find their way in.'

'A passing thief? Out here?' Gabe said doubtfully.

We turned and looked at the drive. We're a good ten minutes' walk from Chesham, set back on a small lane. Apart from the occasional dog walker, it's a rare day when we see anyone at all.

'I guess it must have been, though,' Gabe said at last. He gave Sky a glance, and with a sudden flash of insight I knew what he was thinking.

He didn't mention it until later, when Sky had taken Sandy out for a walk.

'She seems all right today,' he said neutrally.

'That's being young for you.' The truth was, Sky appeared to have suffered fewer ill effects from the night before than me.

'That missing money . . . You don't think she could have had anything to do with it?'

'I don't know,' I said honestly. 'But if she did take it, I don't think we'll gain anything by accusing her of it. And, if she didn't, it will fundamentally undermine her trust in us. After all, why would she *need* to take it? Whenever she wants money, I give her some.'

'Maybe we should think about an allowance. So she can learn to budget.'

'I *like* giving her money.'

'I know,' Gabe said gently. 'Because . . . it's like you're giving her unlimited love, isn't it? But in the long run, she needs to stand on her own two feet. Your friend Adrian has teenage girls, doesn't he? I'll ask him how much he gives them.'

That wasn't quite the end of the money incident, though.

On Monday, Sky came back from school late, carrying a bunch of flowers. 'These are for you and Gabe,' she said, handing them to me. 'To thank you for being so great with me the other night.'

'That's sweet of you,' I said, touched. They were only cheap freesias from the garage, but it was a lovely gesture. 'I'll find a vase.'

'And – look.' Proudly, she pulled down her top to show me her shoulder. It was covered in see-through wrap, but underneath I could make out a small butterfly – blue, the same as mine.

I found my voice. 'You got a tattoo?'

She nodded. 'D'you like it?'

'Sky . . . you're underage. *How* did you get it?'

'Oh . . . I have fake ID. That's how Annabel and I got the vodka.'

I didn't know what to say. Getting fake ID wasn't inherently as bad as tricking us over the beer bottles, but it was still deception. I didn't want to come over all wait-till-your-father-gets-home, but I desperately wanted to discuss it with Gabe before I responded.

But Gabe was in town, at a meeting. So I just said, 'I wish

you'd talked to us first. It's a lifelong decision, after all. And the tattooist could lose his licence if it came out that he'd inked someone your age.'

'I didn't think of that.' Sky looked crestfallen. 'Are you angry with me?'

'Just concerned. Of course, you're a teenager, and teenagers make impulsive decisions. I simply want to be sure that you make them sensibly.' God – I sounded like such a middle-aged prig. I opened my arms for a hug. 'Come here.'

When Gabe came back, I told him about the flowers first, then the tattoo, then the fake ID.

He looked up and saw Sky walking past. 'Sky?'

She came in. 'Yes?'

'How much did the tattoo cost?'

'Um – ninety quid.'

'And the flowers?'

'Ten.'

'And the vodka?'

'Sixteen.'

'Did you take that money from my study?' he asked, without a pause.

Sky chewed her lip. 'Yes.'

Gabe nodded, as if it was obvious all along. I felt dizzy.

She looked from one to the other of us. 'Are you going to throw me out?'

'Well,' Gabe began, just as I said, 'Of *course* not.'

'You don't want me here,' she said fearfully. 'You want me gone.'

'*Why* did you take it?' Gabe asked, baffled.

She shrugged. 'I don't know. It was just . . . there.'

'Isn't it obvious?' I said to him. 'She wants to know how bad she has to be before we turn into the Mulcahys.' I turned back to her. 'Look, Sky. You're safe here and, no matter what happens, we're never going to throw you out. But you have to start being honest with us. Talk to Rowena about this in your next session, will you? I really think there's some stuff here you need to unpick.'

FORTY

Gabe

I'm deeply asleep when I become aware that Sandy's barking. Normally, he's quiet at night, but occasionally he'll be disturbed by a badger or a fox prowling around outside. When that happens, he won't shut up until one of us has been down to reassure him that, yes, we do know about it and everything's fine.

I look across. Susie's sound asleep. Reluctantly, I pull on a dressing gown and trudge downstairs.

Halfway down, there's an uncurtained window. I glance out to see if I can spot whatever it is that's disturbed him. For a moment, I can't work out what I'm looking at – the darkness is full of dancing, glowing motes, like fireflies.

Then I realise – it's burning straw, caught by the breeze. One of our thatched buildings is alight.

I run back to Susie. 'Quick, wake up – there's a fire. Get Sky and Sandy out.' I wait just long enough to see that she's awake, then run downstairs and into the garden.

It's not the house, I see with relief, or my studio. There's an old farm building we use for storage – the hay for Susie's horses is kept in there, along with the tractor we use to cut the grass. The thatch is roaring and crackling, the burning straw streaming skywards in the updraught like a swarm of fiery insects. It's a good fifty yards from the other buildings, thank God. But we aren't out of danger. If it isn't tackled soon, the diesel in the tractor could go up, or some of the burning embers could get blown on to the roof of the main house.

I grabbed my phone on the way out so I could call 999. That done, I turn to check on the others. Susie and Sky are both outside now – Susie's put a lead on Sandy to stop him from bolting. They've put coats on over their night things – Susie a Barbour she uses to walk Sandy when it's wet, Sky an old fishing coat of mine that's far too big for her skinny frame.

What strikes me, though, is how different their reactions are as they look at the fire. Susie looks horrified and apprehensive and appalled. But Sky just seems mesmerised – almost like she's watching a movie, and the flames are the actors, playing out some fascinating scene. At one point, she even takes a few steps forward and raises her hands, palms out, as if to warm them on the flames, before Susie says something and pulls her back.

Then blue lights strobe down the drive as the fire engines arrive, and I run to go and greet them.

FORTY-ONE

Gabe

At weekends, Sky starts meeting up with her new school friends, or going into the West End by train. Sometimes, she and Susie go shopping together, to buy clothes from the kind of cheap High Street chains Susie wouldn't have been seen dead in before. Sometimes, they even come back wearing the same outfits. And when they raid Susie's dressing room for booty from the old days, they pick out clothes I haven't seen for over a decade – denim jackets, leather leggings, tall boots with stiletto heels. When they dress like that, Sky looks about seven years older and Susie seven years younger.

'The Uber driver thought we were sisters,' Susie reports gleefully after one shopping trip.

It's certainly true that they don't seem like mother and daughter. It's not just the closeness in their ages – Susie's in love with Sky, in a way the mothers of most fifteen-year-old girls probably can't be after so long bringing them up, getting to know their flaws and weaknesses, having disagreements with them. This is more like the unconditional adoration she once bestowed on a baby, transferred to a gawky, sometimes tricky adolescent.

Some things are trickier than others. Like the day Sky comes home from school and announces she's now vegetarian. One of the other girls did a presentation about climate change and it's the biggest single difference you can make, apparently.

Providing a vegetarian option at every meal when there are only three of us is obviously impractical. Susie, who isn't a big meat-eater anyway, immediately says she'll go vegetarian too. But I like to cook, and I like meat.

To be fair, we work out a compromise. One third of our meals will be vegetarian, one third pescatarian and the rest will have meat in. As there are three of us, that means the household is reducing its meat consumption by more than if Sky goes vegetarian on her own.

'This is so different,' she says happily, shaking her head. 'With you guys, I can actually have a *conversation*.'

I'm pleased for her, of course. And pleased for Susie, who loves having her around. But, for my part, I'm still struggling with the revelations in the social worker's letter. Having Sky in the house is a constant reminder that Susie lied to me about her past.

Seeing Rowena does help. One of the first things she asked was whether I talked to a therapist after Leah's death. When I said no, we spent our first few sessions discussing that, not the social worker's letter. She helped me to realise that, just as Susie saw in me the possibility of wiping clean the past, in some ways the same had been true for me.

'Is it hard for you,' she asked, 'that Susie's been given a second chance with Sky, while you can never have that with Leah?'

I considered. 'I suppose it is, a bit. Particularly when I see them getting on so well.'

Rowena didn't respond to that.

Something made me add, 'How are Sky's sessions with you going, by the way?'

'I really can't discuss my other clients,' Rowena said with a tight smile. 'Not even when they're members of your household. I'm sure you understand.'

'Oh, I see . . . But, in very general terms, she's good, isn't she? I mean, she seems so well adjusted, given what she's been through. I guess that's the resilience of youth for you.'

Rowena only smiled politely, and I realised even that was going too far for her.

'Of course,' I said, holding up my hands. 'None of my business.'

Somehow, the idea Jack mentioned, of having Sky join the band as a backing vocalist, comes up again.

'Why not?' Susie says. 'If you're serious about a career in music, you might as well see what hard work it is.'

So Sky starts going to rehearsals. It's a while before I drop in on them – I've finished the song I've been writing, now renamed 'Sky's Song', and I want to talk the band through the different parts. When I walk into the rehearsal room, though, I can immediately hear something's wrong. Sky's flat. Not by much, and not all the time – but the rest of the band are professionals. There's no way they can put up with a backing singer who can't actually sing.

Sky's oblivious, though. She looks like she's having the time of her life.

I remember what she said to us, the first time we met her.

My passion's music – particularly singing, but all music really. It seems strange she could have a passion like that, but never realise she wasn't naturally gifted.

I wait until Susie and I are alone before I bring it up. She gives me an agonised look. 'I know, but what can I do? She adores being in the band.'

'Get her some lessons?'

'I'm worried that if we tell her she has a problem, it'll undermine her confidence.'

'Almost every singer needs lessons to begin with. I know I did.'

Susie looks at me imploringly. 'Could you give her a few pointers? Just to get her started?'

I frown. 'Can't she have lessons at school? I thought that was the whole point of her switching.'

'Apparently there's a waiting list. And let's face it, the teacher won't be as good as you are.'

So, slightly against my better judgement, I give Sky some singing lessons. 'Try humming your scales along to a piano,' I tell her. 'If you do that every day, you'll get a sense of what the note should feel like.'

She tries, but she has a light chest and it comes out breathy. I show her how to locate her diaphragm, and how to tell when she's engaging it properly.

'Bizarre as it sounds, one of the best ways to strengthen it is to imagine you're straining on the toilet. Put your hand on your stomach, just above the belly button, and push out. But keep your shoulders still.'

By the end of the first session, I've got her doing lip trills. It isn't that her voice is actually bad. It's more about her ear being untrained. And the truth is, she's probably left it too late to start learning.

She still talks about going to college to study music, though. In her head, standing behind the microphone is the beginning of a glittering career.

More than once, Ian Mulcahy's words come back to me: *Our job is to give them boundaries and consistency and an education that equips them for the real world, not try to be their best friend or encourage them to live in cloud cuckoo land.* At some point, we're going to have to tackle the difficult issue of what Sky will do with her life. Because the truth is, it probably won't be music.

I still think about the Mulcahys sometimes. The more I reflect on it, the more something feels odd about the way Ian Mulcahy gave her up like that – throwing her out of the house so abruptly, without a second thought. I'm no expert on bullies, but don't they usually cling to the power they have over their victims? He'd already succeeded in getting Sky's accusation against him dismissed as fabricated, after all – wouldn't he be able to do the same with the one against Henry? It doesn't quite add up, somehow.

I can't help wondering if we've really heard the last of him, or whether this is all part of some plan we haven't fully understood.

FORTY-TWO

Susie

The record label managed to get us some publicity. Mostly with bloggers to begin with, but, as momentum built behind the upcoming album, with a few professional journalists as well.

I did an interview over Zoom with Fi White, who wrote pieces about women in the industry for *NME*. I was pleased when she said she'd been keeping tabs on Silverlink since we started – she even came to the Roundhouse gig.

'There was one point, a couple of numbers in, where you looked like you'd seen a ghost,' she commented. 'Did you forget the lyrics?'

'No, it wasn't . . .' I hesitated, because, although I didn't intend Sky's existence to be some big secret, I hadn't asked her yet if it was all right to talk about her. 'I'd just seen someone from my past. But I'd need to check in with them before I say any more.'

'Of course,' she said, nodding.

We talked about the album for a while. It was only after that, right at the end, that she said, 'And Susie . . . I have to ask this. What's your reaction to the rumours about Gabe?'

'What rumours?' I said, confused.

'Well . . .' Fi looked a little uncomfortable. 'He's been named on a whisper network as someone who behaved inappropriately with young fans.'

'*What?*' I was so blindsided that for a moment, I couldn't speak. But then I realised I had to – that silence might be taken for tacit agreement. 'That's ridiculous. Gabe would never do something like that.'

'Wandering Hand Trouble had quite a reputation,' she reminded me.

'A couple of them, yes. But not Gabe. And the stories were mostly about the fans, from what I recall – how desperate they were to reach the boys, sneaking into their hotel rooms pretending to be room service, that kind of thing.'

'But that wouldn't excuse sexual contact if the fans were underage, would it?' Fi said evenly.

I felt my blood turn icy. 'I would never condone underage sex. Neither would Gabe.'

'What about using his fame and the platform his music afforded him to get young fans just slightly over the age of consent into bed? Is there a grey area there, do you think?'

'Well . . .' I suddenly remembered what Gabe had said, when I confessed to lying about Sky: *I wasn't always tucked up by nine on tour.*

Oh Gabe, have you done something terrible? Or – because that was almost unthinkable – something that perhaps wasn't thought to be quite so terrible then, but would be seen that way now?

'Yes, there's a grey area,' I said at last. 'And, as a female vocalist who's been around for a while, believe me, I've seen the worst of our industry as well as the best.'

Fi looked up. 'You've had some bad experiences personally? Are you prepared to name names?'

'In those days, we just had to deal with it and move on,' I said limply. 'I'm glad things are changing, but it was a whole culture that was at fault, not just a few individuals.'

Fi wrote that down. 'Got it . . . So, anyway, you're standing by Gabe?'

The phrase was so leading that I almost snapped at her. But, of course, she was only trying to get a soundbite out of me. 'You make it sound like I need to. What's he meant to have done, exactly?'

'I guess that's what I have to find out,' Fi said with a quick smile. 'I'll come back to you for a reaction if I do, of course.'

FORTY-THREE

Susie

No one from the record company was sitting in on the interview, but when I told them about it, all hell broke loose.

Their chief executive and head of PR got on a call with me. 'If we put out a statement now, it'll only make things worse,' the PR guy said. 'Better to wait and see what she digs up, then have Gabe issue an apology.'

'For what?'

'That's what you need to ask him,' the CEO said grimly. 'We'd like to know what we're dealing with here.'

Gabe put his head in his hands.

'Yes, there were fans. Not as many as the rest of the band. But enough.'

'Young fans?'

'All our fans were young when we started – you know that. Christ, I was seventeen when we did our first tour. There was less of an age difference between me and most of our audience than there is between you and me.'

'Could . . .' I hardly knew how to ask this. 'Could some of them have been underage?'

He looked anguished. 'No. I mean, I'd never knowingly . . . But it wasn't like they'd have told me. And I couldn't exactly ask for ID.'

I sighed. 'You do realise how bad this could look?'

'Yes. And I'm sorry if it messes things up for you.'

We both knew that publicity about something like this – even if it related to events twenty years ago – could derail Silverlink's PR launch. Or, just as likely, make the record company decide we were too risky to be worth investing their time and money in.

'Well . . . Let's hope Fi doesn't find anything. She's a reputable music journalist, after all, not some dirt-digging scandalmonger. And Gabe . . . I hope it goes without saying that, whatever happens, I'll support you. I know you'd never do anything toxic.'

'Thank you.' But he still looked troubled. 'Do we tell Sky?'

I thought for a moment. 'We probably have to. After all, some of your fans would have been the same age she is now.'

'OK,' Gabe said. He looked sick. 'But you might have to do most of the talking.'

So we sat Sky down and broke the news that a journalist was digging around in Gabe's past, based on some unsubstantiated rumours.

She took it worse than I'd expected – she burst into tears and ran out of the room. Gabe and I exchanged glances.

'I guess it's all very close to home for her,' he said quietly. 'Given what she's been through.'

'The important thing is that we've been honest.' I put my hand on his, just as Sky came back in.

'There's something I need to tell you,' she said tearfully. 'Those rumours about Gabe . . . It might have been me who started them.'

She'd made some fake posts online, on a website called 'Music Biz Bastards'.

'I just . . . I wasn't sure if you'd turn out to be like *him*. I thought I was being clever . . . I thought, if I posted under a false name saying you'd done something bad, maybe someone would say it happened to them, too. And when there was nothing . . . I thought I should just make absolutely sure. So I added another.'

'And that was it?' I asked. 'Two posts?'

Sky nodded. 'A couple of other people have added to the thread since. But it's nothing. Just a few fans you hooked up with on tour.'

I looked at Gabe. 'It may not look like nothing to the label. Or to Fi White.'

'Well, why don't we tell Fi . . .' Gabe said, then stopped. I could tell what he was thinking. How could we say who wrote those posts, without telling her about Sky and her background?

'I'll delete them,' Sky said quickly. 'I should have done it before. I didn't realise any of this would happen. I'm so sorry.'

She looked so mortified that I took her hand and patted it. 'I'm sure we'll sort it out. We're a family now, Sky. We're in this together.'

SCURRILOUS
The Home of Scandalous Rumours

The Big Question:

Which former boy-band member might be in big trouble as past shenanigans with young fans get dragged into the present? Hint: it's not just trouble . . . it's trouble of the wandering-hand variety. Let's see if The Quiet One needs to talk his way out of this!

FORTY-FOUR

Gabe

So we wait for the results of Fi's investigations. There's nothing else we can do.

But, not for the first time, I find myself wondering about Sky's behaviour. Of course, she's very young, but sometimes the things she does seem . . . well, a bit strange. Just like downloading the spyware app to her phone, and the catfishing of Henry, making fake posts about me seems an oddly elaborate way of checking me out.

Machiavellian, even.

But perhaps that's the result of her time at the Mulcahys, I reflect, and that terrible therapy. It would hardly be surprising if someone who had been through all that was distrustful of everyone but herself.

Most of the time, though, she just comes across as a normal teenager, with a teenager's scattergun enthusiasms. A few days after the Fi White conversation, she gets back from school and immediately starts telling us about some indie band she and her friends are into. She gets footage of a gig up on her phone to show us. Four lanky, spotty teenagers, whose skill at applying hair gel is matched only by their ineptitude at playing their instruments, are making a racket in a reverberating basement. To make things worse, either their drummer's out of time, or, more likely, the whole of the rest of the band are.

'They're playing at Koko on Saturday,' she says excitedly. 'There are still loads of tickets.'

'You amaze me,' I say drily. 'I think I'll sit that one out.'

'I'll go with you, if you want,' Susie offers.

'Really?' Sky looks surprised. 'But what about Gabe?'

'He'll be fine on his own. Won't you, Gabe?'

'I'm sure I can manage an evening without the two of you.' I'm being a bit dismissive, I know, but I'm still trying to come to terms with the whole fake-posts thing. Besides, I tell myself, it'll be more special for the two of them to go together.

On the day, they spend hours getting ready. When they finally come downstairs, I whistle. They aren't wearing identical outfits, the way they did at the party, but they've gone for a matching look – black shorts over black fishnets, white shirts, leather jackets. But it's the make-up which really stops me in my tracks – dramatic cat's eyes of black eyeliner and mascara, making their green irises even more startling.

Susie looked like that when I first met her, I remember, on WHT's farewell tour.

They go off to the station in a taxi, and I spend a quiet and, if I'm honest, rather pleasant evening watching old episodes of *Top Gear*. I cook myself a steak – although a third of our meals are still meat-based, we usually avoid beef, not least because of the earnest conversation that will inevitably follow about whether it's better to cull cows immediately to tackle the climate emergency or keep them alive to avoid animal cruelty. I even let Sandy lick the plate, so at least one animal is content with the deal. Do I wish I was with Sky and Susie in some heaving adolescent mass? Absolutely not. I even feel rather smug about the situation.

I'm asleep when they get home. Dimly, I hear Susie in the bathroom, cleaning off her make-up, before she comes and slips into bed beside me. Still half asleep, I move towards her. Her hair smells of gig, a smell instantly familiar to me – a combination of beer, sweat and London traffic fumes.

And weed. There's a faint, herbal tang of cannabis in her hair. Then she shifts away, and I can't smell it anymore.

'You should have seen her,' Sky says excitedly at breakfast. 'Right down at the front, moshing with the kids.'

'Not exactly moshing,' Susie says, smiling. 'Just dancing.'

'And then, afterwards, when we were at the bar, this guy comes up and goes, "Aren't you Susie Jukes?"'

'You remember Dave, who used to manage it when it was the Camden Palace?' Susie says to me. 'Turns out he's still around.'

'So we got to meet the band!' Sky exclaims. Clearly, it had been the highlight of her evening.

'And were they . . . nice?' I ask.

Sky rolls her eyes. 'They were *cool*.'

I glance at Susie, who looks amused. 'They were very charming. If a little sweaty, by then.'

'Look!' Sky says, holding out her arm. Along her forearm is written in black ink, *KEEP SINGING SKY!!* and an illegible signature.

'Is that Sharpie?' I ask. Hilcham School might foster individuality, but I doubt they'll be keen on indelible marker.

Sky shakes her head. 'Eyeliner. And one of them called Susie a MILF!'

'Well, that's nice,' I say. 'At least, I think it is. I'm married to a MILF.'

'Is it your fortieth birthday coming up,' Susie enquires, 'or your sixtieth?'

'Let's just say, "access all areas" no longer has quite the allure it used to.' I sigh. 'Who was it smoking weed, by the way?'

There's a sudden silence. Sky darts her eyes at Susie for guidance.

'We were with the band round the back, and one of them had a few puffs on a spliff,' Susie says at last. 'It really wasn't a big deal.'

Which, given her own past and the trouble drugs got her into, seems a strange thing to say. But if that's how she wants to play it, I don't really feel I can disagree.

I was right about one thing, though: going to that gig was a bonding experience. They start sharing secrets again, only not by text this time. The two of them have muttered conversations in the kitchen that break off when I come in.

'What was that about?' I ask Susie on one occasion, after Sky gives me a look and hurries out.

Susie hesitates. 'Boys.'

I raise an eyebrow. I'd actually been speculating that they were planning something for my birthday. 'Boys?'

'Given the . . . *situation* at the Mulcahys, she never felt she could talk to Jenny about sex. So I've told her she can AMA.' When I look puzzled, Susie adds, 'Ask me anything.'

'Oh ... I thought kids today already knew everything there was to know about that particular subject.'

'The mechanics, maybe, though there's the issue that what they see online is mostly horrible misogynistic male domination. I just want her to understand that it's really all about the three Cs – consent, contraception, communication.'

'Fair enough.' I put the kettle on, then look around. 'Where's the teapot?'

'Oh ...' Susie looks guilty. 'I dropped it when I was loading the dishwasher. Sorry – I'll buy another.'

'No worries. I prefer teabags, anyway.'

'You know,' Susie says thoughtfully, 'our generation ... we thought we were getting everything right, didn't we? That we were just having fun and, if a few people overstepped the mark, you simply learnt to avoid them.'

'Is this about the whole Fi White thing?' I say, shooting her a look.

'In a way ... And please don't think I'm blaming you for anything,' she adds. 'More ... thinking back to some of the men I slept with. It was all so ... transactional then, wasn't it? I mean, I might have consented, but it doesn't mean I was always enthusiastic or even willing. When #MeToo came along, I supported it, obviously, but you and I were married by then and I never really thought about how it applied to my own experiences. But now I'm not so sure ... Maybe Gen-Z women are right to take it so seriously.'

Given that Sky's been having those chats with Susie, it makes it all the stranger that, as I go upstairs later that evening, I hear a male voice coming from Sky's room. The door's closed, but, as I walk past, I distinctly hear the words, 'Come on, babe. Help me out here.'

I knock on her door. 'Sky? Is everything all right?'

There's the sound of a laptop closing. 'Everything's good, thanks, Gabe,' she says breathlessly.

'Great. Let me know if you need anything.' I move on. There doesn't seem to be much else I can do.

'She was probably on Omegle,' Susie says when I tell her.

'Which is?'

'It's a website where you get connected to random strangers. There's a bit of craze in her year group for it, apparently.'

'But . . .' I'm confused. 'Isn't that *risky*?'

Susie, who's cooking, chops some more salsify before replying. 'There are risks, certainly. But they're mostly risks about what you might happen to see. You can end the chat at any time, as I understand it, and the other person has no way of tracing you afterwards or knowing who you are. So in some ways, it's actually less risky than interacting with someone in the real world.'

'It sounds appalling.'

'Most of the things teenagers do sound appalling to adults. That's what makes them appealing to teenagers.'

'I'm so glad I'm not fifteen again,' I say with a shudder.

Susie smiles, but doesn't say anything.

FORTY-FIVE

Gabe

Susie clearly feels we're navigating the tricky waters of teenage sexuality in a successful way. I'm not so certain – but then, what do I know about it?

I'm fairly sure there are still things I'm not privy to, though. A couple of times, I walk in on silences I don't quite understand, as if the two of them have suddenly broken off mid-conversation. And once, I come in on the exact opposite – Sky shouting at her mother, something about Susie not realising the world has moved on and how she needs space. She storms upstairs when she sees me, so the last bit is delivered from the landing, closely followed by the sound of her bedroom door slamming.

I go over to Susie, who's trembling. 'Are you OK?'

She manages a nod. 'I'm fine.'

'What was *that* about?'

'Oh . . .' She pulls away and goes to fill the kettle. 'Sky's got a boyfriend. One of the musicians in that band we went to see.'

'OK . . .' I say. 'How old is he?'

'Eighteen.'

'And you . . . approve?'

Susie smiles wanly. 'She's made it clear my approval's not required.'

'Well . . .' I search for some words of comfort. 'I guess it's like you've been saying. She's becoming more independent, which in the long run has to be a good thing.'

'She certainly is.' Susie doesn't elaborate.

I can't help thinking that what I heard Sky yell has a grain of truth to it. Susie does tend to think of Sky as a younger version of herself, with similar instincts and desires. And wanting more space is a universal teenage demand. It may not be a bad thing if Sky's pushing her away a little.

None of which I say out loud, of course. Instead, I say mildly, 'Your first row. That must be upsetting for you.'

Susie gives a hollow laugh. 'Not quite the first.'

'Really? I hadn't noticed.'

The kettle's boiled, but, although Susie takes it off the Aga, she doesn't make tea. 'Well, perhaps that's because you're always out in your studio.' She catches my look and sighs. 'Sorry. You're right. I *am* upset. And of course we must let Sky have more . . . space. If that's what she wants.'

FORTY-SIX

Gabe

Sky starts hanging out with Ned, her boyfriend. And that gives a new rhythm to our life, as well – being on our own again sometimes, our evenings filled with music and TV, instead of chatter about Hilcham and who said what to a teacher. It's as if we've gone from childhood to adulthood in the space of a few short months.

Actually, I quite like having more time to ourselves. But Susie misses her, I can tell.

On Saturday, I cook for the two of us – slow-roasted pork with a five-spice rub. Susie comes in just as I'm getting it into the Aga. She reaches up into the cupboard for a glass.

'You've got a bruise,' I say, noticing a purple mark on her stomach.

'Oh . . . Yes. Charlie bit me.' Charlie's her horse, a docile grey who likes to show his appreciation for anyone who grooms him by taking small chunks out of them. 'I bruise so easily.' It's true – her pale skin marks at the slightest bump.

'And how has *this* happened?' I ask rhetorically. The Aga

kettle – a massive, solid thing that wouldn't look out of place in a Victorian scullery – has a dent in it.

'Um . . . I think Sky dropped it.'

I look at the flagstone floor. 'Teenagers, eh?'

It's only later, as I'm lining up a box set on Netflix, that I notice the remote control has been mended with black tape.

'This house is starting to look like a war zone,' I comment. 'Incidentally, what time did you tell Sky to be home by?'

'Well . . .' Susie doesn't meet my eye. 'I suggested midnight.'

'"Suggested"?' I echo. 'And did she agree to your suggestion?'

'She said she'd aim for that, yes.'

'That sounds a bit vague.'

'We have to trust her, Gabe.'

Something about the way Susie's speaking – distant, almost robotic – is ringing alarm bells. 'Have the two of you had another row?'

'Actually, I don't want to talk about it.' Susie gestures at the TV. 'Are we watching this or not?'

By midnight, Sky still isn't home.

The last train from London gets in around one. Add a few minutes for a taxi, and she should be back by one thirty at the very latest.

But she isn't.

I go and wake Susie up – I'd made her go to bed while I waited downstairs. 'She's still not here. Do we have any idea where she might be?'

Susie sits up, then shakes her head. 'No. Sorry.'

'I'll phone her.'

'I've already left three voicemails.' She indicates her phone, on the bedside table. 'And she hasn't been reading my messages.'

'This is taking the piss,' I say angrily.

'I did—'

'The same at her age. Yes, I know.' Ian Mulcahy's words come back to me: *Let's hope Anna doesn't follow the same trajectory.* 'So the bottom line is, we think we know who she's with, but we have no idea where, or what they're up to, or what time she'll be back.'

'She may not be up to anything.' But Susie doesn't sound convinced.

'Do we even have contact details for this Ned? A phone number?'

She shakes her head. 'I did ask, but she doesn't want me contacting him. That wouldn't be cool, apparently.'

I make a decision. 'I'm going to look in her room. Maybe there'll be something there that'll tell us where she is.'

'Gabe, wait—' But I'm already halfway down the landing.

Sky's room looks like a bomb site, the bed strewn with discarded outfits, the floor heaped with dirty laundry. I go over to the dressing table she uses as a desk and pull open the drawer.

Oddly, it's full of food – half-eaten apples, packets of chocolate, bread. Almost as if she's been hoarding it. I spot some of Susie's rings, too.

And condoms. There's an open packet of Durex. With – I check – two missing.

I take the packet back to Susie. 'Did you know about this?' I ask incredulously.

She looks at it fearfully. 'I knew she was thinking about it, yes.'

'And you didn't *stop* her?'

'I tried,' she says quietly. 'Gabe . . . she can be pretty strong-willed when she wants to be.'

'So now what?' I stare at her. 'Do we call the police? Social Services? Or just wait for her to show up?'

Susie starts to cry. 'I don't know. I haven't known what to do for weeks. But you have to remember what she went through. *I* did this to her.'

'I think you need to stop blaming yourself and start blaming her,' I say furiously. I go to the door. 'Try to get some sleep. I'll wait for her downstairs.'

It's five in the morning before she gets back.

'Oh, hi Gabe,' she says when she sees me, as if it's the most normal thing in the world. 'What are you doing still up?'

'Waiting for you,' I say curtly.

She walks past me into the kitchen, clearly a little drunk. 'God, I'm parched.'

I follow her. If anything, I'm getting more, rather than less, angry. 'I found condoms in your room.'

She gives me a sideways glance. 'What were you doing in my room?'

'Looking for anything that might give us a clue to your whereabouts.'

'I was with Ned. Susie knew that.'

'Are you having sex with him?' I demand.

'That's none of your business.' She takes some grapefruit juice from the fridge, unscrews the lid and drinks from the bottle. 'Oh, that's better.'

Susie comes in. 'Let's talk about this in the morning,' she says anxiously. 'The important thing is, she's back and she's safe.'

'The *important* thing,' I say, 'is that she's having underage sex, and we're responsible for her.'

'Oh, come on.' Sky points at Susie. 'She had sex at fifteen. And you clearly slept with underage fans.'

'*What?*' I turn to Susie, dumbfounded. 'What have you said?'

'I was just trying to explain . . . why you couldn't condone breaking the law,' Susie says nervously. 'Because of the rumours.'

Sky wags her finger at me. 'Naughty Gabey. Naughty naughty.'

With an effort, I control my anger. 'Yes. We *will* talk about this in the morning. By which time we'll have worked out what the consequences of this are going to be. Because there *are* going to be some. We've trusted you and you've broken that trust. And to earn it back—'

'*Fuck you*,' Sky snaps. 'You're so pathetic sometimes, Gabe.' Taking a step forward, she hurls the bottle of juice straight at my head.

FORTY-SEVEN

Susie

The bottle didn't actually break, but the blow sent Gabe reeling. By the time I got him to a chair, Sky had vanished upstairs.

'Jesus. *Jesus*,' he said disbelievingly. 'She . . .' He looked at the kettle, and twigged. 'Oh, God. Did she . . . ?'

'She threw it at me,' I admitted. 'She missed, but . . .'

'And the remote?'

I nodded. 'That was the bruise you saw.'

'Anything else?'

'She's . . . slapped me a couple of times. Punched me. And it was her who broke the teapot.' It was a relief to finally tell him, but I felt so ashamed that I started to cry. 'It sounds worse than it is. Please—'

'Don't make excuses for her,' he said shortly. 'No more excuses.'

Already, there was a big lump swelling on his head. I went and got some frozen peas.

'How long has this been going on?' he wanted to know.

'A few weeks, now.'

He stared at me. 'A few *weeks*? And you didn't *say* anything?'

'I should have done, I know. But at first I thought it was an aberration. That she'd somehow snap out of it. If I explained how wrong it was—'

'But she didn't,' he said flatly.

I shook my head. 'She just told me to take some fucking ownership of what I'd done. And once she'd started . . . It was like, before, she was holding it in, but now she can't stop herself. Almost anything seems to set her off.'

'Christ.' He pressed the pack of peas harder against his head and winced. 'But she seemed so happy here . . . Have you told Rowena?'

I took a breath. 'She isn't seeing Rowena anymore. That was one of the first flashpoints, actually – she told me Rowena had "signed her off". Well, I know trauma like that takes years to work through. So I called her . . . She said Sky hadn't turned up for her last two appointments. And the one before that, she walked out of. Obviously, Rowena couldn't tell me what they'd been talking about, but she implied it was something pretty heavy. I tried to persuade Sky to go back . . . She said she was fed up with me using Rowena as a substitute parent and that she knew Rowena reported everything back to me. I said of course she didn't. That was when she threw the remote at me.'

Gabe exhaled. 'You do realise this changes everything, don't you? We'll have to get Social Services involved now. Maybe the police, as well.'

'I don't want to lose her,' I said fearfully. 'I just couldn't bear it.'

He gave me a long look, full of compassion. But I could tell his mind was made up.

'Suze,' he said gently. 'I think maybe you just have to accept that you lost her fifteen years ago. I think that little girl is probably gone forever. And we're completely out of our depth here, dealing with the fallout.'

'There's something else,' I said. 'Something I've been meaning to tell you.'

'Yes? What?'

'Gabe . . . I'm pregnant.'

FORTY-EIGHT

Gabe

She's six weeks.

There'd been what she thought was just an unusually light period, two weeks after our last date night. She only realised when she missed the next one completely.

We don't celebrate pregnancies the way some people do – it only makes it worse when she miscarries. So all I say is, 'That's terrific,' and we hug while she weeps on my shoulder.

As I hold her, I say, 'Let's not tell Sky, though. Not yet. It'll make an already complicated situation even more difficult.' I feel her give a small nod of assent.

'And it makes it even more important that we get these problems with her sorted out,' I add. Susie starts to pull away, protesting, and I shush her. 'I don't mean sending her back to the Mulcahys, although we might need to use that as a threat. But we can't be the first people to have come up against something like this – there must be someone out there who can help us. I mean it, Susie. We can't let this go on. Particularly not now.'

FORTY-NINE

Sky

'What does it feel like?' Rowena asked me. And that's the hardest question to answer.

It's not something I choose. It just happens. And, in the moment, it feels like the only thing that possibly could happen. Like when you know you're about to sneeze, and then, after you do it, you can't imagine how you ever tried to hold it in.

The first time I hit Susie, I felt terrible. I'd thought everything was going to be different with her. That the whole reason I hit Jenny and Ian was because they weren't my real parents. Exploding at people was Anna's thing, not Sky's.

Guess it was to do with me, after all. Not them.

And I hated myself for letting Susie down, but it felt good at the same time. Because now I knew I had a release valve. That I could be my real self again. All those times she'd sat with me on the sofa, watching *Mean Girls* and stroking my hair, or squeezing my hand, or hugging me – it felt good for about a second, but then it made my skin crawl and finally it made me want to hit her in the face.

She can't stop herself from stroking me. I can't stop myself from hitting her. How come I'm the bad one here?

Rowena said, 'Have you tried explaining to Susie that affectionate touch is something you'll need to get used to slowly?'

To which my considered response was, 'Have you ever tried shutting the fuck up?'

She just nodded, like she'd been expecting something like that.

'Sorry,' I added. 'It just comes out wrong, sometimes. Like my brain doesn't know what my mouth's about to say.'

'Can you identify the emotion you feel when you become dysregulated, Sky?' she asked. 'As well as anger, I mean?'

Dysregulated. That's the word she's settled on. Nicely non-judgemental, you see.

I didn't answer her for a bit, because it's actually quite hard. What *do* I feel?

'Do you feel . . . *fear*, for example?' she said gently. 'Anxiety? Panic?'

I shook my head. Because the truth is, no. Not when I'm doing it. That stuff all comes before. What I feel when I hit someone . . ..

'I feel fantastic,' I said quietly. 'I feel like Superwoman. I feel like every single vein in my body is full of honey. That time I smoked weed with Ned and Susie, and my head felt all pumped up, like a balloon? That doesn't even come close to it.'

Rowena leaned forward. 'Sky . . . please understand – you *can* change. I know you don't want to be like this. Your behaviours are the result of trauma in your past, not something that's part of you. But changing *will* mean facing up to everything that's happened to you and working through it, bit by bit. Are you willing to go there with me?'

That was when I swore at her and walked out. Because the last thing I want right now is yet another person trying to understand me.

FIFTY

Susie

I'd been frightened, I realised. Not only of Sky and her unpredictable outbursts, but of telling Gabe, in case he demanded that we throw her out. That he didn't made me even more ashamed of keeping it to myself.

Even so, I'd never seen him so angry, not even when he found out about my convictions. That had been hurt and betrayal and disappointment. This was more like a cold, furious determination. It was because he was protective of me, I realised – because I'd been physically abused. And because I was pregnant.

In the morning, he left a message for Social Services saying he needed to speak to them urgently on a safeguarding matter. Then he called the police on the non-emergency number. He explained what had happened and they promised someone would get back to him.

As he put the phone down, Sky came in.

'Well? Do you have anything to say?' he demanded.

'Not really,' she said quietly. She went to the fridge and opened it. The bottle of juice was back in the door. 'It didn't break, then. That's something.'

She took out some yoghurt and sat down at the table. Gabe glared at her. I was willing him not to escalate this, but I could tell how much she was winding him up.

'I've called the police and Social Services.'

'Good luck with *that*,' she muttered.

'You're grounded for a week. And I'm confiscating your phone.'

'You remind me of someone,' she said wearily. 'Who is it? Oh, yes. Things didn't work out so well for *him*, did they?'

With a sinking feeling, I realised I was going to have to be the one to try to defuse the situation. 'Sky,' I began, 'there's a massive difference between us and the Mulcahys. For one thing—'

'Don't kid yourselves,' she interrupted. 'Take away the fancy house and underneath you're all the same. All wanting me to be your adoring little daughter.'

Did she really think that? I tried again. 'We'll never give up on you the way they did—'

I reached across to put my hand on her shoulder and, so quickly I didn't even see it, her arm flicked back and upwards, pushing me away, catching me in the face. My cry was a gasp of shock as much as pain, but instantly Gabe was there, his fist clenched. 'Don't you *ever*—'

'Please hit me.' She looked at him coolly. 'Please hit me, Daddy.' She gave *Daddy* a horrible, sexual intonation.

Gabe lowered his fist, appalled at himself. And at her.

'Well, if you really won't,' she said. She looked around. There was a knife on the table, a five-inch Sabatier I'd used to cut up a melon for my breakfast. As she grabbed it, I gasped, warning Gabe, who took a step back. But it wasn't him she was after. Holding the knife in her right hand, she raised her left arm and pulled the blade across her armpit.

FIFTY-ONE

Gabe

Susie gets her to the sink. The knife's missed the artery, but it can only have been a matter of millimetres. Within moments, her T-shirt's soaked in blood.

It's a statement, I realise, shocked. A declaration of intent. *I'm the one in control here. Because, whatever you can think of doing to me, I can do far worse.*

How do you deal with someone like that? I feel completely furious and utterly helpless, both at the same time.

While Susie's cleaning her up, the police call back. I take the phone into the study and explain all over again. When I get to the bit about the piece of paper the Mulcahys signed saying they no longer want anything to do with her, the detective stops me.

'If there's a CAWN in place and it hasn't been formally cancelled, you're potentially committing an offence just by associating with her. You need to return her to her legal guardians.'

'That's not going to solve anything. I don't think they'll take her back now, and, besides, she won't stay there.'

'Even so. They're the only people with authority to act in this situation.'

Social Services don't get back to me until that afternoon, but they do at least appear to be taking it seriously – the word 'safeguarding' has clearly acted as some kind of trigger. Until, that is, I explain exactly what's happened.

'So is the young person at any actual risk of harm from someone?' the social worker, who'd introduced herself as Kirsty, wants to know.

'No – she's the one doing it.' I've already explained that. What part of this is Kirsty not understanding?

'If she's not in danger from someone, it isn't a safeguarding issue,' Kirsty says.

'Of course it is. She assaulted my wife.'

'That may be a matter for the police, though without knowing the circumstances, I can't say for certain. But we would only make a safeguarding assessment if – Sky, is it? – might be in danger herself.'

'Well . . .' I say, baffled. I'd expected them to take some kind of responsibility, given that Sky had been adopted, but clearly Kirsty is looking for any chance to do the exact opposite. I remember what Marcus said: *When you adopt, you do it for free, and the state basically says you're on your own.*

I think of something that might fit Kirsty's criteria. 'She's self-harming. And having underage sex.'

'Self-harm isn't a matter Social Services are equipped to deal with,' Kirsty says matter-of-factly, as if that's something she has to explain to idiots like me at least once a day. 'You should speak to her GP. Is her sexual partner of a similar age to her?'

'No – he's a few years older. Around eighteen.'

'Well, then. That's a matter for the police. You could ask them to have a word, although they're unlikely to treat it as a criminal matter.'

Through the window, I see a car reversing at speed into our drive – a silver Golf. There's a bang as our front door slams. Sky runs down the drive and jumps into the passenger seat. The car speeds off again.

I look at the table. On it is Sky's phone, which I'd demanded she hand over while she's grounded.

Susie comes in. 'She's gone, hasn't she?' she says anxiously.

'Yes.' I indicate the phone. 'She must have got hold of him some other way.'

Kirsty's ending the call with a stream of platitudes about how the police will get in touch with Social Services to carry out a multi-agency assessment if they feel the situation warrants it. I'm no longer listening. They think she's just a brat, I realise. They think we're just inexperienced, overanxious parents with a typical rebellious adolescent on our hands. I'd been hoping for – I don't know what, exactly, but certainly for someone to take it seriously, for there to be men in uniforms giving Sky a stern talking to and uttering dire threats. The kind of thing that happened to *me*, in fact, when I was cautioned for hitting Ian Mulcahy.

'So now we've got absolutely no way of getting in touch with her,' Susie says hopelessly.

'I'm sorry. I never thought . . .'

'It's not your fault. This is what she's going to do, Gabe. She's going to twist everything.' Susie looks anguished. 'And no matter what punishments we dole out, her need to punish *us* is always going to be bigger. Because, really, what's the appropriate consequence for what *I* did to *her* fifteen years ago?'

'It isn't your fault, either. You don't deserve any of this.' I put my arms around her. But I know that, whatever I say, the guilt she feels can't be absolved by me. The only person who can do that for her is currently in a silver Golf, speeding into London with no phone.

FIFTY-TWO

Gabe

I go to see Ian Mulcahy.

I take a leaf out of Sky's book – I just turn up at his house. When I get there, I send a text saying I'm outside and need ten minutes of his time.

The answer comes back immediately.

> Not here. I'll meet you at the café.

Which only reinforces my suspicion that there's more to the story of how Sky came to leave that family than either party let on.

Ian comes in, takes one look at my face and nods. 'So you've realised.'

'Realised what?'

'What she's really like.' He sits down. 'It's ironic, I suppose. Her nickname for me is "the monster", but it's her who's that.'

'Please understand,' I say coldly, 'my opinion of you hasn't changed. What you did . . .'

His face darkens. 'Look, that therapy was a terrible mistake – I admit that. But Jenny was at her wits' end. There'd been these blissful honeymoon years after Anna first came to us . . . We'd been so happy. I thought there must be a way to get back to that.' He shook his head. 'I realise now, that wasn't the real Anna. The real Anna was the one who bit and fought and scratched and dared me to slap her face if I so much as remonstrated with her. Who told me every day that she wanted to cut off my head and burn down our house. When we found that therapist, it seemed at long last someone had some answers. And they had all these studies, supposedly backing it up . . . How could I say to Jenny that I was refusing to do the very thing we were being told might cure her?'

'That allegation Sky made about you . . .' I say. 'That was true, wasn't it?'

'Don't be ridiculous,' he blusters. 'I was simply doing what the therapist told me to. Everything else was all in Anna's head.'

But he can't meet my eye.

I sigh. 'Tell me about Henry.'

'Well – that's exactly my point. I couldn't let something like that happen to him as well. No doubt you're aware she tricked him into sending her some photographs – manipulating everything, just as she always does. And if that hadn't worked, she'd have moved on to something even worse. I'm sure of it.'

'So you threw her out.'

He shakes his head. 'I didn't "throw her out". I let her go. There's a difference. Her heart was already set on being with Susie and you.'

'As you knew it would be,' I say softly. 'That was why you gave her the Later Life letter when you did, wasn't it? You knew there was enough detail in it for her to track Susie down. I'm betting you even made those same searches yourself, before you handed it over.'

Ian Mulcahy's silent a moment. 'You've got to understand – I was desperate. Jenny was ... Well, you've seen her. Being constantly torn between love and despair – being beaten up on a daily basis by the child you've opened your heart to ... It's soul-destroying. But Jenny never gave up – she never stopped loving her, even though it was killing her. When I found Susie's Instagram page – when I realised she was married to *you* ... The fact you didn't have children, too ... It seemed like the perfect solution.'

'So you encouraged her to go.'

'Good God, no. I did everything I could to force her to stay.'

'Knowing that the contrast between your inflexibility and Susie's glamorous, easy-going lifestyle would propel her in the exact opposite direction,' I say drily. 'Thanks for that.'

He shrugs. 'What can I say? You'll be that desperate yourself soon. Mind you, it was Anna who did most of the work. Telling you she had a passion for music, and that we wouldn't let her have lessons – you've got to admit, that was a brilliant touch. She knew exactly how to play the two of you.'

I look at him in disgust. For all that he's claiming we're in the same boat, I'm not the one who's schemed and lied to get myself out of my responsibilities. 'So what happens now? Presumably you investigated all the legal options?'

He nods. 'There are proceedings you can go through for failed adoptions – "disruptions", social workers call them. That's one route. Effectively, you have to take the local authority to court and persuade a judge it's in Anna's best interests to go back into care. The problem is, you're unlikely to get costs even if you win, the local authority has bottomless pockets for legal fees, and the judge will take a lot of convincing – it isn't *your* welfare or wishes they'll be interested in, only Anna's. I estimated it would cost me at least thirty grand, with no guarantees of success. And in my case, working in education, it would have been career suicide. It's a small world, and who'd want to employ an educational psychologist who was known to have failed as a parent himself?'

'OK,' I say. 'Next?'

'Kick her out. Put her on the streets.' He catches my look. 'It happens, more often than you'd think. And don't imagine she's coming back to us, either. You've made your bed.'

I sigh. 'Did you try any other therapies? Anything evidence-based?'

'We looked – of course we did. We spent a year on the waiting list for Child and Adolescent Mental Health Services, only to be told it wasn't a mental-health issue. The school decided it wasn't educational, either, so they couldn't allocate any funds to it. Everyone clearly thought we were just bad parents who were reaping what we'd sown, and that if we simply manned up and disciplined her more effectively, she'd grow out of it. Social Services even suggested we got a pet – you know, something for her to love. As if *that* was going to stop her. But we got her a rabbit, anyway. She set fire to its hutch.'

'She burned it?'

'Yes. Anna's always been obsessed by fires. Why?'

'No reason,' I say slowly. The fire service never did establish why our barn caught fire. Their best guess was that an ember from a neighbour's chimney must have carried on the wind. It had never seemed all that likely to me – our nearest neighbours are at least two hundred yards away – but, equally, I'd never come up with a better explanation.

That was the night I'd accused her of stealing money, I recall.

'So we were effectively out of options,' Ian's saying. 'In America, they make big claims for wilderness therapy – camping, hiking, that kind of thing – along with various kinds of residential rehabilitation. But you'll understand why I'm sceptical now about expensive American therapy programmes.'

'What caused her to be this way, do you suppose?' I ask, curious. 'Do you think the seeds were sown even before she came to you?'

He nods. 'I'm certain of it. For one thing, she attached to us far too quickly, given how long she'd been with the foster carers – she tried to come home with us the very first day we went to meet her, despite the fact we were total strangers. I didn't know it at the time, but that's a classic sign something's wrong. There's even a name for it – "mummy shopping". And then, when we were going through the adoption screening, one of the first questions the social worker asked us was whether we'd take a child who we knew had challenging behaviours.' He raises an eyebrow. 'Do you see what she did, there?'

'What?' I say, puzzled.

'"A child we *knew*" – their only concern, legally, is what's in the best interests of the child. So if we said we wouldn't take a child who we knew had problems, an under-pressure social worker might decide it wouldn't be in that child's interest for us to be told about them.'

I'm shocked. It had never occurred to me that someone in a position of authority might be so duplicitous.

'Here.' Ian takes a napkin from the dispenser and writes on it. 'This is the name of a support group for child–parent violence. We found it helped to talk to others in the same boat. As you'll discover, one of the worst things is the sense of isolation. "Battered parents" . . . it doesn't quite have the drama of "battered wives", does it? More like the punchline of some stand-up joke. And, while everyone tells an abused wife to just get out, you can't say that to an abused mother. Or father, for that matter.' He nods at the napkin. 'When you do share your experiences, you find there's no rhyme or reason to it. You can be strict, you can be soft . . . it doesn't seem to make any difference, although we found that having a very rigid system of punishments did at least keep a lid on it. It didn't help us rebuild any bridges with Anna, of course, but to be honest, I was long past caring about that.'

FIFTY-THREE

Susie

While Gabe was out talking to Ian Mulcahy, Fi White called me again on Zoom.

She didn't beat around the bush. 'It seems pretty much all the members of Wandering Hand Trouble engaged in problematic behaviour with fans. Gabe wasn't the worst, by any means. But there's enough there to make it a story I have a duty to tell.'

My heart sank. 'What kind of thing are we talking about?'

'For the most part, sex that was ostensibly consensual but which the fans in question felt they had no choice but to agree to, if they wanted to get close to their heroes.'

'OK,' I said. It didn't sound like the worst thing in the world – not great, certainly, but survivable.

'Then there are some sexts that make for pretty lurid reading, particularly when you consider the ages of the girls concerned. Tell me what you want me to do to you and where, that kind of thing.'

But don't all sexts seem lurid, I thought, when they're released to a world that was never meant to read them? 'Go on.'

'And some instances of potentially illegal behaviour, too. I'm afraid Gabe's implicated in a couple of those.'

I felt my blood run cold. 'Like what?'

'Well...' Fi sounded hesitant, as if she was unsure how to frame this. 'When he was in his early twenties, he slept with a seventeen-year-old in Australia. It was consensual and she was of age, though of course several years younger than him. But later, during the tour, she sent him some nudes. He thanked her and suggested she should send more.'

'Right...' I said, puzzled. 'So, what are you getting at?'

'He was in America by then. Soliciting nudes from a minor is a federal offence there, just as it is in the UK. The maximum sentence is seven years.'

I was speechless. Was she really going to hang Gabe out to dry because of something thousands of teenagers did every day?

'There's more, I'm afraid,' Fi added. 'On one of their first tours, a fan claims Gabe slept with her in Dublin. She was sixteen.' She pauses. 'She was from Belfast, so she may not have realised that what she was doing was illegal. But, unlike the UK, the age of consent in the Republic of Ireland is seventeen. She was underage.'

She was underage. The words hit me like stones. There was no getting away from that. You could make all the excuses you liked – it was consensual, he was only in Ireland for a night or two, neither of them realised it was against the law – but facts were facts. She was underage.

'The wider point is, there was a culture back then for bands like WHT to see their fans as easy meat,' Fi continued. 'The boys gave them attention, sure, but in return they expected sex – or, at the very least, sexual interactions. And, while the fans might have consented, it doesn't mean they really wanted that side of it – even if they thought they did, many later came to realise they'd been taken advantage of.' She consulted a notebook. *'When I was sixteen, this all seemed normal, but once I was a bit older, I saw how fucked up it was.* What's your perspective on that?'

There was a part of me that wanted to snap, *Don't you think I haven't had regrets a hundred times after sex? It comes with the territory.* But there was also a part of me that thought of Sky – how young and vulnerable she was, how impressionable. If I could have stopped her from sleeping with Ned, wouldn't I have done that? Maybe it was the territory that needed to change, and it was Fi and her kind, fearlessly making an example of people like Gabe, who were going to do it.

'It's . . . complicated,' I said slowly. 'I'll have to think about it before I say something on the record.'

'Of course.' Fi left a pause before she added, 'You mentioned you'd had some experiences yourself . . . If you felt able to go on the record about those, it would make the piece much more balanced – more directly about Silverlink, as a female-led group in an industry that's still mostly male-dominated, I mean.'

So that was it. She'd go easy on Gabe if I gave her names and dates from my own past.

I said slowly, 'Not every woman wants to go public with her own story. Other people should respect that, surely.'

'So these were quite traumatising experiences? Ones you find hard to talk about?'

'Not necessarily,' I said, sensing the verbal trap. 'Just very private.'

'OK,' Fi said. She put down her pen. 'But you'll come back to me with a quote about Gabe, yes? My deadline's tomorrow.'

I was sitting at the kitchen table, wondering how to handle all this, when I heard the front door open. I looked up, expecting Gabe.

It was Sky.

'Hi,' she said shortly, going to the sink and pouring herself a glass of water.

'So you've come back.' Then, because I couldn't help but be angry with her, I added, 'I've got to give that journalist a quote about Gabe. Because of those posts you made.'

She shrugged. 'Sorry. But there's no smoke without fire.'

I gave her a disbelieving look and she made a sudden move, as if to throw the glass of water in my face. 'Boo.'

'Sky . . .' I said sadly. 'You've got to stop being like this.'

She stared at me. 'It's Gabe, isn't it? He's the one who doesn't want me here.'

'What on earth gives you that idea?'

'I can tell. He's always wanted me out.' She drank some of the water. 'I'll do a deal with you. Get rid of him and I'll stop. I promise. I'll even go back to that therapist.'

'Of course I can't get rid of him. He's my husband.'

'People change their minds though, right? Relationships break up all the time. You could kick him out if you really wanted to. If you really wanted *me*.'

'It isn't like that. In any case—'

'So what you're saying is, you'd choose him over me,' she interrupted.

'There's no question of *choosing* anyone. I made a lifelong commitment to him and I'd have done exactly the same for you, if the courts had let me.'

'Sure,' she said cynically. 'Everything's permanent with you. Until suddenly it isn't.'

'Sky . . .' I said. 'The way you are right now – it's because of all the changes in your life, I get that. And I get that the only thing that's ever going to make you feel differently is when you understand that, however badly you behave, I'm not going to reject you. But Gabe is here to stay, just as you are.'

She eyed me warily. For a moment, I thought I might have got through to her. Then she took a step back.

'You need to choose,' she said. 'Gabe or me. Don't think about it too long, though.'

FIFTY-FOUR

Gabe

'I can only talk about this in general terms,' Rowena says, 'not the specifics of what Sky and I discussed, because obviously that's still confidential. But I've been reading up in the literature about attachment disorder and I can tell you that, in many ways, she's typical. Fear of being abandoned, which translates into behaviour that's subconsciously – or even consciously – designed to force you into pushing her away. That's how she stays in control. Everything else you've spoken about – hoarding food, sexual impulsiveness, deviousness, the preoccupation with violence, even arson – is textbook, too.'

'It's all my fault, isn't it?' Susie asks numbly.

Rowena shakes her head. 'I'm not sure apportioning blame helps anyone.'

'But she wouldn't be like this if she hadn't been adopted.'

'If anyone's to blame, it's the system that took her away from you,' Rowena says gently.

Susie still looks anguished. 'And I read somewhere – it can also be linked to the mother not wanting a baby in the first place, can't it? As well as taking drugs in pregnancy.'

'The evidence for that is very, very limited.' Rowena spreads her hands. 'The truth is, no one knows why some adopted children attach to their new families and some don't. There are dozens of theories, ranging from the idea that adoptees carry some sort of unhealed primal wound to looking at cortisol levels – the hormone that controls the body's response to stress. From that perspective, acting out is almost like an addiction – it's the only thing that makes the individual feel normal.'

'Is there anything we can do?' I ask.

She shakes her head. 'If you mean medication or some therapeutic magic bullet, not really. There are parenting styles to avoid. Punishment, for example, simply reinforces that they're unlovable and unwanted, so often they actively seek it out – those cortisol levels again. But, equally, praise or affection may make them uncomfortable – it's a reminder that they're not fully in control of the relationship. And avoid time out, or banishing her to her room – that's the exact opposite of what someone with reactive attachment disorder really needs, which is time in, socialising with the rest of the family.'

'Susie and I have realised that we actually have rather different approaches to this,' I say carefully. 'I believe in – well, some system of consequences. Susie takes more of an unconditional-forgiveness line.'

'Well, you clearly need to work out between you how to be consistent, because that's going to be very important. But I'd say those approaches *aren't* fundamentally all that different, are they? There can be consequences, even when you love someone unconditionally. The key is to make them impersonal – to make it clear to the young person that it's them making the choice, not you. And it's very, very important that you never get angry.'

I think with shame of how I reacted when Sky hit Susie. 'Easier said than done.'

'I know,' Rowena says. 'And teenagers with reactive attachment disorder are particularly good at working out how to press your buttons. But if you display any kind of emotion, they'll see it as proof that they're in charge, not you.'

'Anything else?' Susie asks.

Rowena nods. 'There's a model called PACE – it stands for Playful, Accepting, Curious and Empathetic. Keep everything light. Show that you're interested to understand her feelings, without being overdramatic about them. And – yes – give her space. Small, bite-sized amounts of affection or physical touch are much better than coming on too strong. As for boundaries, cut them down to the ones that really matter, the ones to do with her safety rather than being a model citizen.' She pauses. 'For what it's worth, I don't think Sky's behaviour is ever a conscious choice – she'd much rather be like everyone else. When I work with anorexics, they sometimes talk of their illness as being like a bad angel that's taken up residence in their head and is compelling them against their will. I think it might be a bit like that for Sky. Most of the time the bad angel is hidden, even from her, but when it does make an appearance, it's impossible to resist. And she would genuinely have believed that this fresh start with you was going to allow her to cast off all the things that she didn't like or even understand about herself... How has she been at school?'

I look at Susie. 'Funnily enough, we haven't heard from them in a while.'

'Well, I'd make sure you're all dealing with this the same way. She needs to know she can't play you off against them, and vice versa. And, Susie – you and I should book some more sessions together. You're clearly still holding a lot of trauma and guilt about Sky, and I think we need to work through that. This new pregnancy is going to bring enough raw emotion to the surface as it is.'

FIFTY-FIVE

Susie

'We've had absolutely no problems,' Clive Pelling said smugly. 'Quite the reverse.'

Hilcham's head gave us a benign smile, as if it was somehow all his doing.

'So you've seen no . . . acting out?' Gabe asked doubtfully. 'No signs of challenging behaviour?'

Clive's smile became a fraction more concerned. 'Sometimes folk come into this office looking for a label to put on their kids,' he said earnestly. 'At Hilcham, we think every learner is different and we embrace that. Sky's a great example. She's thriving here.'

'What about truancy?' I asked. 'How has her attendance been?'

'Let's see.' Confidently, Clive turned to his computer and made a few clicks with his mouse. A frown crossed his face. 'She's not been participating in afternoon activities as much as we'd hope,' he admitted. 'We give learners a lot of scope to organise their own schedules and sometimes it takes a while for them to step up to that.'

Through gritted teeth, Gabe said, 'Do you happen to know where she's been going? When she's been ... disorganised in her scheduling?'

Clive said vaguely, 'Sometimes learners prefer to work on their projects in the community.'

'So she's been bunking off. And you have absolutely no idea where she goes.'

'Er ... you could try the local library?' Clive suggested.

Gabe sighed. 'Thank you for your time.' His tone clearly suggested that his own time had just been wasted.

'Of course. And, these problems you're seeing at home ... I'm sure they'll pass,' Clive Pelling said brightly as he got to his feet. 'It's so important not to demonise young people, particularly when they're becoming more independent. Rest assured, it's all perfectly normal.'

As we walked back through the mass of students towards the car park, Gabe suddenly called, 'Annabel?'

A teenage girl turned round. It was the friend Sky had brought to our party. 'Oh, hi Mister ... er, Gabe,' she said, a little awkwardly.

'Could we have a quick word? We're just trying to find out how Sky's been getting on.'

Annabel's face clouded as she came over to us. 'We don't see much of each other at the moment.'

'Because of Ned?' I asked.

She hesitated. 'Not exactly ... She went a bit weird on me.'

'In what way? You can tell us, Annabel – it won't get back to her. Or anyone else, for that matter.'

'Well ...' Annabel looked embarrassed. 'To begin with, she

wanted us to spend every minute together. It got a bit much . . . But then she started taking my things. Just odd stuff – like, if I had a sandwich in my bag, you know? Or my calculator, when she's already got one. Eventually I got annoyed with her about it. We haven't spoken since.'

Gabe and I exchanged a glance.

'I'm really sorry to hear that,' I said. 'But, Annabel – it isn't your fault. Sky's . . . working through some problems at the moment.'

FIFTY-SIX

Fi

This article contains details of alleged sexual assaults which you may find upsetting.

The launch of the inaugural album from Silverlink – the prog-folk band fronted by former backing vocalist Susie Jukes – is being overshadowed by allegations involving her husband, Gabe Thompson, formerly of the boy band Wandering Hand Trouble, whose interactions with young fans in the noughties are being described as 'inappropriate', 'toxic' and 'deeply problematic'. It's part of a wider concern about the group, with multiple accusations of sexually exploitative behaviour and a culture of emotional abuse that on several occasions, it's alleged, crossed the line into illegality.

'The boys basically thought they were entitled to have sex with any woman – or girl – they wanted,' one industry insider told me. 'I know for a fact that young fans were often left feeling traumatised and used.'

Through his management, Thompson has issued a statement saying, 'All my relationships were consensual and, so far as I am aware, legal. I am deeply sorry if along the way I have hurt anyone, which was certainly never my intention. WHT's fans were always incredibly important to us and, if we sometimes got too close to them, that was definitely our mistake.'

The same insider told us, 'Gabe used to make jokes about Susie being the groupie he married. She's five years younger than him – it was pretty clear she accepted his mentorship and the strings he could pull as part of the arrangement. That was what he'd got used to in the band, I guess – adoration in exchange for access.'

To date, Silverlink's biggest hit is 'Lullaby for Leah', which Thompson wrote, while their present deal is with Wandering Hand Trouble's former label, Birkenhead. A spokesperson for the label told me Birkenhead takes sexual abuse and harassment 'extremely seriously' and has signed up to codes of practice aimed at stopping 'bullying, harassment, exploitation and discrimination'.

Jukes, who met Thompson when touring with Wandering Hand Trouble, says she is a survivor of music-industry abuse herself, adding, 'In those days, we just had to deal with it and move on.'

Although the boy band has been dormant for almost eight years, rumours of a comeback album persist. Thompson is still a prolific songwriter, penning recent hits for – among others – Jake Croft, Garage Girl and Melissah K.

The online accusations include one from a woman in Australia, 'Alice', who said Thompson had sex with her when she was seventeen, following which she sent him nudes. He subsequently asked her for more, by which time the band was in America. Los Angeles-based attorney Jared Ambrose told me, 'Under federal law, it is illegal for anyone to persuade, entice or coerce a minor – that is, someone under the age of eighteen – into sending sexually explicit photos, which are classed as child pornography. It's a completely different issue from the age of consent. It is perfectly possible to have consensual sex with someone, and for that to be legal in the country where it took place, but to commit an offence if you subsequently ask them for an indecent image, or keep such an image on your phone.'

Jukes told me, 'I would never condone underage sex. And neither would Gabe.' Yet that is precisely what is alleged to have taken place one night in Dublin, on Wandering Hand Trouble's second tour. According to a then-sixteen-year-old fan's anonymous account, Thompson, who was nineteen at the time, had sex with her after a concert. In Ireland, the age of consent is seventeen, and 'defilement of a child under seventeen years' carries a maximum prison sentence of five years.

The allegations concerning other members of

Wandering Hand Trouble are even more extensive, involving emotionally abusive behaviour, misogyny and, in a number of cases, lack of clarity around presumed consent.

'Kai and Danny in particular used to compete to be the first to bed attractive fans. They would denigrate girls the other had slept with in front of the rest of the band and crew,' the insider claimed . . .

FIFTY-SEVEN

Gabe

I've warned the others a journalist is digging around, and send them a link as soon as the article's published. We don't see much of each other these days. Kai's moved to LA, where he's on the judging panel of a TV singing competition; Danny has a huge pile in Essex, with four garages for his collection of supercars; Graham and his husband are in Berlin, dabbling in experimental art; and Rich is said to be in the Lake District, though as he hasn't returned our calls for a while, it's hard to be sure.

The four of us, minus Rich, get on a Zoom. Kai, predictably, is angry. Just as predictably, his anger is directed at Susie. He's never liked her, probably because she never slept with him.

'Couldn't she have kept her mouth shut?' he demands.

'It's not the things Susie said that are the problem,' I point out as mildly as I can – Kai's anger was always contagious, as well as exhausting. 'It's the things you did – that we all did, come to that.'

'We only did what everyone was doing. Those who got the chance, anyway.'

'Do me a favour, Kai – maybe don't put that on your social media?' Danny suggests.

'Of course I fucking won't. Unlike some, I've still got a career.'

'Why d'you even need one? Oh yeah – still paying for all that rehab,' Danny retorts.

On my screen I see Graham shake his head in mock exasperation. He, Rich and I got on really well, and we'd generally got on OK with whichever of Danny or Kai was in the room. It was only when both of them were in the room together that the problems started.

'For what it's worth,' I say, 'the label are pretty confident they've managed to keep a lid on this. We're talking about consensual interactions, twenty years ago, that took place with apparently willing fans – though obviously we apologise unreservedly if that wasn't the case.'

'The label reckon it'll all just go away?' Danny says mockingly.

'That's what they're hoping, yes.'

'Well, that just shows they've still got shit for brains to match their cloth ears.' Danny's looking at something off-screen. 'While we've been talking, Jake Croft's tweeted his half-a-million followers, saying it's so important to really hear all those who speak out about sexual misconduct and that he won't be working with you again, Gabe, or performing the song you wrote together. There's a link to the article. We've all been tagged.'

FIFTY-EIGHT

Gabe

It's like watching dominoes toppling. On Instagram, on Facebook, but particularly on Twitter, an endless stream of retweets and tags surges in, faster than the eye can follow. Susie and I watch the flickering, whirling current, aghast. Occasionally we can pick out an individual comment just long enough to grasp the words:

> i'm so disgusted what the fuck

> They were literally my mums favourite band

> GROSS. first gig I ever went to

> I'm confused what's happening

> I used to kiss Kai's picture on my wall

> @Melissah_K please do not affiliate yourself with these people. Until these claims have been addressed formally we need to support young women and make sure this does not get ignored

omfg this is so disgusting

@spotify @youtube BOYCOTT THEIR TRACKS until this is sorted out

I'm gonna throw up

support all survivors

Just deleted every song Gabe Thompson ever wrote

@apple_music please stand FOR women and join the boycott AGAINST wht

deleted here too

deleted

@garage_girl please do not affiliate yourself with these people. Until these claims have been addressed formally we need to support young women and make sure this does not get ignored

Just deleted all their tracks

@realsusiejukes @silverlinkband how dare you imply survivors are lying

what makes this worse was that they acted as if they were the good guys. we loved and trusted them and this is how they repaid us

deleted here too

> I don't care what anyone says, a 16 yr old is NOT mature enough to decide to sleep with a 21 yr old. Age of consent in UK should be the same as USA
>
> what were the parents doing letting those girls go to concerts? They should take some responsibility
>
> #bringdownWHT
>
> Is anyone surprised? Their f**king name was another way of saying 'indecent assault'. They should all be prosecuted for incitement to rape
>
> #deleteWHT

'This way madness lies,' Susie says at last. She closes her browser. 'Tea?'

'Tea,' I agree numbly. 'Whatever else happens, we'll always have tea.'

As she passes, I put my hand on her belly. 'And this. This is what really matters.'

'Yes.' She puts her own hand on mine, holding it in place.

'For what it's worth . . .' I add. 'Reading that article, I do see why people are angry. I might not have been as bad as Kai or Danny, but it's like that tweet said – the fans thought that, because they loved us, we must surely love them back. But it was all an image manufactured by the label. And when they actually met us, sometimes they were taken advantage of.'

Susie nods. I sense she's about to say something more, but then we hear the front door open.

Sky comes in. It's the first time we've seen her in two days – she barely spends any time with us now. She looks tired.

'Hi,' she says. 'Can I have some money for the cab? It's thirty quid.'

I reach for my wallet. 'Which you'll pay back from your allowance.'

She shrugs. 'Sure.'

Her voice is distant to the point of coldness. Rowena told us to expect that. *A part of her will be scared of the intimacy that discussing her behaviour might bring. If she's stand-offish, don't reciprocate. In a race to the bottom, the reactive adolescent will always win.*

I keep my voice light. 'I take it you've been with Ned.'

She shrugs. 'Maybe.'

'We were concerned. We didn't know where you were.'

She rolls her eyes. '*Concerned.* Right.'

'Anyway, we've had a discussion. In future, if you leave here without us knowing where you are, or without having agreed a time for you to be back, we're going to take away your access to Silverlink – to being the backing singer. The same if you're violent. You can't be part of the band if you're not a functioning member of the family. But the choice is yours.'

Her eyes blaze. 'You can't fucking *do* that!'

'We don't want to, but we have to find some way of motivating you to do the right thing. You need help to change, and putting some rules in place is the best way to do that.'

'Just listen to yourself, Gabe,' she snaps. 'You're such a pompous *prick*.'

'There is an alternative. You could just stay away from Ned altogether. You know we can't possibly condone you having sex before you're sixteen.'

'Which is so damn rich. When *your* band's all over social for doing exactly that.'

'You of all people know that some of those stories aren't true.'

'I know you're a *creep*.' She turns and storms upstairs.

'Well,' Susie says after a moment, 'at least she didn't throw anything. I guess that's progress.'

'What's more . . . I've just had an idea,' I say slowly.

'What about?'

'Ned . . . We can message him, right?'

Susie nods. 'Sure. He's on Instagram.'

Getting out my phone, I find Ned's Instagram account and compose a message:

> Unless you break up with Sky right now, I'm letting the world know you're having sex with a fifteen-year-old. And, given that I'm currently trending with about 500,000 people who think that's not such a great idea, I'd say it'll pretty much end your music career before it's begun. Which would be a blessing for the nation's eardrums, but probably not your preferred choice.

'Are you sure?' Susie says doubtfully, when I show her. 'She's going to go ballistic.'

'Do you really think she and Ned should be sleeping together?'

She hesitates, then shakes her head. 'No. Send it.'

I press *Send*, and we wait for the detonation.

FIFTY-NINE

Susie

It took around twenty minutes. There was a scream from her room, a crash as something hit the wall, then the thunder of feet as she hurtled down the stairs.

'What have you done?' she shrieked.

I was nearest and she threw herself at me. In a flash, Gabe was on her, grabbing her wrists. With her arms pinned, she couldn't hit him, so she lashed out with her feet instead. He looked down, avoiding her kicks, and while he was distracted she sank her teeth into his arm.

Wincing, he pushed her away.

She turned to me. 'I told you! I told you to get rid of him! I gave you a chance! You should have fucking listened!'

Then, as abruptly as she came, she was gone, back up the stairs.

Gabe looked at me. 'What's she talking about?'

I took a breath. 'She had this mad idea I should choose between her and you. Obviously, I told her we're a united front.'

Gabe nodded. But a look of apprehension crossed his face, as if he was wondering just what we'd unleashed.

His phone pinged. He glanced at it, then showed me. It was from Ned.

> She told me she was 16, I swear. And I was going to end it anyway. Things were getting really weird.

'That's something, anyway,' he said. But he shivered.

SIXTY

Sky

He's a fucking hypocrite.

And a pervert and a letch.

If it was just Susie and me, I know we could make it work. Sure, I'd blow up at her sometimes. But she understands that I only do that because we got separated before. That I get panicked when people try to tell me what to do.

Like – *hello?* As if it's some kind of choice I make, instead of the only release I have?

He's a bloodsucking parasite – he'll never voluntarily give her up. Why would he? He's got this beautiful, cool, talented younger woman giving him endless adoration and blowjobs or whatever and making his crappy songs sound good.

Lubing herself for him – which is so utterly gross, now I come to think about it. So she can be his willing compliant sex slave whenever he wants her to be.

It's almost as if he's controlling her. Not violently – it's more subtle than that. But she's been brainwashed until she can't think for herself. I'd be setting her free, as well as me. Not to mention striking a blow for every single one of those women who are totally disgusted by what him and his band got up to on tour.

So, how do I prise his sweaty lecherous fat fingers off her?

The answer's obvious but I have to be careful. I know to my cost you only get one shot at this. I thought I could get rid of the monster once, but that backfired.

This time, I need to get it right.

SIXTY-ONE

Gabe

Over the next week, things with Sky definitely improve. We follow Rowena's suggestion to keep things light-hearted. Instead of making her take time out, we try to limit how much time she spends alone in her room – getting her to do her homework at the kitchen table, for example, or helping to prepare vegetarian meals.

At times, it's hard to believe she's the same person who turned into a screaming, kicking dervish when we intervened over Ned. She's sweet and charming, a pleasure to be around. We even dare to imagine that, by showing her we're prepared to be tough when we have to be, we've got over the worst.

Rowena said we should praise her when she's doing well, but lightly, without making too big a deal of it. So I just say casually one evening, as she's emptying the dishwasher, 'I really appreciate what an effort you're making right now, Sky.'

She looks up. 'Thanks, Gabe. I really appreciate everything you've done for me, too.'

The storm on Twitter rages unabated, but there's nothing I

can do about that except hope it eventually subsides. Melissah K and Garage Girl both follow Jake Croft's lead and announce they won't be working with me again, and several managers let my agent and publisher know the same goes for their artistes, too. I see Kai has also 'stepped back' – whatever that means – from his TV show, 'while historic allegations are investigated'.

So, when the doorbell goes and I see Detective Constable Eddo on the step, with a tall, thin man in jeans and a suit jacket, which he's wearing somewhat incongruously over a white shirt with metal collar points and a black bootlace tie, for one anxious moment I wonder if it could have something to do with all that. Then I realise it can't have – none of the fans involved in Fi's story had any reason to go to the police. It'll be to do with those phone calls I made about Sky.

'Hello, Mr Thompson.' DC Eddo indicates the man next to her. 'This is Gerry Castle, from Children's Social Services. He needs to speak to Sky. Alone, if you don't mind.'

'You're finally going to do something, then,' I say, relieved. 'Good. Come in.'

'I think you may be referring to a different matter,' Eddo says as she steps inside. 'Could you direct us to where Sky is now?'

Susie comes out of the kitchen, frowning. 'She should have an adult with her, surely, if she's going to speak to the police.'

'That wouldn't be appropriate in the present situation,' Gerry Castle says. 'We have to follow procedure and that means me talking to Sky alone. Detective Constable Eddo will wait outside the door.'

'All right,' I say, puzzled. 'You'd better go upstairs. She's in her room.'

*

'What was that about?' Susie asks Sky when they've gone. She'd been closeted with Gerry Castle for over an hour.

'Oh . . . safeguarding stuff,' she says vaguely.

'What do you mean?' Susie asks. 'Is this to do with Ned and you?'

'They've asked me not to say anything, actually. Not until they come back.'

Which they do, less than an hour later, with another police car and a female social worker. The second social worker takes Sky upstairs to pack a suitcase.

'What's going on?' Susie keeps saying. 'Why will nobody tell me what you're doing with my daughter?'

It's Gerry Castle who finally says, 'She's requested to go into an emergency placement for her own protection.' He turns to me. 'We need to speak to you next, Mr Thompson.'

SIXTY-TWO

Gabe

'So tell me more about these guitar lessons,' Gerry Castle says.

'They weren't lessons,' I say patiently. 'It was just a few chords. Four, if I remember rightly.'

He indicates my guitars, propped on their stands next to where we're talking. 'Can you show me?'

I place the six-string across his lap, get round behind him and demonstrate how I'd positioned Sky's fingers on the fretboard. 'Like that.'

'And that was the extent of your contact, on that occasion?'

'Well – no,' I admit. 'She sort of . . . pressed herself against me.'

'*She* pressed herself against *you*?'

'Yes. You can ask Susie – I mentioned it to her at the time. We felt, perhaps, that it was because she was – you know, that she was testing me.'

Gerry makes a note. 'And, later on, when you started giving her singing lessons . . . She says you took her into a soundproof room and touched her belly.'

'I showed her how to locate her diaphragm,' I say through

gritted teeth. 'And we were in my studio because that's where my equipment is.'

'And this was all part of a pattern of dangling musical mentorship in front of her?'

'I didn't *dangle* anything. She asked if we could help her get a career in music. We even let her be part of Susie's band, for Christ's sake. Then it turned out she couldn't actually sing, so Susie asked me to teach her—'

'Hang on. She couldn't sing, but you still let her be part of a professional group?'

'We were trying to be positive. To encourage her.' I realise what the vibe is that I've been getting off that bootlace-tie-and-clasp combo. Gerry Castle is almost certainly a country-and-western fan, and boy bands probably aren't high on his list of musical likes.

He looks at me levelly. 'From a certain angle, Mr Thompson, this sounds an awful lot like grooming.'

'That's ridiculous,' I scoff. 'For it to be grooming, there'd have to be sexual intent. And I never, ever did anything inappropriate with her.'

'Did you wolf whistle at her before she went to a concert with your wife?'

'No, of—' Then I remember. I *did* whistle, but at both of them, at the effect their matching outfits and make-up had made. 'Possibly,' I concede. 'It wasn't a wolf whistle, but I might have made a whistling sound.'

Even I realise that sounds a bit weak.

'She was made up that night to look older than she is, wasn't she?' Gerry asks.

'Well . . .'

'Did you push her into having sex with the guitarist of the band your wife introduced her to?'

'*What?*' I shake my head. 'No – quite the reverse. We made sure the relationship stopped as soon as we could.' But I'm starting to understand, now, how Gerry's looking at all this – as if the relationship with Ned is part of a pattern, one that we're responsible for, for toxic reasons of our own.

Or, rather, of *my* own.

Gerry looks at his notes. 'You told Sky your wife started having sex when she was fifteen, didn't you?'

'No,' I say firmly. 'Susie told her that. She told Sky that she could ask her anything, so she did. It was about things like consent and contraception, mostly.'

'And oral sex, I understand.'

'Really?' I stare at him. 'Well – I've no idea about that. You'd have to ask Susie. But she's a naturally frank person and, if Sky asked her a question, she'd have answered it . . . Do we need a *lawyer?*'

'This is a preliminary fact-finding conversation, Mr Thompson. If it leads to a statutory assessment or a Section-47 investigation, you'll be invited to attend and you can bring a legal or other representative.'

I have no idea what he's talking about.

'Tell me about getting her drunk at a party,' he adds.

'We didn't "get her drunk". She and her friend used fake ID to buy vodka and smuggled it in.'

'But you'd previously told her she could drink alcohol?'

'Two beers,' I say despairingly. 'We said she could have two beers.'

'And when she drank more, you put her to bed.'

'Yes.' I see his look. 'That's "you", *plural*. Susie and I both took her up. Then we took it in turns to stay with her.'

'So you were alone with her?'

'Well – some of the time.'

'Did you undress her?'

'No.' I catch my breath. 'My wife did that. She helped Sky shower after she threw up.'

He makes another note. 'Tell me about the tattoo. And encouraging her to wear revealing outfits.'

With an effort, I control my anger. 'She used the same fake ID that she used to buy booze to con a tattoo artist—'

'*Con*'s a pretty strong word, Mr Thompson. Are you saying she's a liar?'

'Well, since I'm denying every single one of these absurd insinuations, you can draw your own conclusions.'

'So you didn't encourage her to wear revealing clothing, either?'

'No,' I say firmly. 'I think you must be referring to the times she and Susie tried on some of Susie's old outfits. That had absolutely nothing to do with me.'

'She said you made her feel uncomfortable when they showed you. That you stared at her.'

I shake my head. 'Well, I didn't.'

'Have there been any concerns of violence within the home?'

'You know there have. We've been trying to get help for Sky's anger issues for some time. You lot refused to provide any support.'

He shoots me a look. 'My question relates more to *you*, Mr

Thompson. Have you ever been aggressive or violent towards Sky? Or towards your wife?'

'Certainly not. Ask Susie. She'll back me up.'

'I understand you recently accepted a police caution for assault.'

'Well . . .' I'm at a loss for words. 'Technically speaking, yes. But the circumstances were complicated. Someone had insulted my wife—'

He puts his pen down. 'Do you have any naked pictures of Sky on your phone?'

'*What?*' The notion is so ridiculous that I actually laugh out loud. 'Of course not.'

'So you wouldn't mind if I checked?' He's looking at me steadily.

'Yes, actually, I would,' I retort. 'Because I resent the implication that such a thing is even possible.'

'I can wait here with you while DC Eddo organises a warrant, if you'd prefer,' he says, with just a hint of steel. 'But it might take several hours.'

I sigh. 'Fine.' I pull out my phone, tap in my passcode and hand it to him.

Silently, he opens my photos folder and starts scrolling through it, stopping occasionally to enlarge one.

'Have you got *any* pictures of Sky on here?' he asks after a while.

'Not one,' I say triumphantly. 'Like everything else she's told you, it's completely untrue.'

It's actually a good thing, I realise, that I handed over my phone so readily. It will prove this is all made up, and then perhaps we can move on to discussing how to get Sky some proper help.

'Hmm,' Gerry says. 'I'm just going to check the deleted items folder.'

More scrolling. Then he stops. 'So how do you explain this?'

He turns the screen towards me. I look, and flinch. It's a picture of Sky. Sky, smiling apprehensively, sprawled across the bed in the master bedroom. Naked.

SIXTY-THREE

Susie

It turned out to be even worse than we first realised. Because, when the police looked at Gabe's other devices, they found more photographs. One on the Mac in his study, two on the computer in his studio. All hidden in the trash, which he'd never think to check, but which now appeared like a clumsy attempt to get rid of them.

His PIN number and passwords were the same as the ones he used for Netflix and Spotify. Set up back in the pre-Sky days, when it would never have occurred to either of us to be careful about things like that.

As soon as the police had gone, we called our lawyer. It wasn't good. We were still technically in breach of the CAWN, he pointed out – something which was looking more sinister in the light of these new allegations, as if we'd been exerting some kind of malign influence over Sky from the start. Failing to stop her sleeping with Ned, likewise – that could also be aiding and abetting unlawful intercourse, since Gabe gave Sky money for the taxi that time.

The most serious potential charges, though, related to the indecent images. The nudes Gabe supposedly solicited from a fan seventeen years ago were long gone, of course, and without them there was no chance of the police pursuing anything to do with Fi's article. But they were aware of it now, alerted by Sky, and it was all starting to look like a pattern.

The lawyer's advice was to wait and see what the police came back with. 'Even if they do arrest you, the CPS might decide it isn't worth pursuing charges,' he suggested helpfully.

But doing nothing didn't really feel like an option. Gabe might conceivably weather a social media storm about a defunct band that hadn't performed in years, but if that narrative became entwined with one from the present day, his career would be finished.

'Why?' he kept asking. 'Why does she hate me so much?'

To which Rowena's answer, when he put it to her, was, 'She doesn't. She thinks she's a bad person who does bad things, and that's why people push her away. So she does more bad things – the more elaborate, the better. Manipulating a situation makes her feel in control.'

There were only so many times and ways I could say sorry to him. But he knew how terrible I felt for dragging him into all this.

So when I suggested we should get in touch with Sky, to make her understand we still wanted her, he looked at me as if I was completely mad.

'You cannot be serious. The last thing we want is to encourage her to come back, surely? Even just contacting her is another breach of the CAWN.'

'If we give up on her too, we'll be proving she's right – that she *is* unlovable. And then she'll probably be like this for the rest of her life. At the very least, I think we should keep the lines of communication open.'

'Dear God. I can't believe I'm hearing this.' But he agreed we could talk it over with Rowena.

'It's an incredibly complex situation,' Rowena said, when I'd explained what I was thinking of doing. 'On the one hand, Social Services may have commissioned a full psychiatric assessment, in which case she might already be getting the help she needs. But I have to say, I doubt it. And the fact she's focused this latest broadside on Gabe, rather than both of you, suggests that, on some level, she might still be hoping for some kind of relationship with you, Susie ... It's just possible you may have got through some chink in her armour.'

'Or perhaps she simply sees Susie as a soft touch who'll let her do whatever she wants and be her human punchbag into the bargain,' Gabe suggested. 'Sorry,' he added, in my direction. 'But it's got to be said.'

'I think you have to try to separate the disorder from the person,' Rowena said gently. 'Whatever bad things Sky has done, it isn't because she *is* bad, whatever she might think. It's because bad things have happened to her, and she hasn't had the structure and stability and insight she needs to overcome them.' She turned to me. 'As for whether she'll ever be able to share you – that's an open question. But I don't think you can know unless you try.'

So I sent her a text. I was going to say how upset and hurt we were, but Rowena suggested making it less emotional.

Sky – what you did was very wrong, but I think you understand that. I just wanted to let you know that both of us are sorry to see you go and hope you'll decide to come back one day, if Social Services will allow that. You will always be welcome. Love, Susie

She didn't reply.

SIXTY-FOUR

Susie

Sky – how are you? I hope you're settling in at your emergency placement. Just to say that we are always here for you if you need us x

Hi Sky. Hope you're doing OK. Sandy misses your walks! Hope to see you one day soon. Susie x

Hi Sky – if you fancy a vegetarian Sunday lunch one weekend, just let us know Xx

Just to say – hope you're well. Love an update sometime Xx

Hi Sky. Hope all is good and you're sorting through your issues. Still hoping to see you sometime. Susie xx

SIXTY-FIVE

Sky

First impressions: *Actually, it's not that bad here.*

It's a big, detached house on the edge of a modern development. Well, when I say *big*, it's smaller than Susie and Gabe's farmhouse, but inside it's more spacious, with two sitting rooms and a laundry room as well as a functional-looking kitchen – no Aga or bean-to-cup coffee machine here. But everything's bright and colourful and surprisingly well maintained.

It's only on second glance that you notice the little details. The *Fire Exit* sign above the back door. The fact that most of the pictures on those brightly coloured walls have brightly motivational slogans on them (*Liking yourself is the only Like you need! Create your own sunshine! You're braver than you think and stronger than you seem!*). The two washing machines and tumble drier that are always on the go, day and night.

Barry's the house manager – always chirpy but somehow calm, like he's seen it all before. No one messes with Barry, not least because he gets to decide on any sanctions. He's not here much, though, because he also manages two other houses. Most of the day-to-day running of the place is done by Nicole – she's the one who sorts out rotas and helps us plan meals.

The rest of the staff are what they call 'bank'. *This is Lizzie from the bank. This is Sammy – he's bank.* At first, I thought that must be something to do with money, until Maya explained that *bank* just means the pool of zero-hours staff they use. I also thought it was me who was taking a while to get used to all the new faces, but Maya said no, it's the same for everyone. You can come downstairs in the middle of the night and there'll be some random stranger sitting at the kitchen table, staring at you. *Hi, I'm Billy. From the bank.*

Though maybe it does have something to do with money. Apparently they charge the council three grand per teenager a week, and the company that runs it has five more houses like this one. It was started by two ex-social workers, Ken and Cathy, though no one ever sees them. On a luxury holiday somewhere, probably.

Maya's been assigned as my mentor, though she's six months younger than me. She's been here a year. She hardly speaks above a whisper, which may be because she's been through a lot of terrible shit or because she doesn't like drawing attention to herself, I can't work out which. When I asked her what it's like here, she just shrugged and said, 'Better.' Turns out that, before this, her council housed her in a mobile home a hundred miles away. And before that she was in a place where there were no curtains on her window and no sheets on the mattress. But that was an unregulated home, meant for over-sixteens only. Her council claimed it was only temporary, but the school she was at kicked up a fuss and she got moved – ironically, away from the school that had helped her complain. It's like that, apparently – one minute you go off to lessons thinking everything's normal, the next you're standing with a social worker in the car park with all your belongings stuffed into bin bags, waiting for the taxi to come and dump you God knows where.

Then there's Rahmi, Larissa, Jaylen and Rob, my other fellow desperados. Jaylen acts like he's this fourteen-year-old gangster, complete with pimp walk and street attitude. He and Rahmi are an item, although that didn't stop him walking into my room when I first arrived and asking if I had a boyfriend. When I said, 'Not at the moment,' he said, 'D'you want one, then?' – like he was doing me a favour by offering himself, but I'd have to be really quick or the opportunity would be gone. I tried not to laugh, just asked what his girl Rahmi would think. He looked at me and said, 'She ain't my girl, man. She's my ting.'

'Fucked if I know what that means,' I told him, 'but please get out of my room.' Since then, I always make sure to shoot the latch on the Yale lock.

Rob's stick-thin and looks like he couldn't stand up to a goose. Larissa's the opposite – hefty and on a short fuse. I'd been here a week when I first saw her lose her rag – I never did find out what about. The moment she started to lash out, three staff were on her, wrestling her to the ground. She was screaming and bucking and for a moment as I watched her, it was like I was inside her head – I felt myself go hot and I started to tremble. I was back at that fucking therapy centre, being held and tickled until I lost it.

One of the staff asked if I was OK, and when I couldn't speak, he led me away. He probably thought the new girl was just a bit upset because she'd had to watch someone being restrained. I didn't tell him any different. I spent the rest of the day curled up on my bed, shaking and having flashbacks.

But it made me realise – acting like Larissa round here is not going to have a happy outcome for me. So the first time I found myself almost blowing up – I'd gone to put a load of washing on, but Barry and Nicole were in the laundry room, having a conversation, and Barry glanced at the clock and said something like, 'You're too late, Sky, it's five minutes past curfew' – instead of throwing something at him, I forced myself to nod and turn away. I had my room key in my hand and I squeezed it as hard as I could, pressing the sharp edges into the soft skin between my fingers. Somehow, I got myself back to my room and found the blade I'd hidden – a small serrated knife I took from the kitchen my first night here. I nicked the inside of my thigh instead, and the blood dripping out felt like I'd turned a tap and the anger was releasing too – *pfffft*.

Sometimes I kick myself for the way everything turned to shit at Susie and Gabe's. Why did I do that? I'm never likely to have a chance like that again, after all. My own issues aside, the biggest disagreement Gabe and I ever had was over whether he should book Ibiza or Goa for our summer holiday.

But, in some weird way I don't fully understand, that's exactly why I did it. The better something is, the more I need to ruin it.

Maybe coming here will turn out to be the wake-up call I need. Maybe I can finally get my shit together and change.

SIXTY-SIX

Susie

I was sitting at the kitchen table, updating the band's social media feeds on my iPad, when I heard the front door opening. I knew straight away it couldn't be Gabe – he was in his studio.

It was Sky, I saw as she came into the kitchen. So she still had her key. I didn't know whether that was a good sign or not. It was three weeks since she'd left with the social workers, and in all that time we hadn't heard a thing from her, though I'd texted at least a dozen times.

'Hello,' I said cautiously. I was pleased to see her, of course, but I couldn't help being wary of the way she'd turned up unannounced. Then I remembered what Rowena had said. Perhaps that was all part of her trying to control the situation.

Sandy was less circumspect than me, rousing himself from his bed and hurtling towards her, wagging his tail so hard his whole body shaped itself into a circle, first one way and then the other. She rubbed his head. 'Hey Sandy. Good boy.'

'How've you been?' I asked. Keeping it low key.

'All right, actually. I just came back to get some things.'

She looked tired – that lovely teenage innocence jaded, her pale skin mottled with spots.

'Where are you staying?'

'In a home for teenagers.' She went to the fridge. 'Can I have some milk?'

'Of course . . . Do you like it there?'

She pulled out a carton. 'It's all right. There are six of us. The others are all fuck-ups too, so that's something. But there's always a queue for the shower. And I've had to stop being vegetarian. It's just too disgusting.'

'Are you getting to school?' The social workers had barred us from asking Hilcham anything about her, even though we were still paying the fees.

'Sometimes. That's where they think I am now.' She found a pint glass and filled it almost to the brim.

I watched as she chugged the milk down. I felt such a mixture of emotions – love, protectiveness, fear, hopelessness. But perhaps that's parenthood, I thought. Perhaps it's always complicated and painful when your offspring start to become their own person, and this was just a more extreme, surreal version of that. 'Would you like some toast?'

'I can manage it.' She flashed me a smile, and my heart exploded with love for her.

She opened the cupboard where the Marmite was kept. Then: 'What's this?'

Next to the breakfast things, where I'd see it and remember to take one every morning, was a bottle of vitamins: Pregnacare Max, with a picture of a smiling woman cradling her bump.

The penny dropped and she whirled around. 'You're *pregnant*?'

I couldn't deny it – the bottle was already half empty. 'Yes.'

She gasped. The gasp became a bitter laugh that quickly became something else, like she was gulping for air and retching at the same time. 'Well, you didn't waste any time, did you? Throw me out, then get one in.'

'We didn't *throw you out*,' I protested. 'You chose to make all those false allegations about Gabe. And you knew I was trying to get pregnant.'

'You told me you couldn't.' The jar of Marmite hurtled past me and smashed on the wall.

'Sky,' I said, as calmly as I could, 'don't overreact—'

'Don't overreact!' She stared at me. 'You said you wanted me back! You asked me to *lunch*! All those fucking texts! And you never once mentioned *this*!'

'I'm not telling anyone until the second trimester. When you've had as many miscarriages as I have—'

'Maybe you'll miscarry this one.' There was an edge to her voice I didn't like.

Even if I yelled, there was no way Gabe, out in his studio, would hear. I could text him, but my phone was on the other side of the kitchen.

She stepped towards me. 'You don't need another baby. You had me.'

'Sky . . .' I said desperately. 'I've waited five years for this. I don't even know if I'll carry this one to term – I've lost them at eighteen weeks before – but surely you can see that having another child won't affect my relationship with you. Gabe and I will always be here for you—'

'You'll lose this one too.' She shook her head. 'You can't have a *baby*.'

'Look, why not sit down?' I suggested. 'We clearly need to talk about this.'

With a sudden piercing shriek, she came at me. I tried to fend her off, but my chair went over, tipping me on to the floor. Instinctively, I rolled on my side, protecting my stomach. She dropped to her knees, straddling me, her fist raised—

Gabe. Coming into the kitchen, an empty mug in his hand, he took in the situation with a glance. Grabbing her fist, he yanked her off me, sending her spinning across the floor. Then he stood over me protectively, the mug still clenched in his own fist like a big ceramic knuckleduster.

'Get out,' he said icily. 'Just go. I don't care where. But don't come back.'

SIXTY-SEVEN

Susie

Hi Sky, just to say Gabe didn't mean what he said about you never coming back. He spoke in anger and because he was frightened for me. We would love to have you live here again one day but you would have to promise to get help for your anger and violence issues. Susie xxx

SIXTY-EIGHT

Sky

Hi Susie, just to say your life won't look so fucking perfect by the time I've finished with you xxx

SIXTY-NINE

Gabe

'It's come to our attention,' Gerry Castle says, 'that Mrs Thompson may be pregnant.'

'Has it, indeed?' I say coldly. 'And may I ask just how this confidential medical information reached you?'

'I'm not at liberty to reveal that. The important thing is, is it true?'

We're in a small glass-walled meeting room at the Social Services offices, a hideous 1970s block in Aylesbury that makes Gerry's clothing choice look almost normal. Today, he's wearing tooled leather cowboy boots under his suit trousers.

'That's not something we'd share with other people until the baby's viable,' Susie says. 'I've had a number of late miscarriages, if you must know.'

'I'm sorry to hear that.' Gerry looks down at his notes. 'The thing is, if you *are* pregnant, it may affect the scope of any safeguarding investigation.'

'Why?' I say, shaking my head. 'How is Susie being pregnant even remotely relevant to what's been going on with Sky?'

'There are a number of issues here. Your wife had a baby taken into care by the family courts – the judge found that, on the balance of probabilities, the infant was likely to suffer significant harm. It also appears that Mrs Thompson is in contempt of court in relation to those proceedings, having shared information about the child's identity. And now there are these new allegations of possible offences against the same child ... We'd be remiss if we didn't widen our assessment to consider a PBA.' We must look blank, because he adds, 'That's a pre-birth assessment. To determine if this baby could also be at significant risk of harm. If there's any possibility it is, we may need to apply for another Placement Order.'

SEVENTY

Susie

Instinctively, my hands went to my belly. It was as futile as if I'd put them there in the face of an oncoming bus, but I couldn't help myself.

'That's . . . *obscene*.' Gabe had gone white. 'You can't possibly think . . . that's . . . that's like state-sponsored *abortion*.'

'Our only interest is the well-being of the child. Of both children, now.' Gerry spoke calmly, but his eyes flickered to where his colleagues sat, just a few feet away, on the other side of the glass. I realised now why this meeting had taken place in their offices. There was probably a panic button under the table.

Gerry turned to me. 'You'll remember some of the process from last time, but there are considerably more steps these days. We do try to support parents to have a positive outcome, so cooperation is key. The more engaged you are, the more you can demonstrate that you've addressed any concerns.'

'I don't understand,' I said. 'What concerns can there possibly be?'

'That's what the assessment will have to determine.' He glanced at Gabe, and I realised that, in the light of Sky's accusations, at least one of the concerns was going to be him.

SEVENTY-ONE

Susie

There was so much to deal with, my mind couldn't process it. There was a constant feeling of panic in the pit of my stomach – which, to add to everything else, made me wonder what I was doing to our baby. I googled 'effect of stress in pregnancy' and discovered that it increased the risk of miscarriage. Great.

Because I was already an at-risk pregnancy, I was under the care of a consultant. He told me he could prescribe antidepressants, but that they might increase the risk of miscarriage too, even as they reduced the risk from anxiety. Instead, he recommended bed rest and hydration. Bed rest and water . . . I realised that medical science had no answers for people in my position. There was no drug or treatment that could keep my baby inside me, not if my body chose differently.

Just as there was no legal process that could make the social workers go away. It was best to cooperate, our lawyer confirmed breezily. Yes, they were effectively obliged to do an assessment because I'd had a previous baby taken into care, but every case was judged on its merits. Even if the allegations against Gabe were ultimately judged to be substantive enough for Sky to be kept away from us, that didn't necessarily mean we couldn't care for another child.

He made it sound as if what the social workers were doing was completely normal, which I suppose it was, in his world. But then I googled 'can Social Services take my baby' and the results were terrifying – a cascade of first-hand accounts by people to whom exactly that had happened. Stories of biased social workers, twisted reports, parents tricked into making admissions carefully designed to sound bad when quoted in court. When the stakes were this high, how could anyone stay calm?

SEVENTY-TWO

Gabe

I find Susie in a state of panic. She's been on all these websites telling her we should refuse to speak to the social workers, or that we should even leave the country.

'We could go to Goa. We've always said it would be great to have a house there. I've checked – the extradition arrangements are so complicated, you have to have done something really bad—'

'Suze, listen to yourself,' I say gently. 'Running away – that's crazy. Besides, it would look like we'd done it because of those photos of Sky – that I'm guilty and trying to escape justice.'

'We need to take this seriously, Gabe.'

'I *am* taking it seriously. But I also know we've done nothing wrong. Sky might have managed to make Social Services suspicious of us, but you can't entirely blame them for that – just look how much evidence she faked. The truth will come out eventually.'

Susie gestures at her iPad. 'The internet is full of people who thought that way.'

'And we of all people know that what's on the internet isn't always the whole truth, right? You heard what the lawyer said – they'd have to prove we're unfit parents, when the truth is you'd clearly be a brilliant mum. Your life is nothing like it was when Sky was taken away – you're married, you're not facing a possible trial, we have a stable home life, you've been clean for fifteen years—'

'That's what I'm trying to tell you,' she says despairingly. 'I'm not. Not exactly.'

I frown. 'What do you mean?'

'I smoked dope with Sky and Ned. Just the once, but . . .'

I stare at her. Then I remember – that night after the gig, when she smelled of weed.

'I don't think she can have told them yet, or they'd be all over it,' she adds. 'But it's only a matter of time. And when you put that together with my conviction . . .'

'So we deny it,' I say. 'It's just another lie she's telling.'

Susie shakes her head. 'They'll do a test on my hair – it shows whether you've taken any drugs at all in the last three months. And if it confirms I've lied about that, the implication will be that we've lied about everything. We can't risk it.'

'OK. But one joint is hardly the crime of the century. If they took away the kids of everyone who'd done that, there'd hardly be any families left.'

I say it reassuringly, but I can't help feeling uneasy. Smoking weed is one thing, but smoking weed with your fifteen-year-old daughter and the boy she went on to have sex with . . . In Gerry Castle's parallel universe, this could be made to look very bad indeed.

'That's another problem – I don't think they'll be able to tell it was just one joint,' she says miserably. 'The smaller the amount, the less accurate the test is.'

'Jesus.' We're going to be painted as a paedophile and a junkie, I think disbelievingly. For the first time, I find myself wondering if we could be in real trouble here.

But Susie is pregnant with our child, and the last thing she needs right now is for me to voice those worries out loud. I say firmly, 'We're not running away to Goa. We'll sort this out. If your daughter thinks she can destroy this family, she's got another think coming.'

Susie nods. But I can see the hurt in her eyes when I talk about Sky like that. I can't help suspecting that, even if we do manage to get through this somehow, for her, that chapter isn't yet closed.

SEVENTY-THREE

Gabe

'You were right,' I say heavily. 'We should have walked away.'

Marcus shrugs. 'Hindsight's a wonderful thing. But Susie was in an impossible position and you both wanted to help Sky.'

We're in a pub in Hillingdon, where Marcus is attending a two-day conference on fostering. I'm surprised his local authority think he has any more to learn after almost twenty years, but he's told me they put just as much time and money into making sure people already doing the job keep up to date as they do into training new foster carers. Once again, I can't help reflecting on the difference between the support available to people like him, where the state is legally the child's parent, and adopters, who take on the responsibility themselves.

He gives me a sympathetic look. 'It can't have been easy, though.'

I shake my head. 'It really wasn't. There were times . . . It was like Susie was fixated with her. When they started wearing the same clothes, I felt I hardly knew her anymore.'

'Being a parent does change you. And for Susie, losing a child then having it come back fifteen years later must have been mind-blowing.'

'Yes. Of course.' I take a pull of my Guinness.

'Gabe, mate . . . Is there something else that's bothering you?' Marcus asks.

I sigh. 'It's clear to me that we've got to choose between trying to get Sky back and fighting for our own baby. If Sky decides she's had enough of whatever children's home they've got her in and just turns up on our doorstep again, how could Susie ever be safe? But I'm not sure Susie agrees. I think she still wants to find a way of ending up with both of them.'

Marcus is silent a moment. 'I don't disagree – you'll have to decide what your priority is. But there is another way of looking at it. Living with you hasn't turned out to be all that great for Sky, has it? She's ended up exhibiting exactly the same destructive behaviours as before. Maybe you can persuade Susie to see it that way – that being with you isn't the best way to break the cycle.'

'Last time we met, you mentioned a kid you fostered who had reactive attachment issues,' I say, curious. 'Do you know what happened to him?'

He nods. 'Yes, as it happens – years later, he turned up at one of my Christmas lunches, totally out of the blue. He was one of the lucky ones, depending on which way you look at it. Things got really bad for him, but eventually a judge ordered that he should be given a placement in a specialised therapeutic community. Places like that cost hundreds of thousands a year, though, so you have to be a very extreme case to justify the expense.'

'What did he do to qualify?'

'Tried to kill his foster parents. He set fire to their house while they were asleep.'

'Ah.'

Marcus nods again. 'Not a club you really want to be part of.'

'Especially not with a baby on the way.' I take another pull of my pint. 'You know . . . talking to Rowena about what happened with Leah, I realised it would have been almost impossible for me and Donna to have survived her death. It was easier to feel shit if I wasn't around someone else who was also feeling shit, and she felt exactly the same way, so we ended up just . . . pushing apart from each other. A bit like when you swap around two magnets that have been locked together, and suddenly you can't get them to even touch. If the worst does come to the worst, and Social Services take this baby . . . I don't think Susie and I could survive it, either. After all this time, to finally have a child – for her to give birth to it, and hold it, and breastfeed it – and then to be forced to hand it over to some social worker to take God knows where, all over again . . . I think it would probably destroy us.'

Marcus looks at me sympathetically. 'Social workers aren't bad people, Gabe. They just have a process they have to go through.'

'I think you see them in a more positive light than we do. And you've never had Sky, lobbing her missiles from the sidelines.'

'True,' he agrees. 'Once the process has started, there's always a risk. Which is why I think Susie's right about one thing: you *do* need to take this more seriously.'

'We've got a solicitor.'

'Advice from some family-law generalist at the firm that did your conveyancing is not enough. If you really want to fight this, you need a lawyer who specialises in stopping child removals.'

He hesitates. 'Look, I probably shouldn't be saying this, but a few times now, I've been on the other side of the fence, fostering kids who were the subject of contested Placement Orders. There are a couple of lawyers who the local authority are reluctant to go up against, because they know they'll make them look useless in court. Just having one of those people on your side will make them realise they've got a fight on their hands. It'll cost you an arm and a leg, but you might as well spend all that money you made writing crappy power ballads on something, right? At any rate, if I thought I was facing the removal of my unborn child and quite possibly the loss of my marriage too, that's what I'd be doing.'

'You're right,' I say after a moment. I push a beer mat towards him. 'These lawyers – write down their names, would you?'

SEVENTY-FOUR

Susie

At twelve weeks, we went for our first ultrasound. The waiting room was full of happy, excited couples, most of them years younger than us. Only Gabe and I sat tense and silent, unable to speak. I clutched his hand so hard I could feel his knuckles crack.

When we went in, the sonographer already had a colleague with her – in case she needed a second opinion, I realised; they always had to double-check the findings before they broke bad news, and on that terrible occasion when they hadn't been able to find a heartbeat, there'd been an agonising wait while the one who'd done the first scan went and looked for someone who was free.

I got up on the couch without waiting to be asked, my throat so choked I could hardly breathe. They started straight away – just the usual murmured caution about the gel being cold before I felt the sensor pressing into my belly. Was she pressing so hard because she couldn't find anything? That was just paranoia, I told myself. It was always like this. Even so, I turned my head away. The monitor was at an angle to me, but I didn't want to glimpse anything accidentally, not if my baby might be lying inside me lifeless.

'That's the heartbeat,' the sonographer said quietly, and I immediately burst into tears of joy and relief.

'Do you want to see?' she added.

Next to me, Gabe was crying too – we both had to wipe our eyes before we could look at the screen. Even then, there was actually no heart to see – not to my untrained eye, anyway – just some vague blurry outlines. But, as if by magic, a wavy line started to flow along the bottom of the screen and the distorted, underwater sound of a pulse came out of the speaker.

'Oh my God,' I said. 'Oh my God.' I was trying not to get carried away – I'd been here before, after all, only to miscarry weeks later – but it was real, now. We'd reached the first milestone.

The sonographers smiled at each other. 'I'll leave you to it,' the older one said. She slipped out.

The sonographer doing the scan had gone straight to the heartbeat without making the usual preliminary measurements, so she went back and did those now. For the first time, I saw the outline of a foetus, etched in shades of grey and black like some old charcoal drawing. Through our joined hands, I felt Gabe stifle another sob.

'How sure are you about your dates?' the sonographer asked as she worked.

I nodded. 'Pretty sure.'

'We were on a schedule,' Gabe joked. He still sounded dazed.

'If so, the baby's very slightly smaller than normal range,' the sonographer said.

I was instantly alarmed. 'What does that mean?'

'Most likely nothing,' she reassured me. 'It's within the margins of error, but it's something we'll want to keep an eye on. We usually schedule second scans at twenty weeks, but, in your case, we'd probably want to do one sooner anyway. I'll make sure it's in your notes.'

Yet another thing to worry about, I thought. Then something else struck me. When I first started having investigations to try to find out what might be causing my miscarriages, the consultant asked if I ever smoked cannabis.

I answered – truthfully – that I hadn't touched it for years. 'Why? Is it relevant?'

He shrugged. 'There's some evidence it can be linked to a higher risk of miscarriage. As well as lower birthweight.'

I knew Social Services would want access to my medical records. I also knew that, although in theory I had to give my consent, in practice they'd simply ask a judge to issue a court order for them if I refused.

At the thought of Gerry Castle poring over the picture of our baby that was whirring out of the ultrasound's printer, my skin crawled. But it was more than the horrible invasion of privacy that was making my guts contract.

If you were trying to build a picture of a woman who still hadn't learnt the lessons of fifteen years before, the tiny little figure on the screen – the head so much bigger than the body, but already recognisably, undeniably human: *our child* – might not simply be the near-miracle it was to Gabe and me. It might look like yet another piece of evidence.

SEVENTY-FIVE

Sky

Cutting myself with the knife I've hidden keeps me going. But it isn't going to last forever. Already Maya's getting needy and Jaylen's getting annoying and Nicole's trying far too hard to be my mum. Like I haven't had way too many of *those* already. I need to get out of here before someone pins me down like they do Larissa, and that means coming up with a plan B.

A plan, let's face it, that doesn't involve Susie and Gabe. They're not going to want me now. Besides, I only have to think about that *thing* inside her and I feel myself turning red with rage and panic. It's like I literally turned my back on her for one single moment and – *bang* – she's replaced me.

I keep checking Facebook to see if she's announced it yet. But there's been nothing, only a few lame pictures of Sandy.

I scroll through them anyway. I do miss Sandy.

Idly, I try Susie's login, to see if she's changed her password since I hacked into Gabe's computers and phone. To my surprise, she hasn't.

I shake my head in disbelief. *Asking for trouble.*

Then I do another search, for a name I've never looked up before. It's a bit harder to find, but maybe some algorithm or other susses the connection, because Google helpfully puts it on the second page of results.

I stare at it. Am I really desperate enough to do this?

But it's not like I have any other options.

Time for a fresh start. Yeah – another one.

SEVENTY-SIX

Susie

Sally Davis didn't look like a lawyer the local authority was going to be frightened of. She looked like a sweet little granny you'd meet walking the dog. But we'd checked her out and she got glowing reviews.

When I told her I'd seen some websites that suggested we shouldn't cooperate with Social Services, she nodded patiently.

'I've met some of the people behind those sites at various conferences. All I'd say is that it's a high-risk strategy – you'll almost certainly end up in court, in an adversarial situation where you're effectively challenging the judge to find reasons to take your baby away. Whereas, if you can just gather the evidence to show what's really happened, the most likely outcome is that the social workers will simply close their files.'

'What sort of evidence?' Gabe asked.

'At this stage, anything and everything. They can't start formal care proceedings until the baby's born, so time is actually on your side. You need to prove, first, that Sky's accusations against Gabe are baseless, and, second, that you're perfectly capable of bringing up a child. I can't advise you on the first – you'll need to speak to a specialist sexual-offences solicitor – but I can definitely help with the second. It's all about creating a picture of yourselves as competent parents. It could be really simple things, like showing how well you look after your dog. Or, conversely, if you've got a dog who might be a danger to the baby, that you've planned ahead by getting rid of it.'

I thought of poor Sandy. How would he be with a toddler? Pretty good, I hoped, but how would we ever prove that? And, if we had to make some token sacrifice to show Social Services how committed we were, could I really just get rid of him?

'The original charges against Susie were outrageous,' Gabe was saying. 'Presumably we can go back and unpick those?'

Sally shook her head. 'Outrageous or not, a court upheld them. Far easier to work with Social Services to show they're not relevant anymore.'

'What about the cannabis?' I asked. 'And the possibility the baby might be underweight?'

'Well, they don't help our case, but neither do they do much to undermine it. If that was the only evidence being presented to the court, I might be concerned. But I'm hoping that, if it does ever come to proceedings, there'll be a whole raft of things pointing the other way. That's your primary task, now – to prove that their concerns are unfounded.'

SEVENTY-SEVEN

Gabe

'Today,' Gerry Castle says, 'we're going to work on your genogram and ecomap.'

'Sounds great,' I say brightly. 'Er . . . what are those, exactly?'

'Diagrams of the baby's family and social networks. There's evidence that parental isolation is one of the biggest risk factors for a child, so we need to get an understanding of all the people who could support you.' He glances out of our window. 'You're quite remote here, for example. Have you thought about how you'd get the baby to the park? What about antenatal classes? Which neighbours or relatives could you call on if you needed to go out urgently and your baby was asleep?'

'We have a lot of friends,' Susie says weakly. 'But they're mostly other musicians, rather than relatives or neighbours – it's a close-knit world.'

Gerry regards her loftily. 'We find that sometimes people confuse a plethora of social media contacts for genuine support.

When we do the initial family network meeting, we'd hope to have at least a dozen people there.'

'Hang on,' I say. 'The *what*?'

'After we've drawn up the ecomap, we'll invite your relatives and other significant people on it to a meeting,' he explains patiently. 'We'll then facilitate the group to write danger statements about specific areas of concern, along with matching safety goals for you to work towards.'

'But we haven't even told people Susie's pregnant yet,' I object. 'And I'm not sure we'd want to tell our friends and family that we're being investigated by Social Services.'

He gives me a disapproving look. 'One of the benefits of involving a naturally occurring network around the family is that it breaks the taboo of secrecy that typically surrounds child-abuse situations.'

'*Child abuse*? That's a pretty—' I catch Susie's expression and swallow my words. *Cooperation and collaboration, Gabe.* 'Of course. If that's what we need to do.'

'Many people find it's a very positive process, if you engage with it constructively.'

'Then I'm sure we will, too,' I say.

I remember a phrase Susie came across in her endless online research: *disguised compliance*. Being accused of that is a real black mark, apparently. It isn't enough to go along with what these people want; you have to convince them that you genuinely see the error of your ways, like some Maoist re-education programme. If you don't do that, you're *pre-contemplative*, which is the worst thing of all: it means you haven't yet accepted that there's anything wrong with you.

'It'll be good to reconnect with our family in any case,' I say, nodding eagerly. 'I'm sure they'll have loads of useful suggestions.'

SEVENTY-EIGHT

Susie

After Gerry had gone, we sat and stared glumly at the ecomap we'd drawn up. To be perfectly honest, it looked a bit thin. My parents both had new partners and were living abroad – my father, Tim, in Rimini, and my mother, Leilah, mostly in the South of France. Gabe's parents were still in the same three-bedroom house in Leicester where he grew up, but they were less and less inclined to leave it and we only saw them a couple of times a year. I got on pretty well with his sister and her husband, but they were the other side of Cambridge and the effort of getting all their kids into the car for the near two-hour journey to us meant we didn't see them much. As for parks and so on, I'd always thought that, if I did manage to have a baby, we'd cross those bridges when we came to them.

Good God, were we going to have to move house as well, to convince Social Services we were serious about this?

I googled 'danger statements' to see what Gerry wanted us to work towards. Needless to say, the results did nothing to make me feel better.

> Grandparents are worried that: Mum does not always put Zoe's needs first. For grandparents not to be worried, they need: to see Mum responding whenever Zoe cries…

'You've got to stop doing that,' Gabe said, seeing what I was doing.

'I know. It's just so hard not to.' I put the iPad down. 'You do realise this means we're going to have to tell our families about Sky?' So far, we hadn't said anything – we'd wanted to give her a chance to settle in before subjecting her to that.

'Oh, Jesus.' Gabe had gone white. 'I'm going to have to tell my parents I've been accused of exhorting naked pictures from a teenager they don't even know about yet.'

'It could be worse. You could be having to explain that your wife has been done for sex and drugs offences and has already had one child taken away by the courts. Oh, wait – you *are* going to have to tell them that.'

I'd always got the impression that, in some vague, unspecified way, Gabe's parents disapproved of me. Well, now they were really going to have something to get their teeth into.

SEVENTY-NINE

Gabe

Our second hotshot lawyer, the one dealing with Sky's allegations against me, is a man called Mark Fraser.

'Ordinarily, I'd be saying you shouldn't worry too much,' he tells us at our initial meeting. 'The images are category C, the lowest level. Even in the unlikely event you were charged and convicted, that would only mean community service or a suspended sentence. It's far more likely that the police and CPS will close their files with a *No Further Action* note.'

'But this isn't an ordinary situation,' Susie says quietly.

Mark shakes his head. He's a young man, about thirty or so, with the plump, pinkish face of a choirboy. 'They'll only do that if they analyse Gabe's devices and find, first, that those are the only indecent images on them, and, second, that there's no indication he's searched for anything similar online. Unfortunately, there's a backlog of tens of thousands of devices to be analysed that way. It could take up to a year.'

'By which time our baby will have been born, and potentially removed by Social Services,' I say, realising.

He nods. 'Exactly. In order to get this resolved before it influences any care proceedings, you need to tackle it head on.'

'So how do we do that?'

'Well, I don't think you want to focus too much on the fact that Sky's been violent. Social Services might argue it's an additional reason for removing the baby.' He catches our puzzled expressions. 'I know it seems bizarre. But the court won't be interested in who's in the right, only whether the baby's safe. And, from what you've told me, this baby *could* be at risk from Sky – she's already tried to make Susie miscarry. If removing it means it would be in less danger, that's something the judge is obliged to take into consideration.'

'But that's . . . crazy,' Susie says, appalled. 'They should be getting her help to control her violence, not punishing us because of it.'

Mark shrugs apologetically. 'It's a catch-22, I'm afraid. On the one hand, criminal law says they can't arrest her until she's committed a crime. On the other hand, family law says they have to look into the future and predict whether she might commit that crime.'

'So we park the violence,' I say, sighing. 'What *do* we focus on?'

'We need to show there's a pattern of deceptive behaviour here and, ideally, that there's a plausible explanation for it in the shape of reactive attachment disorder. You said she also obtained nude images of her adoptive family's son?'

I nod. 'Henry. He was duped into sending them to her.'

'Do you think the Mulcahys would sign an affidavit to that effect?'

Susie and I exchange a doubtful look.

'We could try,' I say. 'They haven't exactly been cooperative so far.'

'Do you remember – she said she sent the picture to her school email account, so he couldn't simply get hold of her phone and delete it,' Susie says to me. 'Maybe it's still there. After all, she moved schools soon after.'

Mark makes a note. 'That could be useful. Apart from anything else, if she sent it by email, she'll have committed an offence. Technically, that's distribution.'

'Hang on,' Susie says anxiously. 'This is my daughter we're talking about.'

'We're not trying to get her arrested,' Mark reassures her, 'simply discrediting her evidence against Gabe.' He pauses. 'But I'm afraid it *is* going to mean roping in the ex-boyfriend.'

'Ned?' Susie says, puzzled. 'What's he got to do with it?'

'From what you've told me, she lied about her age in order to have sex with him. And he said in his text to Gabe that he wouldn't have slept with her if he'd known how old she really was. Section 74 of the Sexual Offences Act says a person has to be able to give informed consent to intercourse. So if someone lies about having had a vasectomy, say, or says they're single when they're actually married, they can be guilty of obtaining sex by deception, which English courts treat as rape. So far as I know, it's never been used against a minor claiming to be over the age of consent, but there's no reason why it shouldn't be. Fifteen is still well over the age of criminal responsibility.'

There's a silence as Susie and I process this. Susie's the first to speak. 'We are *not* going to accuse Sky of rape. We're simply not.'

Mark nods. 'I understand how you feel. But, again, we're not trying to put Sky in the dock, just keeping Gabe out of it – as well as giving Social Services, and potentially a family court if it comes to it, enough background so they don't take away your baby.'

Susie's face has gone pale. She puts her head in her hands.

'We'll also subpoena Social Services to disclose the paperwork from their investigation into the allegation she made against Ian Mulcahy,' he adds.

'Why do we need that?' I ask.

'First, it will show that she has a good understanding of the process – this time around, she'd know exactly what kind of evidence it would take to get someone charged. Second, given that she was judged to have been lying on that occasion, it shows a track record of making false allegations.'

Susie looks at me, stunned, then back at Mark. 'But she *wasn't* lying that time. Ian Mulcahy faked some evidence that suggested she was, but she was actually telling the truth.'

Mark spreads his hands. 'Possibly. But if Social Services believed him, it's a powerful corroboration of Gabe's story.'

Susie's too shocked to reply.

'I'm afraid there's something else,' Mark adds. 'I appreciate you've been trying to make Sky feel that your door is always open if she wants to come back – and from a therapeutic point of view, that may well be the right thing to do. But it doesn't help *us*. Looked at a different way, you're trying to entice her back to the place where she alleges a serious sexual offence took place. At the very least, it could be construed as witness-tampering.'

'You want me to stop texting her?' Susie says, appalled.

'More than that. I want you to change the locks and install a CCTV system that records to the cloud. And if she does turn up, I want you to call the police. They're unlikely to do much, but they'll log it. It'll create an evidence trail that could bolster our case.'

'This is *grotesque*.' Susie stands up. 'We're not doing this. *Any* of it. I thought we were fighting the allegations against Gabe, not painting Sky as something out of *The Exorcist*.'

'But what if it's actually the same thing?' I say quietly. 'What if, to make our case, we have to make a case against *her*? Which is ultimately more important? Protecting her, or our baby?'

Over the course of our marriage, I've seen Susie miserable, and angry, and horrified, though rarely all at once. What I've never seen, though, is the look of pure hatred that flashes across her face as I say those words.

'Can you not *see* what that will do to her? If we – of all people – appear to side with *him*?' She shakes her head. 'I'm going outside. I need some air.'

I get up to go with her, and she gestures angrily at my seat. 'And *time*, Gabe. I need some time on my own.'

Mark waits, unperturbed, as she strides out. I suppose he witnesses scenes like that quite often.

She'd been like Sky, I think. As Susie left, I'd been reminded of Sky, storming out of our kitchen.

I push the thought away. 'Sorry about that. It's very difficult for her.'

Mark nods. 'I can imagine. But it does bring me to a couple of final points. First, this journalist, Fi White. I'd like to hit her with a cease-and-desist, and also make clear to her she mustn't write anything that could prejudice potential legal proceedings against you. It's unfortunate the police take so long to process indecent images, of course, but the silver lining is that it should keep her from writing anything else for at least a year, by which time the fuss will hopefully have died down. We can also try to get confirmation that it was Sky who posted the original allegations on the whisper network, and that they were made up, which will all contribute to the picture of someone using false allegations to manipulate people's perception of you.'

I nod. Susie won't like that last part, I know, but it's clear that she and I are going to have to have a serious talk about how to handle this in any case.

'Then there's the question of what actually happened. We've been talking as if you're completely innocent of these charges, and of course I respect that. But, equally, if there *are* any other indecent images on your devices, it's best I know now, so we can plan your defence. There are some very good therapy centres, for example, and if you were able to say that, while you were waiting for the police to analyse your phone, you went and got help, the CPS would take that into consideration before deciding whether or not to charge you.'

I shake my head. 'There's nothing. Or, at least, nothing put there by me.'

'Right. Which leads me to the last thing.' Mark looks a little discomfited. 'I understand why this must be difficult for Susie. But I'm going to have to get my assistant to draw up a formal letter of engagement, and it seems to me that it's you I should be acting for, not the two of you. I don't think I even *could* act for both of you, given that the criminal allegations are against you, rather than her. And it's clear to me that, if we do end up having to fight any charges, there could be a conflict of interest.' He pauses. 'That's to say, in order to clear your name, I might need to advise you to do things that Susie won't be happy with.'

EIGHTY

Susie

'We're not using him,' I said when Gabe finally appeared outside. If anything, my anger had only grown while I'd been waiting. 'He's *odious*.'

'And highly recommended by our other lawyer,' Gabe said firmly. 'Besides, it was you who wanted us to take this more seriously, remember? You were right, I can see that now. We've constantly been on the back foot, while Sky's been able to make all the running.'

'Will you please stop painting her as some kind of *perpetrator*.'

'But she *is*,' Gabe said, with just a hint of impatience. 'She wants to get our baby taken away. She wants to break up our marriage. These are the facts, Susie – she's said so herself.'

'She can't help herself. She's damaged.'

'Yes. And she's going to damage *us*, if we don't stop her.'

'What happened to "in this together", Gabe?' I said acidly. It was the most wounding thing I could think of, and completely unfair, but I wanted to provoke him. I wanted him to stop being so maddeningly reasonable and to stop agreeing with horrible lawyers and to find us a way out of this mess where no one got hurt.

'That was below the belt,' he muttered.

'You haven't *got* anything below the belt.' I knew I was just hurling pathetic playground insults now, but I couldn't stop myself. 'You should have grown a pair months ago, before everything got this bad. And if you'd only put a decent passcode on your phone in the first place, none of this would have happened.'

'This is *my* fault?' he said, astonished.

'What sort of person becomes an indecent-images specialist, anyway? I bet there's some dodgy accusation in *his* past.'

'Look,' Gabe said patiently, 'you're understandably upset –'

'Too right I am!'

'– but even you must be able to see that we have to stop centring our whole lives around Sky now. She's very nearly an adult. She needs to start taking responsibility for her actions, instead of constantly being allowed to play the victim.'

I stared at him angrily. Truth be told, it was that *even you* that whipped my fury up still further – the knowledge that there was more than a grain of truth in what he was saying, that I'd been so blinded by my love for someone I barely knew that I'd sleepwalked into this.

I reached for something – anything – that might wound him still further.

'Is that what you said to your teenage groupies, Gabe? What you'd have said to their parents? That they were *almost adults*?'

His face clouded. I could see him making a gargantuan effort not to get angry. 'We have a baby on the way. It's what we've always wanted. What *you've* always wanted. You have to prioritise, Susie. *Our* child, or . . . or . . .' He made an exasperated gesture. 'It's obvious, surely?'

And that made it even worse, because the echo of Sky was ringing in my ears – *You need to choose* – like a feedback loop, a howling crescendo of turmoil and frustration and anger. There was only one way out, and right there in the car park of some bland prefab business park, with people hurrying past us into the law firm's offices and wondering no doubt who the crazy couple shouting at each other were, I let him have it – the very worst thing I could say.

The thing I'd been trying to avoid even thinking.

'What if I don't want a baby with you anymore, Gabe? What if Sky's more important to me than any of that? What if I'd rather have a termination?'

EIGHTY-ONE

Sky

Rahmi and Jaylen have a row and break up, and afterwards Rahmi runs away. There's a bit more staff activity than usual, then two uniformed police officers turn up to talk to Barry. They seem remarkably relaxed about the situation – 'All right, Baz? Hear we're back on the frequent-flyer programme. Any more call-outs and we'll have earned a toaster.'

Frequent flyers – that's what they call repeat runaways, Maya tells me, as Barry takes them into his office. They'll do a sweep of a few obvious places – the town centre, bus shelters, a particular playground where the local glueheads nod out – then basically give up and wait for her to come back.

I give Maya a sideways look. 'Where do you think she is?'

'She went off in a car with two older guys. It'll be the usual thing. They'll have given her ket.'

'In exchange for having sex with them, you mean?'

Maya shrugs. 'Or with their mates.'

'Have you told Barry?'

She shakes her head. I get it. You don't snitch. The one thing all of us here want is to be in control of our own lives. Even when we're quite clearly not.

'What if she doesn't come back?' I ask.

'The feds always give it twenty-four hours before they put out an alert. That's when Barry has to change the notification from *absent* to *missing*. But the people who've taken her know that. They'll make sure she's back before then.'

I'm silent a moment. It occurs to me that Maya knows the system here pretty well. She might be able to help with plan B.

But that means trusting her – a little bit, at least.

'If someone wanted to get out of this place,' I say casually, 'and they didn't want the feds coming after them, how would they do it?'

She gives me a look. 'They'll always come after you. You've just got to make sure they don't look too hard. You want to be NAR – no apparent risk.'

'And how would you manage that?'

She shrugs. 'Leave a note saying so.'

I do a double take. 'Is that it?'

'Pretty much. I mean, there'll still be reports and all that, but if you've left a note saying you're not in danger and you don't want them looking for you, you're not exactly going to be top priority, are you? Not when they've got people like Rahmi to look for.' She gestures at the police car outside. 'Even then, that lot'll probably decide it's a *lifestyle choice*. Which is another way of saying, you went off with some men one day and they didn't bring you back, but no one gives a shit.'

Again I find myself wondering what strange roads have led Maya to this place. 'OK. Thanks.'

'You gonna do that, then? Run away?' She asks it casually, but I see the look in her eyes and I know exactly what's going on in there, because it's familiar to me as well. It's the look of a shutter coming down as yet another person in your life decides you're not a keeper.

'Maybe.' I shrug. 'Haven't decided yet. Might stick around for a while.'

'Cool,' she says in her soft, whispery voice. She doesn't bother to say that I'm lying, even though we both know it.

EIGHTY-TWO

Susie

Gabe drove us home in silence. But as my anger slowly subsided, it was replaced by the realisation that I'd gone too far this time. Even if we needed to have that conversation, which we did, throwing it at him like that in the middle of a car park was unforgivable.

We almost never fight. That's one of the things I love about him – however emotional I get, he stays calm. But sometimes his very lack of anger can be infuriating, and sometimes I know I push his buttons just to get a reaction.

He pulled into our drive and cut the engine. As he reached for the door handle, I stopped him.

'Gabe . . . I'm sorry.'

'Sorry for what you said? Or the way you said it?' His voice was flat.

'Both. But . . .' I took a deep breath. 'I *have* been having second thoughts. Or perhaps that's putting it too strongly . . . Doubts, maybe. Fears. I just couldn't find a way to tell you.'

'But *why*?' He sounded genuinely confused. 'Because of Sky?'

'Not exactly. Not the way that sounds.' I was struggling to put this into words, but I knew it was important to try. 'If I have this baby, and they take it away from us, there's a chance its life could be like hers has been. I don't think I could bear to do that to a child of mine, not a second time. And then there's the possibility that we might go through all this, only for me to lose it anyway. But if I had a termination . . . there'd be no arguing then, would there? It would be the biggest *fuck off* we could possibly give them. We'd be out of their clutches for good.'

'You mean . . . you'd be in control,' he said, frowning, and I silently blessed him for trying to understand.

'Yes.' I gestured up at the farmhouse. 'We have a nice life, don't we? This place, Sandy, the band . . . And now we're thinking of adding another person into the mix. It's all just so terrifying. I'm not even sure I can do it.'

It had started to rain, but with the engine turned off the windscreen wipers didn't come on and the drops made a pattern on the glass, *tap tap tap*.

'Because, if I'm honest,' I said quietly, 'the judge was probably right to rule that Sky be taken away from me, back then. I've never admitted that to myself before – not in fifteen years. I've always told myself I was the victim of some terrible miscarriage of justice. But I wasn't. I was an out-of-control, spoilt, twenty-year-old cokehead who'd have made a terrible mother.'

'But you're not anymore,' he said softly.

'I'd like to think not. But look at the evidence – I've just done it again, haven't I? Having Sky come to live with us has been a horrible failure. And that's got to be partly down to the way I've parented her.'

'Don't beat yourself up. She was damaged before she came here.'

But he didn't disagree.

We were silent a moment, each lost in our own thoughts.

'You said, back there, it was me,' he said at last. 'That you didn't want to have a baby with me anymore.'

'I was trying to provoke you. Sorry. First trimester hormones and all that.'

He acknowledged the apology with a nod. 'But there *is* a grain of truth in what you said – I can tell. We've not been getting on the way we used to. Not since . . .' He sighed. 'You know, when you suggested pausing the schedule that time, I was relieved.'

I glanced across at him. 'I hadn't realised.'

'I was going to say something. But you got there first.'

'So . . . Is there a part of you that also thinks termination might be a good idea?' I was finding it hard to get my head around this. I'd always taken Gabe's commitment to having a baby with me for granted.

He shook his head. 'No. I mean – whatever your decision is, I'll support it. Even a late termination, if that's really what you decide you need. But there's never a perfect time to have a child, is there? And, let's face it . . . if we don't take this opportunity, there may not be another. Besides, I think we can do it – I think we can beat Social Services *and* create a human being who's kind and loving and tries to do good in the world. Someone who's as beautiful and amazing and fearless as you are.'

I put my hand on his. 'As *you* are, you mean. But thank you. It's good to know you'd support me, if the investigation really did get too much.'

He didn't answer. I knew how big a deal that would be for him. But I also knew he wouldn't go back on his word.

And I knew then there was absolutely no way I could pass up the opportunity to have a child with this man. I'd needed to hear him tell me I had the freedom to choose, but it was the very fact he'd said it that made me sure I didn't want to.

'And Sky?' he said at last. 'Do I have your permission to fight her allegations tooth and nail?'

'Oh . . .' I said desperately. 'I don't know, Gabe. I just don't know.'

He waited. His response lay between us, unspoken: *I'd support you, even if it meant not having a baby together. What about you? How deep is your support for me?*

'Do what you need to do,' I said, and promptly burst into tears.

EIGHTY-THREE

Sky

Dear Barry and Nicole,

Thank you so much for making me feel welcome here. I have greatly enjoyed my time in this home. However, I have recently been contacted by an old friend from Edinburgh who has offered me a place to live and I have decided to go and stay with her instead. I just wanted to reassure you that I am perfectly safe, not in any trouble, and do not need anyone to come looking for me.

Kind regards,

Sky

EIGHTY-FOUR

Gabe

'I need something from you,' I say to Ian Mulcahy. 'And I'm not going to take no for an answer.'

He glances at me suspiciously. 'What is it?'

We're sitting on a park bench near the council offices where he works. He's grudgingly given me five minutes.

'Sky's made some allegations about me that are remarkably similar to the ones she made against you – except that, in my case, there isn't a grain of truth in them. My lawyer needs you to sign something explaining the similarity.'

He looks away. 'I've got no interest in raking all that up again.'

'But you'll do it, all the same.'

He snorts contemptuously. 'I don't think I will.'

'Look,' I say patiently. 'It's very simple. I don't want to use the investigation into you as part of my defence, not least because it sticks in my throat to use something I know full well you lied about. But I will if I have to. And if I do, it'll be part of a narrative about what a terrible, toxic parent you were. You told me education's a small world and you don't want anyone to know that Sky's adoption failed. Well, unless you help me, they *will* know – I'll make sure of it. At the very least, we can produce that note you signed, proving you threw a fifteen-year-old out of your house. What sort of educational psychologist thinks that's an appropriate way of dealing with a troubled child's problems?'

Ian Mulcahy considers me thoughtfully. 'I didn't take you for a blackmailer.'

'I'm starting to surprise myself. Call it payback for sending me those documents about Susie.'

'That? I did *that* to protect you.'

Now it's my turn to snort. 'Really.'

'Yes.' He catches my look. 'Think about it. Anna – Sky – knew all about Susie's past and you didn't. If I hadn't sent you those papers, she'd still be using them as leverage over Susie now. It was mostly self-interest, I admit – I thought it better that you knew the full picture from the outset, so you'd be more inclined to make allowances when things got tough. Allowances for Anna, that is, not Susie.' He pauses. 'It might not have seemed like it at the time, but I really wanted living with you and Susie to work out for her – as much as anything *can* work out for Anna, anyway. How is she, by the way? Jenny's desperate for news.'

'We don't know. They've got her in a children's home for teenagers.'

He nods, unsurprised. 'Well, you can tell your lawyer I'll give you your statement. But you know something? I don't think it'll do you any good, not in the long run. Anna's uncontrollable and she's not going to change.'

EIGHTY-FIVE

Sky

I strip my bed, gather my possessions and place the note on the bedside table. Before I leave, I reread it one last time. Like a polite letter from a well-brought-up young lady, I think, thanking her hosts for a lovely weekend. I can imagine the police and social workers passing it round their multi-agency meeting and scratching their heads. *She even left her room tidy*, Barry informs them. *What sort of runaway does that?*

The sort with a plan, I tell him silently.

It's just before dawn when I go downstairs. There's meant to be a member of staff around all night, but usually they're asleep or watching TV. The front door's locked on the inside to keep intruders out, but they're not allowed to lock us in. That would be deprivation of liberty. We have to have the freedom to make bad decisions, apparently.

Not that this *is* a bad decision, I remind myself. Quite the reverse.

The first train to London leaves at 5.45 a.m. On the platform, there are just a few bleary-eyed commuters, a couple of nurses and some workmen in high-viz jackets. No one gives me a second glance. There'll be CCTV, but I don't worry about it. If I was really going to Edinburgh, I'd be going via London anyway.

At Marylebone, I have a pastry, killing time, then go to St Pancras and walk around a bit. From there, I head across Regent's Park to St John's Wood. It's almost eight now and everything's getting busier. I pass a smart school that has security guards on the doors, like it's a nightclub that needs bouncers, then turn into a road where almost every house has some kind of tradesman's van parked outside – gardeners, builders, decorators, security consultants. Everyone here's busy spending money.

Except number sixty-seven. Number sixty-seven is quiet. But somebody's home – the Mercedes G-Wagon and Porsche parked on the drive tell me that.

I press the intercom and wait. It's the sort with a camera, and I position myself in front of it, selfie style, waiting to announce myself.

But then the door's pulled open and a man comes eagerly on to the steps, bouncing on the soles of his feet with excitement. He's about Gabe's age, but short and muscled like a bodybuilder, with cropped greying hair and a stud in one ear.

'I don't believe it,' he says, beaming at me. 'I don't fucking believe it. You made it. Come on in and give your old man a hug.'

EIGHTY-SIX

Sky

Hi Jason. My name is Sky and I am 15 years old. If you might have had a baby with a woman called Susie Jukes in 2007 could we perhaps speak? I believe you may be my birth father.
Best wishes
Sky

EIGHTY-SEVEN

Susie

'Does the baby have a name yet?' Gerry Castle asked, his pen poised over a legal pad.

'No,' Gabe said. 'We don't even know if it's a boy or a girl. Why?'

'I need to open a case file for this meeting.' Gerry sounded uncharacteristically apologetic. 'If you don't have a name, the file will just be called "Unborn Thompson". The thing is, we can't rename it later – the files are stored on a separate secure system.'

Gabe made a couldn't-care-less gesture, as if to say that file names were the least of our worries. But then he saw my look. *Cooperation and collaboration.*

'Unborn Thompson is fine,' he said brightly. 'In fact, that might even be a contender, when it comes to it. Musicians have given their kids worse names, after all. How do you take your tea, Gerry?'

'I think I'll change mine to hibiscus,' Leilah said. 'Would you mind, Gabe? As you're up.'

We'd managed to scrape together twelve attendees for Gerry's family network meeting. As well as Gabe and me, there was his sister Hannah and her husband Nick, my mother Leilah and her new husband Matias, and Gabe's parents, Bill and Christine. I'd also roped in the band – Jack, Marlon, Stu and Chrissie – but, to be honest, they were only there to make up the numbers.

Gerry had brought along an easel and a large flip-pad, on which he now wrote, *Areas of concern*.

'First, we're going to come up with some statements about risk,' he said as he wrote. 'Then we're going to write some matching statements about what Susie and Gabe will need to outcome, in order to make us all feel less concerned.'

Oh dear, I thought. He was going to use *outcome* as a verb, which would totally wind Gabe up.

'Well, *my* main concern –' Hannah began.

Eagerly, Gerry uncapped his marker. 'Yes?'

'– is that this baby might be taken away by Social Services.' Hannah looked around. 'I mean, that's why we're all here, right? To try to stop that happening.'

'And this is a very important part of that process,' Gerry assured her. He pointed the end of his pen at my mother. 'Leilah, why don't you go first? What specific worries might you have for your grandchild?'

Leilah considered. 'Susannah's always found it very hard to stick at things. Even when she was little. Schools, for example. I suppose one might worry she'll get bored of it.'

Says the woman who's on her third husband. I forced myself to beam and nod, as if grateful for this pearl of maternal wisdom.

Gerry wrote down *Bored of the baby* with evident satisfaction. 'Christine?'

Gabe's mother looked anxiously at her husband. 'What do we worry about, Bill?'

'Drugs,' he said crisply. 'If she went back on the drugs, that would be really bad.'

I nodded cheerfully as Gerry wrote down *Drugs*.

'And prostitution,' Bill added.

Even Gerry had the grace to hesitate before he wrote that.

I am a thirty-five-year-old pregnant woman with a husband and a career, I wanted to shout. *Not a chaotic twenty-year-old trying to coax a scumbag into handing over an eight-gram bag of coke.*

I didn't, of course. I just kept smiling.

Gabe, coming back with Leilah's hibiscus tea and Gerry's – rather surprising – peppermint, caught the end of this and raised his eyebrows at me. I thought about the two of us laughing about it when they'd all gone and felt slightly better.

Gerry turned to my stepfather. 'Matias? Anything to add?'

'I am sure they will be excellent parents,' Matias said in his serious, near-perfect English. 'However, I have two concerns. One is whether they will be able to get staff, out here, so far from London. The other is having a wild dog in the house.'

'*Rescue* dog,' Gabe murmured. 'Not actually *wild*.'

Somewhat doubtfully, Gerry wrote down *Staff*, then put *Remoteness* next to it.

'I'll tell you something else for free,' Bill said. 'Having kids is bloody hard work. Christine didn't get a moment's rest from the day Hannah was born. Susie's never even had a proper job.'

I let my mouth fall open at that. Gabe said mildly, 'I think most people would call being a professional singer a proper job, Dad.'

'Singing!' Bill pronounced it like it was two separate words – *sing-ging* – for extra scorn.

'We've done all right from our sing-ging,' Gabe said. 'Both of us.'

'Well – in your case, you were more of a professional sex object,' Hannah said.

'Thanks for that, sis,' Gabe said.

'Any more concerns?' Gerry asked, with the air of a man who was starting to enjoy himself. 'Chrissie? Jack?'

Jack considered. 'I'd be worried if the baby came to rehearsals without ear defenders. My new kit's pretty loud.'

'The right school is so important, too,' Matias murmured.

'I don't want to point out the obvious,' Bill said bluntly, 'but these two have already proved they can't discipline a teenager effectively.'

With a flourish, Gerry wrote down *Parenting style*.

'I don't think *that's* true,' Leilah said, frowning. 'They simply tried to make the poor girl welcome.'

'Oh, here we go,' Bill muttered. 'Jordans and all that.'

'What's wrong with Jordans?' Leilah said, puzzled.

I gave Gabe a helpless look. How did we ever think this wasn't going to go badly? We might have arrogantly assumed that, just because none of us lived on council estates, we were somehow less dysfunctional than other families, but the truth was, we were simply affluent enough not to have to see each other very often. What should have been a simple tick-box exercise to prove how normal we were was actually proving the exact opposite.

'Good,' Gerry said. 'I think we've generated some useful areas of concern, so thank you for that. Now we'll focus on what addressing those concerns might look like.'

Through the window, I saw a police car turning up our drive. 'Were the police invited to this?' I asked.

Gerry kept writing on his flip-pad. 'Not that I'm aware of.'

Gabe got up. 'I'll see what they want.'

Gerry was saying something about the importance of sustaining safety goals over time. I was barely listening. My attention was on Gabe, outside – his expression of concern, then disbelief, then anger – as he talked to the two police officers. Gradually, everyone else in the room followed my lead, until we were all staring out of the window.

Gabe came back in. 'You won't believe this,' he said furiously. 'She's missing.'

EIGHTY-EIGHT

Sky

The house is amazing. Not Gabe-and-Susie's-house amazing – that's like something out of a style magazine, all tasteful colours and understated shabby-chic furnishings. This is more bling. My bedroom has a massive TV that rises on hydraulic motors out of the foot of the bed. The bath has whirlpool jets and a switch that makes them light up with different colours. In the basement, there's a swimming pool with underwater speakers, and the fitness room has a huge screen linked to a virtual gym.

'Not bad for someone who spent four years banged up,' Jason says proudly when he shows me round.

It's not only him who spends a lot of time in the fitness room. Tabitha does too. She's his girlfriend, though sometimes he calls her 'wifey'. She used to be a model – she's blonde and very thin. She goes shopping roughly every other day, to places that are all within a few hundred yards of each other. Selfridges, Gucci, Tiffany, Chanel.

'She'll take you, next time,' Jason says to me, nodding. 'Go on – put a dent in my plastic, princess. There's nothing I like better than seeing my girls come home with all them Bond Street bags.'

He's already given me a fat wad of cash 'for expenses' – not that I have any, living here. And a box containing the latest iPhone. I can't believe it. They cost almost a thousand pounds.

'And I'll take your old one,' he says with a wink. 'Lock it somewhere safe. We don't want anyone knowing you're staying over, right?'

One of the sitting rooms is reserved for his work. Every morning, he lays out a row of phones on the glass coffee table – not iPhones, just cheap pay-as-you-go mobiles. Then, every night, he takes the SIM cards out and disappears into the back alley to hide them.

'Safely off the premises,' he says when he returns. 'Can't be too careful, in my line of work.'

What that work is wouldn't take a genius to figure out. Sometimes, hard-looking men with Eastern European accents and girlfriends who all look like Tabitha come round for dinner, and at some point in the meal all the women have to get up and leave them to talk, like in some period drama. And sometimes, when there's a problem that can't be sorted on the phones, young men with elaborate tattoos slip into the garden by the side gate, the one he usually keeps bolted, for muttered conversations.

Sometimes, I overhear him on the phone. Occasionally, he'll even wander near me as he talks, winking or pulling comic faces that don't show in his voice. It's all done in a kind of code – but, again, it's not rocket science. *Tops* and *bots* are uppers and downers – cocaine and heroin. Sometimes, he changes it to *lemo* and *bobby*, just to mix things up. *Shardy* is ketamine and *jackets* is skunk. *The flat*, where most of his supplies come from, is Amsterdam. *How much the tops in flat, buddy?* might be followed by, *That won't even buy me a drink. But if you wanna send over a scratch . . .*

When he has those conversations in front of me – trusting me – it feels good. It isn't like Gabe and Susie trusting me not to take money, or Hilcham letting me set my own timetable. It's more like the thrill of being welcomed into his world.

His neighbours think he runs a haulage company. 'Which, in a way, I do, princess. Besides, it's good like that round here. Everyone's moody in their own way, right?'

Translation: whether you're a Canary Wharf banker working all hours, or a reclusive celebrity avoiding the paps, no one here's got much interest in residents' associations or street parties.

When we first started messaging, he was suspicious. Which was interesting, because usually for me it's been the other way round. It took a week or so before he agreed to talk, then another week of FaceTiming before he asked if I wanted to come and stay with him. To see how we got on, as he put it.

Even now, I can sense him watching me. Sizing me up.

I've got no illusions. The fact I've been in care clearly helps – there's no family in the background who might cause problems. And the fact I'm too young to be a police informant is a bonus, too.

Since it's expected of me, I do a bit of shopping with Tabitha. It's nice to have new clothes, but to be honest my heart isn't in it – not at her kind of shops, anyway. In the end, while she does her regular beat up and down Bond Street, I go round to Oxford Street. Juicy Couture, All Saints, Miss Selfridge.

'Christ, you're a cheap date, princess,' Jason says when he sees the receipts. 'Tabs, why can't you try some of these places?'

I've been there a week when he asks me what I want to do with my life.

'Cos, if there's any way I can help . . .' he adds.

I tell him I want to go to uni to study music. He sucks his teeth.

'Uni? Which one?'

'I haven't decided yet.'

'What about Manchester?'

'Why Manchester?'

'It's big. Lots of students, good scene. Good *music* scene, I mean.'

We both know that isn't what he means, or not only that.

And then he clearly goes away and mulls it over, because it's another day or so before he says casually, 'Tell you what, princess. How would you feel about running a few errands for me while you're here?'

EIGHTY-NINE

Susie

Gabe was incandescent with anger. 'Did you know about this?' he kept asking Gerry. 'Did you know she'd absconded from the place where you were supposedly keeping her safe?'

'I was aware there were concerns,' Gerry said defensively. 'And we don't actually know she's absconded. Just that she's absent.'

'And the police have absolutely no idea where she's gone.' Gabe gestured at the police car, still parked outside. 'They thought she might be here, for Christ's sake. We're listed as the last place she ran away to – that's how up to date *their* information is.'

'Most absentees do turn up safe and well eventually. She left a note, I believe, saying she might go to Edinburgh. To visit a friend.'

'She doesn't have any friends in Edinburgh,' I said flatly. I felt numb and panicked at the same time. 'And, as you keep reminding us, she's still a child. Why aren't you doing more to find her? Why isn't this all over the news?'

Gerry hesitated. 'When young people go missing – young people in care – and it's of their own choice, the media aren't always very interested. I'm sorry.'

'You *took her away from us*,' Gabe said. 'She's vulnerable – in so many ways – but we trusted that, at the very least, you'd keep her safe.'

'We take the safeguarding of looked-after children very seriously,' Gerry said feebly. 'But it's not as if we can lock them up.'

We gave the police a list of all the places we could think of – Annabel's, Ned's, even the Mulcahys' – but they'd already tried most of them.

When everyone had gone, Gabe and I sat and racked our brains for more ideas.

I glanced at him. 'Thank you for caring about her. Some people in your position might have been relieved she's gone.'

'Of course I care – she's your daughter. She's also psychologically troubled and has a history of making bad choices. They should have been watching her like a hawk.'

We were silent a moment.

'There must be somewhere,' Gabe said at last. 'Or some*one*, more likely. Unlike the police, we know Sky and how she thinks. I keep remembering that phrase Marcus used – "ghost kingdoms". Who else might she have constructed a fantasy around, the way she once constructed one around us?'

'Beats me.'

But even as I said it, an awful thought slid into my head. A thought so horrible I didn't even want to contemplate it, but which couldn't entirely be dismissed.

'Oh my God,' I said slowly.

Gabe looked at me. 'What?'

'She might be with her father.'

'Her . . .' Gabe began, then stopped. 'You've never actually said who her father is.'

'I . . . I didn't think it was relevant. I wasn't deliberately keeping it from you, Gabe, I promise, not once I'd told you about the court case. Somehow it just never came up – he was always an irrelevance, even then.' I took a deep breath. 'But one day Sky asked me a direct question, so I told her. It was the man I was arrested with – the dealer. He and I were together briefly – at least, I was sleeping with him, until I realised he was having sex with his other female customers too, when he got the chance. I told Sky he was a scumbag who'd never had anything to do with her, and she seemed to accept that. But I remember she asked me what his name was, and I told her.'

NINETY

Sky

It was Maya who'd explained to me how the drugs business works.

'It's all run from the big cities – London, mainly. Sometimes, when they go into a new town, they set up a base – what they call a trap house – or they might do it all by runner. Either way, they get kids to ferry the gear and cash around.'

'Why kids?'

She shrugged. 'They're less likely to get stopped and searched. Girls are even better than boys, that way.' She gave me a sideways look. 'Posh white girls are best of all. They got people out looking for that sort. However many they get, they always need more.'

'Why? Because the first lot get arrested?'

'Not even arrested. Matrixed.' She saw my puzzled look. 'It's like this list the feds have. Anyone they think might be involved with the lines, they put them on the matrix. They're no use to the crew then, cos they can get stopped any time.'

I couldn't help wondering if Maya had ever been matrixed. 'What happens to them after that?'

'If it's a girl, she might end up as a giftie. You know – made to have sex with the elders. If it's a guy, maybe they'll arrange a fake mugging with another crew. So then they'll be like, *You owe us now, that's three grand you've gotta pay back*. But if the kid's done a good job, shown some balls, they might get to be an elder themselves.'

'Girls too? Or just the guys?'

Maya nodded. 'Sometimes girls. They gotta be able to handle themselves, though. Most of these crews carry blades.'

I thought of the knife in my room, the one I used when I needed to let the anger out. How it felt in my hand, the power.

Jason takes me to a flat in an estate behind Marylebone train station.

'Airbnb,' he says succinctly, as we wait for the door to be opened. 'Not in my name, obviously. The owner's not meant to sublet, so she's sweet with it.'

Inside, two young guys – one my age, the other about twenty – are weighing white powder into small bags. A third is on a computer.

'Lewis, K-Man,' Jason says, indicating the ones with the scales. 'They look after distribution. That's Pauly on the web, and Jonny's out doing full service. Boys, we're now a family business. This is my long-lost daughter.'

Neither Lewis nor K-Man reacts much to that. Pauly looks up and nods briefly.

'K-Man, take her out on a couple of runs,' Jason instructs. He turns to me. 'Mix it up. Train's good, but not every day. Don't use Uber – they can track your data. Black cabs are all right, but they cost, so don't go crazy. Can you handle a moped?'

I'm about to point out that I'm too young to ride a moped, but then I catch myself. I'm about to ferry cocaine down a county drugs line. Of course no one here cares if it's legal or not for me to ride a moped.

'You'll pick it up quick,' he says, nodding. 'But get a decent helmet, yeah? Don't want my princess banging that beautiful head. And keep the visor down, or the CCTV'll get you.'

NINETY-ONE

Gabe

We give the police Jason's name. When we don't hear anything back, I call them.

'According to the file, that gentleman's been spoken to,' a bored voice says. 'He's not had any contact with her.'

'What if he's lying?'

'Why would he do that?' the voice says patiently.

I relay this conversation to Susie, who says, 'I literally cannot think of a single other person she could have gone to.'

'I get that, but . . . she was only in our lives a few months. There must be loads of things we don't know about her.'

She frowns. 'You make it sound like she's gone for good.'

'I didn't mean that. She'll turn up, for sure.'

I hope that'll be the case, of course. But I can't help remembering Ian Mulcahy's words: *Anna's uncontrollable and she's not going to change*.

Mark, the lawyer, won't be drawn on what her disappearance means for me. 'On the one hand, they no longer have their only witness. On the other, she may simply reappear at any moment ... I think we continue as we are.'

So I call Ian Mulcahy again and get the address of Jill and Mike Fletcher, the foster carers who looked after Sky when she was first put up for adoption. Their front door is still just as the social worker described it in her letter, with a pane of wavy glass. It isn't an excited three-year-old who comes to open it, though, but a teenager of Sky's age with glasses.

'Amazon?' she says doubtfully.

I shake my head. 'I'm looking for your parents. Are they in?'

'Mum?' she calls over her shoulder. 'It's for you.'

After a short while, a woman in her fifties comes to the door, wiping her hands on a towel.

'Could I have a few minutes?' I ask. 'It's about a little girl you fostered around twelve years ago.'

'Sky?' She looks anxious. 'You'd better come in.'

We go into the dining room. Jill carefully shuts the door before we sit down.

'Rosie knows she was adopted, of course. But she doesn't know much about Sky. Are you a social worker?'

'No.' Briefly, I explain why I've come.

Jill sighs. 'Oh, that poor girl. It was an awful time – we'd fully intended to adopt her as well, but the local authority kept asking us to take more and more children. First there was Rosie, then Sky, and then they asked us to foster Morgan, too. He was seven. They weren't meant to tell us why any of them had been taken into care, but they usually gave us some idea. So we knew he'd been abused, but not the exact details.'

'Ah.' Suddenly, I can see exactly how this conversation is going to unfold – the awful inevitability of it, cycles of horror and neglect repeating themselves down the generations.

Jill nods. 'He never gave any signs of being abusive himself. Quite the opposite – he was introverted, almost mute, terrified of his own shadow. We were concentrating on making him feel safe . . . It was an uphill struggle, particularly with two boisterous three-year-olds around. We probably neglected the girls a bit. But they always seemed perfectly happy, playing together with their dolls.'

She stops for a moment, unable to go on.

'It was a teddy bear they used to play with that first made us realise. Mike noticed someone had picked apart the seam where its legs joined and poked a pencil up there. Rosie told us it was Sky, and, when we spoke to her, she told us what Morgan had been doing to her. It had been going on for weeks.'

'Oh my God,' I say heavily.

She nods. 'We tried to make it work, but it was so hard. Mike slept in Morgan's room to make sure he didn't get out, while I slept with the girls. Sky was in a bad way by then – bedwetting, refusing to eat, going up to total strangers and being inappropriate . . . We were exhausted. Social Services did try to help, but at the end of the day it was just us and these poor damaged kids in this house. So, in the end, we had to ask them to take him away.'

She's silent for a moment.

'By then, we were going through the adoption process with the girls. Endless meetings with the social workers, home visits, little diagrams of all the people we were supposed to be able to call on for support –'

'I know about those,' I say with feeling.

'– when the truth was, we never saw anyone else. How could we, when Sky might . . . Well, I won't spell it out.'

'So you decided to keep Rosie, but not Sky.'

Jill looks anguished. 'Put like that, it sounds so brutal. But we thought it was the only way for her to get the help she needed. If we'd adopted her, all the support would have stopped, and where would that have left her? That's when they found the Mulcahys . . . They asked us not to say anything to them about Sky's problems, though. They said it was best done through the proper channels.'

'What happened to Morgan?'

'He went to a children's home. I heard he was in a young offender institution at one point.' Jill starts to cry. 'It's awful, I know, but what could we do? It was either give one of those kids a decent home, or fail all of them. At any rate, that's what it felt like.'

'You mustn't blame yourself,' I say gently. 'You adopted a child. That's an amazing thing to do. And Rosie seems like she's doing really well.'

'Yes.' Jill slides a tear from one eye with her finger. 'She is. Tell me, did we do the right thing? Did they get Sky some help? Social Services were under such strain then . . . But the Mulcahys seemed like decent people. He was a psychologist, too, so we assumed that was why they'd chosen them – because he'd know what to do with her.'

'I'm afraid . . .' I stop, unsure how to put this. It wasn't only Susie who was affected by Sky's adoption, I realise. Jill has also been tormenting herself about whether she made the right choice.

But equally, I can't lie to her.

'It was good for a while,' I say gently. 'I think, for a time, they were all genuinely happy. But once she hit adolescence, it got tough.'

Jill nods. 'You know, it wasn't always plain sailing with Rosie, either. There was a period when – well, I won't go into details. But we got through it in the end, and now she's just lovely to be around. So perhaps there's hope for Sky, too.'

'I hope so,' I say. 'I really hope so.'

NINETY-TWO

Sky

All I ever wanted was to be left alone.

Nothing bad happens when you're on your own. It's being with other people that fucks you up.

Either they get angry or they try to be nice. Of the two, being nice is the one I really hate. Being nice just leads to more bad stuff.

But there's a trick to dealing with that. When I want people to stop being nice, I make them angry. They might shout a bit, but sticks and stones and all that. Pretty soon they end up leaving me alone after all.

It's funny, but when people are nice I get anxious and confused. But when they're angry, I feel comfortable. Like everything's back the way it should be.

Mum and the monster, Susie and Gabe, Annabel, Maya – all of them so fucking needy. All wanting me to love them. If they really want me to be happy, why can't they just leave me be?

Is Jason any different? Probably not. I mean, I know what he wants from me, which makes things simpler. But pretty soon he'll either get bored of me or do a Susie and get soppy. Probably the former. He doesn't strike me as the sentimental type.

So when he casually says one day, 'K-Man tells me you're doing well out there,' I pretty much guess what's coming next.

I shrug non-committally. But, as it happens, I *am* doing well. Turns out there's only one real requirement for being a drug gang's courier: don't panic. Don't panic when you see a police car. Don't panic when some stressed-out customer threatens to stab you. Don't panic when Blado and Dash, K-Man's minions, bundle you into the back of a van and threaten to kill you, then laugh and say they're only messing you around.

I've learnt to ride a moped. It's a buzz, actually, weaving in and out of traffic on the A41, a backpack of drugs or cash on my back. Or *food* and *Ps,* as the crew call them.

Sometimes they get me shotting – making deliveries direct to the customers. To be honest, that's not as exciting as being the courier. But it's all part of the job, and I want to learn.

I had a lot of preconceptions about this work. I thought I'd be dealing with crackheads and junkies, but that couldn't be further from the truth. Maybe it's the area we cover, in the London commuter belt, or maybe it's because of the type of drugs Jason prefers to deal in, but our customers are mostly middle-class professionals. They want coke, mainly, plus a few pills. Almost nobody wants downers. Everyone wants to feel good.

So, yeah, I'm doing well out there. And Jason's been pleased with me, I can tell.

But now he hesitates, like he's got bad news. I force myself to keep my face unreadable.

'You know you can't go on staying here, don't you, princess?' He watches me carefully, judging how I'm taking this.

I nod. 'I understand. It's too risky for you.'

'Too risky for us *both*. It's been great having you, but I can't chance you bringing the old bill to me. And *you* can't risk being here if they come looking for you, can you?'

I shrug. 'Guess not. So that's it? You're chucking me out?' I feel the familiar wave of rejection and anger washing over me. Nothing fucking lasts. Why did I ever think it could?

'Whoa!' he says. 'Course not! Come here, princess.' He puts his big, muscled arms around me and squeezes me hard, his chest as solid as breeze blocks. 'What I'm thinking is, I'll set you up in a nice little apartment somewhere on that patch you've been working,' he says as he steps back. 'Not a bando – some posh development where the neighbours don't give a fuck. Kind of like a family franchise, delivering full service for me. As high-end as this business gets. What do you say?'

Full service – that's the other angle to this, the part the elusive Jonny mostly takes care of round here. First, you hang out somewhere where there are plenty of potential customers – Camden Market, say – handing out business cards offering *Full-service party supplies – immediate delivery*. Then you wait for the phone to ring – or, rather, to ping. When it does, you get the drugs over to them super quick. It's designed for people who think an hour's wait for an Uber or Deliveroo is way too long, and are prepared to pay more for a faster service.

'I reckon that's the future on that line, anyway,' Jason adds. 'Nice middle-class kid like you turning up on a scooter, everything clean and friendly and unthreatening. Who wants to think their party gear's been stuffed up some roadboy's sweaty arse? This way, you'll blend in, they'll get their stuff nice and quick, and you'll still have K-Man and Dash around to back you up if there's any trouble.'

I think of living on my own. No one trying to stroke my hair or wanting to be nice to me or asking me how I feel. Just respect, cash, freedom.

When the alternative's some scummy children's home, it's really no contest.

'Yes, please,' I say. 'I'd like that.'

'Great,' he says. 'That's my girl.' He eyes me thoughtfully. 'But there's something I'd like you to do for me first. A bit of a favour. From what you've told me, you might actually enjoy it.'

NINETY-THREE

Susie

We were out walking Sandy when my phone rang. It was Stu, Silverlink's bassist. Assuming it was something to do with the rehearsal later, I let it go to voicemail.

Within moments, though, there was a text from Chrissie, the keyboard player.

WTF?????

Followed by a WhatsApp from Jack.

Are you serious?

I tried to pick up Stu's message, but reception was bad, and by the time I managed to catch any of it we were almost home. Something about Facebook and Instagram. He sounded furious.

I found my iPad and got Silverlink's page up. The most recent post apparently went live just after nine that morning. It had my name on it, just like all the other posts.

But I didn't write it.

It is with great sorrow and regret that I announce the end of @silverlinkband and also of my marriage. The recent allegations of sexual misconduct against my husband and mentor, Gabe Thompson, have unfortunately turned out to be all too true. I want to express my deepest sympathy to his victims and to all those affected by the toxic culture around @WHT.

What is even more shocking is that those victims now include my own 15-year-old daughter, who was groomed by him when she came to live with us. The police are investigating indecent images of her found on his phone and computers. Please respect my need for privacy at this difficult time.

NINETY-FOUR

Susie

I looked for the *delete post* button, but for some reason there wasn't one. Then I tried to write something to say it wasn't true. At first, I thought the reason nothing was working was because my hands were shaking, but then the *Login to Facebook* box came up and I had to re-enter my username and password.

Login failed.

'Shit,' I said frantically. I tried again.

Login failed.

'She must have locked you out.' Gabe was watching over my shoulder, horrified.

'How can she do that?'

'Either she knows your password and she's changed it, or she's guessed your security questions. Did she ever ask where you grew up? The name of your first pet?'

'Jesus . . . Almost certainly. We talked about my past all the time.'

I looked at the page again. Already there were dozens of shares, comments and gasping-face emojis. There were no words to express how violated I felt.

I should have changed all my passwords after what happened to Gabe, I realised. But it never even occurred to me that she'd do something like this.

I grabbed my phone and called Stuart. 'Stu, it's all fake. Can you post something to say I've been hacked? And you'd better take me off as an administrator, at least until we get my login back.'

'Sure.' He hesitated. 'Do you know who's behind it?'

'In a way. It's Sky. She was behind that article, too.'

'Sky?' he said incredulously. 'Our so-called backing singer? You've got to sort that little bitch out, Susie.'

I sighed. 'It's gone way beyond that. I'll explain next time I see you, but for now, can you just deal with Facebook? And, please – I understand you're upset, but can you also not call my daughter a little bitch?'

I rang off. While I was talking, Gabe had been on my iPad.

'I've reported the hack to Facebook. I think they have to check it out before they give you back control, though.'

'Why would she do this?' I said. 'She knows how much the band means to me.'

'Yes,' Gabe said desolately. 'And I think that's precisely why she's done it. She knows there'll be no coming back from this. I think it's her way of burning her bridges.'

NINETY-FIVE

Sky

Two last things to do before I move out of here and into the apartment Jason's bought me. Two messages to send. Both anonymous, from some gibberish account with no posts.

The first is to Susie and Gabe. I've watched the implosion on Facebook – *Boom! Boom! Boom!* – with mixed feelings. On the one hand, it's nice to see a plan falling into place so beautifully – like watching something burn, something big and precious and solid, all because of a single match. And Jason's glee is infectious – at one point, we were actually dancing round the room, high-fiving each other and laughing. But on the other...

On the other hand, there's this little voice inside me saying, *Susie did try. She tried her very best.*

Fuck it. I promised to destroy her whole fake-perfect life and I will. And I know from experience there's no point in half measures. If you chicken out even a little bit, people start telling you that you've changed, and suddenly you're not the one who's in control anymore.

I send her just ten words.

> This is what you get when you fuck people up

The next is to Maya, even shorter.

> Do it

I take the SIM card out and go downstairs, where Jason's waiting.
'Ready, princess?' he asks.
I nod. 'All ready.'
I hand him the SIM and he hands me a pay-as-you-go. 'Look after that, won't you? That's your business, now.'
'Got it,' I say. 'Let's go.'

NINETY-SIX

Gabe

The police ask me to attend another interview. Of course, I take both my solicitors – my legal team, as I've started to think of them. Between them, they charge over a thousand pounds an hour. Looks like I'll be selling the Banksys after all.

Before the interview, the two of them go off to have a disclosure meeting with the detectives. They come back looking perturbed.

'There's no fresh evidence as such,' Sally Davis explains. 'Just a new allegation to put to you.'

'What kind of allegation?'

'They've been contacted by the manager of the home where Sky was placed before she went missing.' Sally pauses. 'Apparently, she told another girl she was going to meet *you*.'

I shrug. 'Well, she wasn't.'

'Yes, but you can see why they have to speak to you again, can't you?' I must look puzzled, because she adds. 'If you were the last person to see her, and the police are investigating naked images of her on your phone – well, there's one interpretation that's potentially quite sinister. Gabe, you should prepare yourself – they're wondering if you could somehow be connected to her disappearance.'

DC Eddo has a more senior officer with her this time, a detective inspector. DI Hoare says very little, which makes his presence even more ominous.

Eddo shows me Sky's note.

'Does she have any friends in Edinburgh that you're aware of?' she asks.

'None whatsoever. But as I was saying to Susie just the other day, we've only known her a few months.'

'Is there anything else that strikes you as strange about this?' DC Eddo taps the note in its plastic folder.

'Well – yes. It's very oddly worded.'

'Almost as if someone had written it for her, you mean? Someone older?'

Too late, I see where she's going with this. 'If so, it wasn't me. I haven't been in touch with her since the day she came to our house and attacked Susie.'

'That may technically be true,' Eddo says. 'But it appears she has tried to contact you. When we checked her phone records, we could see she sent a text the day she left the children's home. It was sent to your phone – the one we already have in custody. And when we looked at the device, we were able to see what that message was.'

I frown. 'But why would she text that phone, given that I didn't have it anymore?'

'Perhaps she didn't know the police had taken it.'

'Well, of course she did. She'd planted those photos on it, then told Social Services about them.'

'So you say. But she didn't tell the social worker the full context around those photos, not initially. It was only when she was re-interviewed by a specialist sexual offences officer that she did that.' DC Eddo pauses. 'An "affair", she called it. Needless to say, an "affair" isn't what the law calls an ongoing relationship between a grown man and a fifteen-year-old child.'

I gape at her. Sally Davis says calmly, 'For the record, my client denies ever having any kind of sexual relationship with Sky. Perhaps you could show him the text. Then he can tell you whether it means anything to him.'

'Of course.'

Eddo slides another folder across the table. Inside is a photograph of my phone. On the screen there's a message:

On my way. Can't wait!! xxx

'Her own phone was turned off an hour or so afterwards,' Eddo adds. 'It hasn't been turned on again since. She hasn't used her bank card or contacted any of her friends. And the last CCTV images we have for her are at St Pancras railway station, near the platform where the trains to Chesham depart. That's where you live, isn't it? If she was going to Edinburgh, she'd have gone to King's Cross.'

'Well, I haven't seen her,' I say desperately. 'Or heard from her, unless you count an anonymous message Susie was sent after her Facebook and Instagram accounts were hacked. We're pretty sure it was her. But we can't prove it. Maybe your technical wizards would like to look into that, when they're done with my phone.'

Eddo looks at me thoughtfully. 'You've got a lot to lose, haven't you, in this situation. Your career has already been affected by allegations of sexual misconduct with minors.'

'Just to be clear,' Sally interrupts, 'none of those allegations involved the breaking of any UK laws, apart from the posts Sky herself made, which she later admitted were made up.'

Eddo nods. 'Noted. But those images on Mr Thompson's phone would still be illegal even if Sky was two years older.' She turns back to me. 'You maintain the allegations were started by Sky?'

'I know they were.'

'You must have been angry with her.'

'I suppose I was, a little.'

'And let's say, for the moment, that you're correct and the indecent photographs were placed on your devices by her.' She shrugs. 'She's only fifteen, after all. Perhaps she hoped your wife would find them and everything would come to a head. I don't suppose *you* wanted that, though. You must have been hoping this would somehow all go away.'

'That's just ridiculous,' I say wearily.

'Do you own a dark blue Audi estate, registration LX77 ANU?'

Taken aback by the change of tack, I nod. 'Yes. Why?'

'We have a warrant to take it into police custody. It'll be examined by our forensics specialists.' She glances at the clock. 'A transporter should be at your house any time now to collect it.'

'But . . . what are you looking for?' I say, bewildered. 'I mean, of course there'll be traces of Sky in it – I gave her lifts to school.'

'We'll be searching it for any signs of violence. At the moment, this is still a missing-persons inquiry, but given this new information, and the fact she's vanished so completely . . . we have to consider the possibility that Sky's been murdered.'

I stare at her, astonished. DC Eddo doesn't need to say any more for her meaning to be clear: *And we think you may have done it.*

NINETY-SEVEN

Gabe

'She can't stay hidden forever,' Susie says. 'Sooner or later, she's got to turn up.'

I shake my head glumly. 'I thought so too, initially. But, according to the lawyers, thousands of people go missing every year who are simply never seen again. And the majority are young people from the care system.'

I'm back at home, trying to come to terms with this new development. It was bad enough when I was suspected of extorting nudes from Sky. To be suspected of having a sexual relationship with her, and then killing her to cover it up . . . It's unthinkable.

Susie and I have both been hopelessly naive – I can see that now. And over-trusting, particularly in Susie's case. But how could anyone blame her for wanting to take in the daughter she'd lost for fifteen years? She'd been in an impossible situation.

And now we're trapped in a nightmare that only seems to get worse with every hour that passes.

At least Susie's still carrying our baby. Her consultant has booked her in for fortnightly scans – 'reassurance scans', she called them – and every time I hear that heartbeat, and glimpse that little stranger curled like a tiny boxing glove inside Susie's increasingly swollen belly, it becomes more real.

Her doubts have eased, as well. It's almost as if, now we're being assailed on so many sides, having a baby is the one thing she can cling to, the only thing that might come right in all of this.

Whether that certainty would survive the baby's father being formally charged with murder is another matter, of course.

'What will definitely clear me is if she's found,' I say. 'They can't say I murdered her then.'

'Well, at least the police are searching for her now.' Susie shifts in her chair, her hand smoothing her twenty-week bump.

'Are they, though? The more they focus on the possibility that *I* might have killed her, the less likely they are to put resources into any other lines of inquiry.'

We're silent a moment, both lost in thought.

Susie says, 'That Facebook hack . . . Do you suppose there's any way of tracking where she was when she did that?'

'Interesting . . . I've no idea. But I bet you Stu will know.' Like many guitarists, Susie's bassist spends as much time tinkering with amps, pedals and other gadgets as he does playing his instrument. He's our go-to guy for anything technical.

Susie makes a decision. 'Let's try him. Pass me my phone, will you?'

When she gets through, she puts Stu on speaker and explains what we're after.

'Sure, that's possible,' he says. 'Every time there's a new login, Facebook automatically records the device's location.'

I look at Susie, surprised. 'Really? It's that simple?'

Stu talks us through how to find the information in Susie's Facebook settings – and, sure enough, there's a login on the day of the hack, listed as being from a device in Westminster.

'So she's not in Edinburgh,' Susie says. 'I knew it.'

'Stu, can we make it any more precise?' I ask.

'Not from the login, unfortunately – that's just the IP address they're tracking there.'

'Damn.' Westminster is too large an area to be much use.

'I'm assuming you've disabled location tracking on your account, Susie?' he adds.

'Location tracking?' she echoes. 'What's that?'

'OK . . .' Stu says, as if explaining to an idiot. 'So, unless you tell it not to, Facebook monitors the precise GPS coordinates of its phone app, right down to around five metres. That information's very useful to them – if you visit a car showroom, say, they can sell ads on your feed to a car manufacturer, particularly if they put it together with all the other information they're collecting, like how much your house is worth or how many kids there are in your photos. The difficulty for the user is accessing that information. At one time, you could call it up on a regular browser, but then there was a big fuss about privacy, so they turned that feature off. They didn't stop collecting the data, though – it's way too valuable. They just mostly keep it to themselves. If she'd sent you a message—'

'Hang on,' I interrupt. 'She *did* message us. It was anonymous, but it was definitely her. Are you saying there might be a way to get her location from that?'

'Well . . . maybe. The data will definitely be attached to it, but whether I can decipher it is another matter. There are forums where people help out with stuff like this, though . . . Forward me the message and I'll see what I can do.'

It's a couple of hours before he calls back. 'I've got a location you could try – 67 Barwell Place, in St John's Wood. According to the register at Companies House, it's also the address of a haulage company, Miller Logistics.'

I look at Susie. She's gone white, but she manages a nod. I turn back to the phone. 'Thanks, Stu. It looks like you've found her.'

'Jason Miller,' Susie says when I've hung up. 'That was his name. Now what? Do we tell the police?'

'We could – but, realistically, what are they going to do? It's one anonymous message, sent from the house of someone who claims not to have seen her in fifteen years. And we've still got no proof that hack was her.'

Susie thinks. 'Let's go there ourselves, then. If we see her going in or out, they'll have to believe us.'

'You mean, stake it out?' From the little Susie's told me about Sky's birth father, he doesn't sound like the kind of person who'd be happy to find us camped outside his home.

Susie nods. 'We'll find somewhere unobtrusive to watch from. C'mon, Gabe. It's like you were saying just now – if she's there, it's the only way.'

So we get into Susie's car and drive into central London. Barwell Place turns out to be a short residential street a stone's throw from Abbey Road Studios, and number sixty-seven is an ugly brick building with white pillars lining the front. A red Porsche and a black Mercedes G-Wagon are parked on the driveway. Clearly, Jason Miller has done all right for himself.

We park a discreet distance away and wait. But even after an hour has passed, no one has gone in or out.

'This is agony,' Susie says with a sigh.

Just then, a thin woman with expensive-looking blond hair and a Chanel handbag comes out, arranges some dark glasses on her head and looks expectantly at her phone. A Prius with an Uber sticker pulls up and she gets in.

A little later, a short, muscular man with a shaved head comes out of the house. He's wearing tracksuit bottoms, a hoodie and running shoes.

Susie stiffens. 'That's him. That's Jason.'

I look at him, curious, as he does some stretches. I've met a few of Susie's exes, and although they weren't the sort of people I'd necessarily be friends with, I could see why she'd been attracted to them. They were front men, usually – big personalities who liked that she was always up for a good time. Jason Miller looks very different.

'Don't judge,' she adds. 'I was eighteen when I met him. He was very . . . confident. You didn't come across people like him at my parents' dinner parties. Or at Jordans, come to that.'

'I'm sure.'

After a few more stretches, Jason flips his hood up over his head and jogs off in the direction of Regent's Park, throwing a few air-jabs and uppercuts as he does so.

'What now?' Susie asks. 'Should we try the house?'

'Let's give it a bit longer. Maybe she'll come out.'

We wait, but Susie's getting more and more tense. 'Screw it,' she says at last. 'I'm going to ring the bell.' She gets out and strides towards the house, with me following her.

She presses the button on the videophone half a dozen times, but there's no response.

'This is hopeless,' she says, grimacing with frustration. 'OK, I give up. Let's go.'

As we turn back towards the car, Jason Miller steps on to the drive.

'Well, look what the cat brought in,' he says softly. 'Susie fucking Jukes.'

'Jason.' Susie's gone rigid. 'This is Gabe, my husband.'

'Yeah?' he says, looking me up and down contemptuously. 'Forgive me if I don't shake your fucking hand.'

'We're looking for Sky,' Susie says defiantly. 'We know she's here.'

'What makes you think that?'

'She messaged us,' I say.

He keeps his gaze on Susie. 'You never told me she was my daughter, that time we got busted. I had to find out from Social Services when I was inside. Maybe I was a mug for not working it out. But you were such a slag back then, I thought it could have been anyone's.'

'Now, wait a minute—' I say angrily, stepping forward.

'Yeah?' He looks at me, amused. 'What you gonna do, matey? You come to my house, you stand on my property, you tell me I'm some lowlife scum who's kidnapped her daughter ... You think anyone's going to care if I beat the shit out of you? But if you really want to have a go, be my guest.'

When I say nothing, he nods contemptuously. 'Thought not. Pussy.'

'She was here,' Susie says. 'I know she was. She hacked my band's Facebook page from here.'

'Did she now?' Jason puts on an expression of mock sympathy. 'That must have been so upsetting, to have the whole world know you married a kiddy-fiddler.' He flashes me a look. 'No offence, *Gabe*.'

'That was *you*?' Susie says incredulously.

'Me?' He shakes his head. 'Nah. I don't know the first thing about computers. Never have done.'

'You and Sky together, then,' I say. 'So you *do* know where she is.'

He looks at me, utterly unfazed. I can see why Susie described him as confident.

'Look, matey,' he says patiently. 'I've no idea where Sky is. But put it like this – if I *did* know, she'd better be careful. Because nothing would give me more pleasure than to make her pay for the fact her slag of a mother got me sent down for a four stretch. Now fuck off, before I do something I might regret.'

'I never realised,' Susie says when we're back in the car. 'It never even occurred to me that he'd blame me for his conviction. I thought he'd understand that cooperating with the police was my only chance of getting Sky back.'

'He didn't strike me as a very understanding person,' I say drily.

'He *does* know where she is. And he'll put her in danger, just to get back at me.'

'He may have only said that to frighten you. He's still her father, after all.' But I say it more to comfort Susie than because I really believe it. I'd looked into Jason Miller's eyes and seen nothing there – no spark of warmth or humanity, just cold self-interest.

Now that I've met him, it isn't hard to guess where the funds for the Porsche and the G-Wagon and the ugly house came from. If Sky's got herself mixed up with that, she could be heading for prison, too.

Or something even worse.

'Well, at least we've got something to tell the police now,' I say. 'He's an ex-con, after all, with a conviction for drug-dealing. He must be on someone's radar.'

Susie nods. 'I'll call them when we get home.' She looks out of the window. 'Oh, Sky . . . What have you done?'

NINETY-EIGHT

Nicky

So this is great. Basically, I'm running my own small business.

First, I go on a printing website and order a bunch of business cards with *Full-Service Party Supplies – Immediate Delivery* on them, along with my new pay-as-you-go number. No point in changing a winning formula – round here, most of my customers will work in London and already know what those words mean. It's not that different from Deliveroo or Uber Eats dropping a flyer through your door announcing they now cover your postcode. People will be like, *Great! What took them so long?*

I'm a bit more targeted than they are, though. Once the cards arrive, I go to the train station and slip them to twenty-somethings doing the urban commute – millennials stuck in the office grind who'll be desperate to blow off steam at the weekend. A few other select groups, too. Nurses – nurses love drugs. Students. A few of the slightly cooler sixth-formers.

Mid-morning, when the station gets quiet, I go into the town centre and look for young mums with pushchairs. I give a few to older people who are dressed a bit more stylishly than the average. An estate agent quietly asks for a handful. Delivery drivers, a stressed-out executive or two, some young chefs in whites having a fag break outside their kitchen.

Not one person has a go at me or threatens to call the police. The opposite, in fact. People thank me as they tuck the card away. Like I'm the fourth emergency service or something.

By six p.m., WhatsApp's starting to ping. People want to know how quickly they can get their stuff.

By the end of the week, I'm turning over a grand a day. And I'm on twenty per cent, which is a whole lot better than if I was in some franchise scheme selling toiletries. Jason's set up a bank account in the name of Bucks Hospitality. I deposit three grand at a time, in cash, just as he told me. My share gets transferred into a second account under a new identity he's made for me – Nicky Mason.

Saturday's my busiest day – I zip around on the scooter, delivering to pubs, golf clubs, farmers' markets and housing estates. There are two nightclubs in town and, although I'm too young to get in, I'm constantly selling to those who can. Sometimes they don't order until they're actually standing in the queue. A hen night calls in for five grams of coke and twelve Es, to be handed to them as they get into their stretch limo.

But mostly it's a gram here, a few pills there. Plus some weed for the Sunday climbdown.

On Monday, I take the day off. The apartment is nice, but it needs brightening up. I order a load of stuff from a furniture store in High Wycombe. I get some fake Banksy prints, too. Going for a bit of a Susie-and-Gabe vibe.

Susie and Gabe . . . When I think about them, I feel a twinge of regret. Do I hope Gabe's going through hell because of what I did? Not really. I thought it would feel good to mess him and Susie around, but now it comes to it, I realise I've grown up and moved on.

On Tuesday, I call K-Man for more gear. It won't be him who brings it, of course – that's what the youngers are for. So when the bell goes with the coded ring, I'm just expecting some random kid.

It's Jaylen – Jaylen from the children's home.

'What the fuck are you doing here?' I ask.

He gets over his surprise. 'Working. Same as you.'

He looks past me into the apartment and his eyes widen. 'Whoa – this place is proper. Who you smashing to get this, Sky?'

'No one,' I say. 'Now, give me the stuff and fuck off.'

He hands me the backpack and leaves. But I can't help feeling uneasy. He's the first person here with any links to my old life. He's surely too smart to snitch on me. But I make a mental note to mention it to K-Man, all the same.

NINETY-NINE

Susie

After that, everything went quiet. Nothing from the police. No news of Sky. Even the social workers seemed to be engaged in some phoney war, their core groups – multi-agency meetings about the unborn baby – endlessly rescheduled.

I got to twenty-four weeks, which felt like a massive milestone. Theoretically, the baby was viable now. It was further than I'd ever got before.

At my next scan, when the sonographer asked if we wanted to know the baby's sex, I surprised myself by saying yes. I looked at Gabe to make sure he was OK with it, and, after a moment, he nodded.

'You're having a little girl,' the sonographer said.

A little girl ... Neither of us really minded which it was, but somehow I could always see Gabe as a father of girls. They'll adore each other, I thought ruefully, and, far from being jealous, the thought made me smile and reach for his hand.

But my smile was tinged with sadness, because twenty-four

weeks was when I'd discovered my first baby was going to be a girl, too, all those years ago.

Even as I looked at the image of my other daughter on the screen, I couldn't help thinking about Sky. It increasingly felt as if some kind of tragedy was going to be inevitable for her in the end. And, while I reluctantly had to accept that there wasn't really much more I could do for her, having another little girl inside me – one who'd be loved and cherished and spoilt rotten from the moment she was born – wouldn't wipe that slate clean. I'd always be the mother who failed her firstborn.

Two days after the scan, out of the blue, Fi called.

'Susie, look . . . This isn't really a professional call,' she said, after we'd exchanged guarded pleasantries. 'You know I can't write anything about Gabe at the moment. But someone's contacted me who I think you ought to meet.'

'Why? What's it about?'

She hesitated. 'I think it's better you wait until you see her. But, put it this way . . . you should come alone. I don't think she'll talk if Gabe's there.'

We arranged to meet in a Costa on the Euston Road. Sitting with Fi was a woman about my age, with short, stylishly cropped hair and a leather jacket.

'This is Ella,' Fi said, introducing us.

'Hello,' I said cautiously as I took the seat opposite her. My heart was beating like a hammer, but I tried to sound calm. 'You want to talk about Gabe, I understand?'

Ella nodded nervously. 'I think so. I've agonised over whether to do this. I must have changed my mind a hundred times.'

She still seemed undecided. 'You were a fan, presumably?' I prompted gently.

She shook her head. 'An assistant on the video crew. We were filming the European leg of WHT's tour for MTV.'

'When was this?'

'Twenty eleven.'

I did a quick calculation. So at least she wouldn't have been a minor. That was something.

'I was twenty-five,' she added. 'It was the first time I'd been abroad for work.'

She hesitated again.

I said, 'Look . . . take as much time as you need, but whatever it is you're here to say, please understand that I'm here because I want to hear it. I'm not going to be angry or refuse to believe you. If Gabe did something bad, I want to know.'

It felt unreal to be hearing those words coming out of my own mouth, but they seemed to have the desired effect because she nodded.

'OK. I'll try.' She took a deep breath. 'It was common knowledge that Gabe and Donna had separated. Everyone was talking about it. He seemed really quiet and withdrawn. Not like the others – Kai and Danny were always so loud and obnoxious. But Gabe seemed . . . nice. I really wanted to get to know him. I suppose I fancied him, too.'

'Go on,' I said, even though every cell in my body was dreading what might come next.

'This one time . . . I found myself in a lift with him at the hotel.

Just me and him. He said hi . . . The next night, we were in a different city, at a different hotel, but the same thing happened. He said something about how he promised he wasn't stalking me – which I thought was sweet of him, because he was the big star and it might easily have looked like it was the other way round.

'I explained I was with the crew . . . He asked if I wanted to have a drink. I thought he meant in the bar, but then he said there were fans down there. So we went to his room.'

She fell silent again. This time, I waited for her to continue.

Eventually, she shook herself and went on: 'He poured us both huge drinks. There was a bottle of bourbon that was already half empty – I think he must have been drinking earlier. We talked for a bit . . . And then he just said, "Are we going to have sex?"

'I didn't know what to say. Because I hadn't actually decided, at that point. I mean, it was obviously on the cards, but I'd only been there for about five minutes. It was as if he simply assumed that was all we were there to do – almost like I was a hooker or something. And the way he said it – it wasn't flirtatious or anything. Just really peremptory and curt.

'But then I thought, This is one of the band, and maybe this is what they're used to – with the fans, I mean. And I thought . . . If I say no now, he's going to be pissed off. I didn't know if I'd be able to stay on the tour after that.'

'You felt you had no choice,' I said quietly.

She nodded. 'I thought . . . Well, it's partly my fault. I'd got myself into a bad situation without thinking it through and the easiest thing was just to go along with it. I didn't want to come across as one of those women who makes a big deal about things like that. And I suppose I didn't want all the hassle it might involve, either. You know – maybe getting called a prick-tease, or having to face him getting angry.'

Now it was my turn to nod, because that could describe many of my own sexual encounters at twenty-five.

Ella started to cry silently, tears streaking her cheeks.

'He said, "Or you can leave, if you want." But his voice – it was really flat and cold. Like he was *dismissing* me. And I . . . I said no, I'd stay. I still don't know why I said that. I should have just got out of there. But I suppose I still thought we could salvage something – that maybe we'd get the sex over and then we could get back to talking.'

She took a deep breath. 'So we started . . . He got behind me and he was really . . . I don't know, *impersonal*. Like I wasn't even there. I told him to stop, that I wasn't into it anymore. And he did . . . but then he just suddenly went crazy. He was striding round the room, shouting and swearing. At one point, he picked up the glass I'd been drinking from and threw it at the wall.'

She stopped again.

'I think I screamed when the glass broke. And he just . . . changed back again. Almost like he'd woken up. He kept saying how sorry he was, that he didn't know what had happened. I was crying – I was just so shocked. He said he'd walk me to my room. I could tell he wanted me out of there, so I said OK and we both got dressed. When we got to my door, he said sorry again and asked if I was all right. I said yes. It was all so awkward. I said something like, "Please don't tell anyone." I don't know why I said that, either – I think because I thought he might be wondering if *I'd* tell people. Anyway, he said he wouldn't.

'I didn't sleep all night – I was worried about how difficult it would be the next time we ran into each other, and about my job. Then, a couple of days later, I heard some people talking and I realised it wasn't just his marriage that had ended – his daughter had died, too. I thought maybe that was why he'd been so weird. So I didn't tell anyone, I just avoided him. And then my eating disorder came back and I had to stop work anyway. I was really messed up for a while.'

She was silent a moment. 'I still don't know how much of that was him and how much was me. I mean, I was probably less healthy than I thought I was when I went into that room. But it took me a long time to get better.'

'Ella, I'm so sorry,' I said gently. 'It must have been awful.'

She nodded. 'When I saw that article of Fi's . . . I was reassured, in a way. Because I've sometimes wondered if what happened to me was a one-off, or if he was that way with lots of women. That's why I contacted her. I wanted to be sure there wasn't other stuff – stuff she hadn't printed because of defamation or whatever.'

'I haven't heard this from anyone else,' Fi added. 'Though a couple of people have told me how much Gabe was drinking around then. Alone in his room, mostly.'

'For what it's worth, what you've just told me is completely unlike the Gabe I know,' I told Ella. 'Not that I'm doubting a single word of what you've said, or trying to excuse him. But I think he must have been in a dark place.'

'Yes,' Ella said. 'I think he was.'

All three of us were silent after that.

'I won't be printing this,' Fi said at last. 'Not even when it's possible for me to. That's Ella's choice.'

'Thank you, Ella. And Fi . . . this period when Gabe was behaving that way – when did it stop?'

'From what I understand, it was one of the reasons the band decided to call it a day – they could tell how unhappy he was. So the next tour was going to be their last.' She paused. 'That was when he met you, wasn't it? Right at the beginning of that final tour. By all accounts, he's been a different person ever since.'

ONE HUNDRED

Gabe

Susie and I talk late into the night.

The horrible truth is, I'd all but forgotten that particular encounter. Despite what Fi said to Susie, there had been others that were almost, if not equally, as bad – ones she hadn't found out about. But they've all melded together in my memory, a blur of bodies, bottles, blackouts. Fans pulled into hotel rooms for half an hour of distraction, then pushed out again. I was doing pills, too. The same runner who kept Kai and Danny in coke had a standing order to keep me in Xanax and temazepam. Everything was fuzzy and imprecise. But never quite fuzzy enough.

One detail I do remember: crying silently even as I had sex with a fan, unable to stop the tears.

That was my ghost kingdom: I thought that, by pushing my own flesh into some fresh-faced young body, I was somehow resetting the clock on everything that had happened. When the truth was, I was simply blotting it out for a few minutes.

Not that the bodies *were* particularly young, by then – it was almost fifteen years since the band formed, and our audience had aged along with us. So at least it wasn't schoolkids I was being a complete dickhead with.

Which doesn't excuse anything, I know. I used women the way some people use weed or booze or betting. And they *felt* used, I could tell. The look of disappointment when they realised you didn't want to talk or kiss or hug.

I remember one who actually said to me, as she stood by the door of my hotel room, preparing to leave, 'Well, I guess it's true what they say. Never meet your heroes.'

I told myself those women were only getting what they'd wanted. I certainly never realised that some would feel traumatised by the encounter. I told myself that, of all the things I could do, sex was probably the least harmful. But even so, I was eaten up with shame. And the next night there was always another city, another hotel. Another attractive face offering herself up.

I was trapped in a horrible spiral of self-loathing and despair. And none of it was helping, anyway.

But then, nothing could have helped. It was way too late for that.

Leah was two when Donna and I first noticed something was off. At first, we thought it was great she was sleeping late. Then we wondered if it was really normal for a two-year-old to sleep quite so much. And sometimes, when she woke up, her skin was clammy.

We took her to the GP, who thought she had an infection, probably viral. Then her tonsils became inflamed, so he started her on antibiotics. Her temperature went on spiking, but he told us not to worry, these things take time.

When spots and bruises started appearing on her skin, we did the meningitis test – rolling a glass over them – and panicked when they didn't disappear. The doctors in A & E were sure it wasn't meningitis, but, since they didn't know what it was, they did a blood test anyway.

After six hours, the results came back. She had a high white blood count and low platelets. It was almost certainly leukaemia.

We had no idea then, but there are dozens of different childhood leukaemias. Acute lymphoblastic. Myeloid. Juvenile myelomonocytic. A bunch of almost unpronounceable Latin names, but which one you have is what decides whether your particular case is possibly curable or probably incurable.

Leah had a bone-marrow biopsy, CAT scans, X-rays – all of them under general anaesthetic. She was in the moderately curable category, but almost the very first X-ray revealed a secondary tumour in her lung. She had a permanent line put in her chest so she could have regular chemotherapy sessions. Sometimes the line got infected, which meant the chemo had to be paused.

When we asked how long her treatment would take, the doctors talked in terms of years, not months.

But we coped. You go into survival mode. It's made easier by the fact there are other families on the ward, all going through the same thing. And in any case, you have no choice, no time to do anything but manage. Manage the vomiting, manage the rashes, manage the mouth ulcers and the constipation and the diarrhoea and the nosebleeds. Manage the hair loss – the first time I found a cluster of her beautiful eyelashes on her pillow, I cried.

By the entrance to the ward, there was an old-fashioned ship's bell, known as the NED bell. Doctors don't talk about cancer being cured. They talk about remission getting to the point where eventually there's 'no evidence of disease'. When a kid came back for a check-up and was told they were now NED, they got to ring the bell on their way out to signify no more treatment, and everyone stopped what they were doing and cheered. It didn't get rung often, but when it did, I thought about the day when Leah would ring it too. I hoped she'd still be so little, I'd have to lift her up so she could reach.

When the chemo didn't work, they started giving her stronger drugs via a lumbar puncture. Each fortnightly session meant a general anaesthetic. Every time we left the ward to go home, I would carry her, tired and floppy, past the NED bell, and I'd look over and imagine us ringing it. Sometimes I'd even go and tap it quietly with my knuckle, so I could hear the note it made. A middle C.

Gradually, Leah lost her fine motor skills. Her skull changed shape. But that was because she was getting such a powerful treatment, we told ourselves. We willed it all to come right.

And, slowly, it looked as if it would. The platelet numbers rose, the white blood cell count dropped. We started to, not relax, exactly, but we were no longer in a state of perpetual high alert. She went back to having her chemo through a central line.

Two days before her third birthday, she had a very slight temperature. We gave her Calpol and put her to bed.

When I checked her, half an hour later, I noticed her breathing was abnormally fast – in-out, in-out, all in the time it took me to make a single breath. When I put my hand on her forehead, it was burning. I could feel her heart hammering through her chest.

We called an ambulance. The paramedics immediately got

more lines into her, to give her fluids. I was shocked to see that nothing seemed to cause her any pain – even when they put a cannula in the back of her hand, she was unresponsive.

They radioed ahead to tell the hospital her blood pressure – fifty over twenty. By the time we got there, it was too low to measure.

It was septic shock. I couldn't fault the doctors – often, septicaemia gets missed, but in her case they realised instantly what it was and did all they could to save her. But in the race between the medics and organ failure, organ failure won.

At her funeral, we had an old-fashioned ship's bell. As the undertakers carried her tiny coffin out, I rang it. The note reverberated around the church. A middle C. No more treatment.

Right from the start, Donna and I grieved differently. She was tearful and wanted to talk about it – endlessly looping on every episode in Leah's illness, picking over each minute of her septicaemia, as if by repeating the details we could somehow make sense of it all. I was angry – and, in an effort to keep a lid on my anger, I suppose I became distant and cold. But sometimes the anger erupted, and when, after six months, she decided to go back to New York, it was a relief that she didn't ask me to go with her. In any case, I had a tour coming up. Singing fatuous pop songs was hardly a comfort, let alone a pleasure, but at least I could slot back into the old routines. And, yes, new vices. That was the beginning of the dark time.

When Donna told me she wanted to make our separation permanent, my rage against the world turned – I'm ashamed to say – into something more destructive. I know I should have been bigger than that. I should have got therapy, kept away from any kind of relationship until I was able to cope with one. But, apart from a few hey-that-really-sucks conversations with the band, I spoke to no one.

Until the first day of our final tour, when I found a beautiful backing vocalist in tears backstage and stopped to ask what was wrong. If she hadn't told me about Sky, I would never have talked about Leah. And, in that moment of unburdening, everything changed for me.

It's stayed that way ever since.

ONE HUNDRED AND ONE

Susie

By the time he'd finished telling me, Gabe was in tears. And my emotions were complicated, too. Because, while it wasn't my place to forgive him – only Ella and the other women he behaved badly with could do that – there was something so incredibly intimate about watching the man I loved confessing his most private sins that I desperately wanted to give him some kind of absolution.

For what it was worth, he was pretty sure he didn't do anything illegal during that period. When he asked Ella if they were going to have sex, or told her she could leave if she wanted – phrases she heard as being cold and dismissive – he was almost certainly trying to make it clear she really wasn't obligated to stay with him, given the state his head was in. And his outburst, which she'd interpreted as anger at her asking him to stop, was, he thought, directed at himself, for letting himself succumb to yet another meaningless encounter.

But both of us knew that wasn't the real issue. When you have casual sex with someone, you enter into an unspoken contract not to treat that person's feelings casually. Two people quite literally strip themselves bare and make themselves as vulnerable as it's possible for human beings to be. At the very least, you owe your partner consideration and tenderness and kindness and appreciation.

All the things that Gabe has always shown me, in fact. Which is why his actions with Ella seemed so completely out of character. But perhaps that's another difficult truth about human beings – that, as Rowena once said to us in a different context, good people can do bad things, particularly when bad things have happened to them.

'This is why you were so understanding when you found out about my convictions,' I realised. 'Because, in a way, you'd been there yourself.'

He nodded. 'I tried to talk to you about it. But it wasn't the right time – your mind was still running on Sky, which was understandable. You just sort of brushed it aside.'

'We're both such fuck-ups, aren't we? Look at us.'

He reached out and touched my bump. 'Do we even deserve to have a child?'

'No one does. That's the extraordinary thing about it.'

He hesitated. 'And me? Does all this change how you feel about me? Because I could completely understand if you decided I wasn't the man you thought you'd married.'

I put my hand on his. 'There's a lot to grasp, and of course it'll take me a while to process it. But you know the way you acted was wrong, and, frankly, you're already paying for it, given how the band's been cancelled. I think we can work it through.'

'Thanks,' he said quietly. 'I should have known from the way you've stuck by Sky that you'd do the same for me.'

He was silent a moment. 'You know . . . when we were talking, I realised something. Sky's the same age as Leah, isn't she? They were born in the same year. If Leah had lived, she'd be fifteen too.'

'I'd never thought of that.'

He nodded. 'And I thought . . . what would I want for her? If she was in trouble the way Sky is now, I mean. And the answer is . . . I'd want someone to be looking out for her. Someone who'd stop at nothing to make sure she was safe. Who'd see past the bad things she'd done to the good bits underneath.

'I'd have done anything to save Leah – absolutely anything. I can't do anything for her now, of course. But I can support *you*. So, what I'm saying is . . . don't give up.'

ONE HUNDRED AND TWO

Nicky

Five grand in notes makes for a pretty full backpack.

It's more than the money-deposit safe outside the bank will accept, so I take the train into Marylebone to drop it off at K-Man's flat. I stick the bag under my seat, tucked behind my legs where it's safe, and watch the countryside go by.

The door to the next carriage opens and a policeman with a dog comes in. For a moment I freeze, but then I force myself to relax. I'm clean. There's nothing in the rucksack but money.

The dog looks a bit like Sandy. As they pass, I lean out of my seat and stroke his head. 'Good boy.'

The dog turns towards me, licking my hand. But then its nose goes down to the backpack, snuffling at it frantically as if it's full of meat or something. It stiffens, then starts to bark.

'Is that your bag, miss?' the dog handler asks.

We're just pulling into Gerrard's Cross and, in a flash, I'm out of my seat and running. He and the dog are facing the other way and, in any case, he has to choose between me and the backpack. I sprint into the next carriage, then the next, waiting for the doors to the platform to unlock. I'm almost at the front of the train now. I look back and see him coming down the aisle towards me, the backpack slung over his shoulder. He says something to the dog and lets it off its leash. It races towards me. But I'm in luck – the doors are opening. Already, people are crowding forward to get on the train, blocking the dog's way. I push through them and hurtle up the walkway towards the exit.

As I vault the ticket barrier, I look up – right at the CCTV camera over the entrance.

Shit.

I get away from the station and catch my breath. I know this is bad – really bad – but I can't put off making the call.

'Hello, princess,' Jason says when he answers.

I tell him what's happened.

'So they've got my five grand,' he says flatly.

'Yes. But I'll pay you back. I won't take any commission until you've got it all—'

'Doesn't work like that,' he interrupts. 'Cos now you're gonna be matrixed, aren't you? You go on working, you'll put the whole line at risk. And you could lead them to me.'

'I'd never do that. I swear I wouldn't.'

'You think? I've already had your mum and her nonce coming round, asking after you. Turns out that thing you did with Facebook wasn't quite as untraceable as you promised. Sorry, princess. I think you've just made yourself redundant.' He pauses. 'We're going to have to think of another way for you to earn back my five K.'

'What do you mean?' I say slowly.

'There are ways. I mean, you've already got a nice little set-up with that classy apartment. I'm thinking escort work.'

He's so matter-of-fact that it's a moment before I take in what he's saying. 'That's not . . . I don't want to do that.'

'Yeah,' he says. 'A lot of girls say that, until they find out what the alternatives are. But we can start you off gently. Bit of camming. Put on a nice show with one of the boys.'

I don't say anything. My head's spinning. I thought he wanted me in his life. I didn't kid myself that he was ever going to love me, but I thought I was more to him than some disposable runner.

I feel sick at the realisation that, for him, it was only ever about the money. He simply wanted me for what I could do for him.

I've been such an idiot.

'Besides,' he's saying, 'you'll like sex work. Your old mum did, didn't she? And the apple never falls too far from the tree. Go back to the apartment and wait for instructions. Someone'll come round and tell you what to do.'

I've got nowhere else to go, so I do as he says. But after twenty minutes of numbly pacing up and down, I realise this is all wrong.

Whatever way Jason decides I'm to earn his money back, it's not going to be pleasant. And I have to face the fact that he's been manipulating me from the start.

I get a bag and start stuffing clothes into it. I've no idea where I'm going, but I guess I'll have to figure that out on the way.

As I cross the room, I glance out of the window. Jaylen's walking towards the building. He's carrying his coat in his hand and it looks to me like he's got something wrapped up inside it. Something long and heavy.

I go and pull open the front door. When he sees me, he stops.

'What have you got there, Jaylen?' I ask. 'A blade? Acid? A gun?'

A little shamefaced, he pulls out a machete. 'This.'

'And you're meant to scare me with it? Well, consider me scared.'

He says nothing. Of the two of us, I think, he's the one who looks more terrified.

'Or do *I* scare *you*?' I add. 'Boo!'

He doesn't move, just looks at me. And I suddenly realise it isn't me he's frightened of.

It's what he's been told to do to me.

'Are you here to shank me?' I say slowly.

He raises the machete. He's shaking so much, the whole blade waves around, the tip twirling small circles in the air like a baton.

'Tell them I wasn't here,' I say. 'Tell them you saw me running off. That way, you'll still get the respect, but you won't have to do it.'

He shakes his head. 'They said you're gonna snitch to the feds. They said I have to make sure you can't talk.'

'They're lying. Someone wants me dead in case I lead the feds to him, but it isn't because I'm snitching.' I take a deep breath. 'It's the face who runs this line. He's my dad.'

'Fuck,' Jaylen breathes. 'Your *dad* ordered this?'

I nod.

'That's some proper shit.'

'I know.'

When he doesn't move, I add, 'I'm going now. I know you don't want to kill me, Jaylen.' I have to get past him, so I keep my voice calm and low. I really want to go back inside the flat to get my things, but something tells me that, if I break eye contact, he'll change his mind.

There's twenty pounds in my pocket. It'll have to do.

Very slowly, I edge around him, then turn and walk backwards, my eyes fixed on his. Still holding the machete, he starts to cry.

'You're too good for this,' I tell him. 'Take care.' Then I turn and run.

As I near the street, I see K-Man and Blado jump up from the wall where they're sitting. Of course – they'd hang around to make sure Jaylen went through with it. I pelt through the estate, with them running after me. They're big guys and I can sense from the sound of their trainers that they're gaining on me. I reach the moped just in time, the engine spluttering into life first go. As I weave off, I see K-Man's other minion, Dash, at the wheel of a black SUV, pulling forward so the others can jump in. But what the moped lacks in speed, it makes up for in manoeuvrability, and pretty soon I'm cutting through a long queue of mothers waiting to pick their kids up from school. A few minutes after that, I'm on the road to London. The petrol tank's showing empty, but that's the least of my problems – the most pressing being, *Where next?*

ONE HUNDRED AND THREE

Gabe

I'm at home when I get a call from the police.

'We've had a confirmed sighting of Sky,' DC Eddo says. 'Yesterday, by a police dog handler, on the train from High Wycombe into London. She ran away from him, but she was caught on CCTV.'

'So she isn't dead,' I say, relieved. 'Which means I can't have killed her.'

'We've informed your solicitor that you're no longer a suspect in a possible murder investigation, yes.' Eddo pauses. 'However, we do urgently need to talk to Sky about a different matter.'

'Why? What's she done?'

'When she ran from the dog handler, she abandoned a backpack containing five thousand pounds – the dog had been trained to alert to large amounts of cash. We believe it's drug money.'

'Drug money?' I echo. I'm not entirely surprised, but even so, it's not good.

'We also need to speak to her about the death of a fourteen-year-old youth called Jaylen Harris. It happened close to where we believe she may have been living under an assumed name, in a flat that had recently been purchased by an offshore company.'

'You think Sky could have been involved?'

'Not directly, because someone matching her description was seen leaving the area shortly before he died. But his death also has the hallmarks of drug-trafficking – he'd been stabbed and he was carrying a large weapon himself, not that he ever got to use it. Our hypothesis is that his murder and the money are connected.'

'This must be down to her father – her birth father,' I say immediately. 'He's been in prison for drug offences.'

'Well, that's one possibility. But there's currently nothing that would justify us interviewing him under caution, let alone applying for a search warrant. Sky may be able to tell us more, of course.'

'So that's why you want to speak to her?'

'I'm afraid it's a bit more serious than that.' Eddo hesitates. 'When the police seize a large amount of cash, the gang will often make an example of the person who lost it. Sometimes through an act of retributive violence.'

Retributive violence . . . It takes me a moment to work out what she means.

'You're saying . . . she might be in even more danger now,' I say slowly.

'Let me put it this way: we do have serious concerns for Sky's welfare. If she makes contact with you, or with Mrs Thompson, please let us know immediately.'

She rings off. I stare at the phone in my hand, feeling sick. If it was Jason Miller's money that Sky lost, will the fact she's his daughter protect her? Almost certainly not, I realise. And he'll be worried she could lead the police to him, as well. He'll be looking for her, using his network of runners as his eyes and ears.

I think back to the contemptuous way he looked me up and down – *Thought not. Pussy* – and a shiver runs down my spine.

ONE HUNDRED AND FOUR

Sky

I've been homeless five days now, and it really, really sucks.

I ditched the scooter at a Tube station and mingled with the rush-hour crowds to avoid being caught on any more cameras. But once I got into London, I had nothing. Nowhere to go, nothing to do, not even enough money to sit in a café. And it was raining.

I remembered how, when I wandered round St Pancras to lay a false trail that time, I ended up in the Eurostar station. It was warmer down there, and there were rough sleepers in some of the alcoves. So, on my first night, that's where I went. I lay down on a bench and tried to get some rest. I had nothing with me – not even a sleeping bag, just the clothes I was wearing.

About three in the morning, a member of staff woke me up and told me to go home. I think he assumed I was just sleeping off a boozy night out.

I wandered the streets, steering clear of anyone who might conceivably be one of Jason's minions, until I came across some homeless people queuing at a soup van behind Marylebone Road. At first, they were aggressive – they thought I was scrounging a meal that by rights was theirs – but then one took pity on me and told me about a day centre that could give me bedding and a hot meal. There are hostels specifically for first-time homeless, apparently, but they have long waiting lists, and the other places are pretty rough.

'What about the police?' I asked. 'Do the day centres have to give them your name?'

He gave me a sideways look and shook his head. 'Nah.'

In the morning, when the centre opened, I went there and got given a sleeping bag, some warm clothes and a rucksack. There was a beanie in the bag of clothes and I pushed my hair up under it, so I didn't have to worry too much about CCTV. Then I was back on the streets.

The thing people don't realise is just how tiring being homeless is. You don't sleep at night, because you're terrified. Even if I manage to stop thinking about the gang finding me, there's all the everyday shit to contend with as well. Rough sleepers get pissed on, beaten up, or have boxes of half-eaten takeaway thrown at them by groups of drunk young men who think that's pretty hilarious at two o'clock in the morning. The only time it feels safe to sleep is during the day. But the ground is hard and cold, and it's demeaning. You peer out of your sleeping bag and all you can see is feet. Other human beings are these faceless gods who tower over you, heads in the sky, going about their important business. You imagine how, if they were going to notice you at all, they'd look down their noses and dismiss you as just another piss-stained junkie.

So you feel tired. And scared. But mostly what you feel – what I've been feeling, anyway – is anger. All these tossers who think they could never be where I am now. When the truth is, it only takes a few bad decisions and a bit of bad luck.

On my second night, a man in a suit offered me fifty quid to suck him off. He held the note out to show me. Then he tore it in two and dropped half in my lap. 'That's to prove I'm serious. You'll get the other half after.'

'Nice,' I told him, tearing my half into pieces and scattering it on the floor.

He called me a skanky cock-sucking cunt and walked off. Which is nicely ironic, when you think about it.

At the day centre, an outreach worker told me that I'd get priority for a refuge if I was a victim of sexual abuse. 'A lot of teenage girls on the streets are running away from homes they don't feel safe in,' she added. 'Was there abuse in your home, Sky?'

I opened my mouth to tell her the whole slick narrative about Gabe and how he'd groomed me, but for some reason I couldn't be arsed anymore.

'Yeah,' I said. 'There was abuse. From me, mostly.'

As I said it, I realised it was true. Strange place to have a revelation like that, wandering round London with no money.

So now I do a bit of begging. Yes, that's demeaning too – people assume you just want the money to get high – but, fuck it, it's not as demeaning as wearing the same underwear for a fortnight. And the economics are OK. If you can pester someone every couple of minutes and just one person in twenty gives you a tenner, you'd still be making more than minimum wage.

So – still a businesswoman, in a way.

With my hard-earned funds, I sit on buses and aimlessly ride around London, killing time. I like the way double-deckers are so warm and humid – that smell of cappuccino and KFC and damp coats. When you fall asleep against the window, you get wet hair from the condensation.

But even there, the lowest place I can possibly be, I'm not wanted. People stare at me and move away. Schoolkids make sarcastic remarks to each other about the smell. A mum with a baby sits down with a sigh, too tired to properly check out who she's sitting next to, then realises and quickly gets up.

I doze off and fantasise. About how I'd like to go back to all the places where I grew up and burn them down, mostly. I've always liked fires, but now the urge takes hold of me like an obsession. The monster's prim little semi. Gabe and Susie's oh-so-perfect farmhouse. Even that fake-cheerful children's home, and Jason's palace of bling. It would be so satisfying, such a fucking *mission*, to raze them all to the ground one by one, the flames leaping up big and powerful and destructive like my furies.

One final *fuck you* before the inevitable.

Fitting, too. I'm homeless. They've still got their homes. Let's even things up, people. All those commuters who look down their noses at me – they've no idea how dangerous, how determined, I really am.

ONE HUNDRED AND FIVE

Susie

We plastered London with posters – *HAVE YOU SEEN SKY?* above a photo of her. We got in touch with a missing-people charity, who helped escalate the appeal with media organisations. And, after I posted a desperate appeal online, Silverlink's thousands of followers – if anything, even more loyal since they'd learnt I'd been hacked – joined in, sharing and reposting Sky's details.

'You'll find her,' everyone told us. 'Her looks are so distinctive, someone's bound to recognise her.'

But what those people didn't know, because we weren't publicising it, was that she didn't want to be found. All the time we were looking for her, it was a sure bet Jason's crew were too. We veered between hoping she'd be spotted and hoping she'd manage to stay hidden.

There were sightings, of course – dozens of them. From Southend to Southampton, well-meaning members of the public got in touch to tell us they'd seen her. One lady even described in detail the school uniform Sky had been wearing and the science books she'd had in her hand. Another was convinced she'd seen her wearing a niqab – she'd recognised her by her eyes, she said.

But as the days went by, even the false alarms tailed off. People's attention spans were so tiny, you only really got one chance. Then they moved on, to the latest funny video clip.

'I think I mishandled this,' I told Gabe miserably one evening, after yet another fruitless day of putting up posters and chasing dead-end leads.

'The appeal?'

'No . . . This whole thing with Sky. I think I wanted it to work so much, I ended up setting it up to fail. We both wanted something that was actually impossible – to wave a magic wand and somehow make it as if the adoption had never happened. But it *did* happen. And I think Sky realised before I did that no amount of unconditional love was ever going to wish away the last fifteen years. If I'd only kept a bit more distance, taken it slower, we might have been able to work out some kind of relationship. Instead, I tried to be the one thing she didn't need – another parent. And, as a result, everything's imploded.'

'Come here,' he said gently, pulling me into his arms. 'You mustn't blame yourself. There's no playbook for this situation, after all – you were trying to figure it out as you went along. We all were. And you had your own trauma from the adoption to deal with.'

'What if she's already dead?' I whispered into his shoulder.

'Shh. She's not. We'd have heard. Besides, she's smart.'

'But even if we *do* find her – what then? She'll still be in trouble with the police for drugs. And I'm living proof that a conviction for something like that can really fuck up your life.'

'You're proof that someone can turn their life around, as far as I'm concerned,' Gabe said, still holding me. 'But of course – when she's found, we'll get her the best help we can. She won't be facing it on her own.'

ONE HUNDRED AND SIX

Sky

I'm outside the farmhouse. It's dark and freezing, but I'm so used to the cold I hardly notice it now. In my hand is a plastic jerrycan of petrol. There's a cigarette lighter in my pocket.

It feels like a long time since I was last here.

Through the window, I can see Gabe and Susie in the kitchen. Susie looks troubled. Gabe reaches out and pulls her into his arms, speaking reassuringly into her ear, and she smiles gratefully. With a shock I realise that, even after everything – everything I've done, everything she's found out – she still feels the same way about him.

Still choosing him over me.

And now I have a choice to make, too.

I unscrew the top of the jerrycan.

Raising it above my head, I pour the petrol over myself in a long, glugging stream. And it feels good. Like I'm finally coming home.

Somehow, I always knew it was going to come to this, that I was going to return to blackness, my hair plastered to my head by the stinking amniotic fluid, my clothes drenched and slimy and primed.

My hand slides into my pocket for the lighter, so that I can be born.

ONE HUNDRED AND SEVEN

Gabe

Operator: Emergency. Which service do you require?

Gabriel Thompson (GT): Fire. Our property's on fire—

Operator: Connecting you now.

[Ringing tone]

Call handler (CH): Fire service. Can you confirm your full address for me, caller?

GT: Yes, it's [redacted]. Please hurry. It's a thatched building and the roof's already gone up. And we need the police as well – the person who started it's still here.

CH: The fire service are on their way. And you believe the fire was started deliberately?

GT: I know it was. She's watching the flames right now with a can of petrol in her hand. I think she wanted to kill us.

CH: The police have been alerted too. Is everyone safely out of the property?

GT: Yes. We're all outside. If they come quickly, they'll get her. But they need to be careful. She's covered in petrol.

CH: They'll be there as soon as they can. Is everyone at a safe distance?

GT: [Indistinct – shouting.]

CH: Caller, are you still there? I need to take some details.

GT: She's walking away. They need to hurry if they're going to stop her.

CH: Stay on the line please, caller.

GT: [Sirens.]

CH: Are the emergency services at the scene?

GT: Yes, they've just arrived. They've got her. Thank you.

ONE HUNDRED AND EIGHT

Gabe

'So she just stood there,' Detective Constable Eddo says, 'watching the flames.'

I nod. 'Almost as if she was mesmerised. And when your colleagues walked up to her, she let them simply lead her away.'

Eddo makes a note. 'And by this time, the barn was fully alight.'

'That's right – completely ablaze. I had over a hundred grand's worth of equipment in there. It's insured, thank God, but this is devastating for us. That studio was my livelihood.'

'Why do you suppose she targeted the studio?' Eddo asks curiously. 'The logical thing would have been to set fire to your house. That was where you were, after all –' she glances at her notes – 'when you happened to wake up to go to the bathroom, and you realised your dog was barking at someone outside.'

I shrug. 'Who knows? Nothing Sky has ever done has made much in the way of sense. She was doused in petrol herself. Rowena – the psychotherapist she's been seeing – thinks she probably meant to burn down both buildings, and herself along with them, but at the very last moment felt some kind of responsibility or remorse. It's partly why she believes Sky could respond well to treatment.'

'Yes, I've read her report.' DC Eddo looks down at her documents. 'And I see Sky has consented to it being given to the court as evidence.'

'Her lawyer – Mrs Davis – thinks it's a compelling part of her case.'

'Indeed.' Eddo regards me thoughtfully. 'A Placement Order in a therapeutic community won't be cheap, though. I'm amazed the local authority are supporting it.'

I shrug. 'It's the only thing that might help her – they can see that just as much as we can.'

At least, they could after we said we'd withdraw our legal action over the unborn-baby proceedings if they agreed to back Sky getting the help she needed. Once she'd admitted making everything up, it was clear they'd been far too swift to rush to judgement on us, and far too slow to get any help for her.

'And you're paying for all this.' DC Eddo clearly isn't going to let it go. 'You and your wife. Sky's therapist, the experts' reports, the expensive family-law solicitor . . .'

I spread my hands. 'What can I say? She's still family. Blood is thicker than water.'

Eddo gives a tight smile. 'Her birth father might not agree.'

'Well, no. And that's another reason why this Placement Order's so important. After he was arrested, she'd have needed to be in some kind of witness protection anyway. A secure community might even be a cheaper option.'

DC Eddo says nothing. But neither does she say the interview's over.

I add, 'The county-lines unit have said they'll tell the judge how useful her evidence has been. They fully agree that she was a victim of child exploitation, rather than a criminal herself.'

'But she still put those pictures on your phone,' Eddo says. 'That's definitely a crime. And that's the crime I'm investigating.'

'Category C indecent images – the lowest level,' I agree. 'Motivated by the same deep-seated psychological issues for which she's now agreed to seek help. So if, rather than criminalising her further, you were also to support the therapeutic placement . . .'

'You'd have a full set of endorsements. All the professionals telling the judge the same thing.' DC Eddo nods. 'And the remarkable thing is, it's only come about because of that fire. If she hadn't set your studio alight, and you hadn't seen her and called it in, she'd probably be lying dead in a gutter somewhere. Rather than getting the most intensive help the state can offer someone like her.'

I shrug again. 'She was careless, I guess.'

'Or careful.' DC Eddo gets to her feet. 'I don't know why, but I get the feeling someone's been very, very careful about all this. I just hope that person knows what they're doing.'

Relieved, I stand up too.

She holds out her hand. 'Goodbye, Mr Thompson. I don't suppose we'll meet again. Not unless they move me to insurance fraud, anyway.'

ONE HUNDRED AND NINE

Susie

It was a crisp, cold day in February when Gabe and I went to see Sky. Studley Court turned out to be an old Edwardian manor house near Aylesbury, with nothing outside to suggest what its real function was – it could have been a run-down hotel or a small boarding school. Only the fact that the lawns on either side of the drive had been turned into vegetable gardens, where a few teenagers in thick coats were turning over the soil with spades, gave any clue.

We waited in a large room that looked as if it might once have held a snooker table. At one end, chairs were arranged in a small circle – for group sessions, presumably. A teenage youth wandered through with cartons of milk. Everything about the place felt unhurried, calm, friendly.

When Sky appeared, she gave us a big smile. 'Oh – wow! It's so good to see you.' Then she saw Lily, asleep in her papoose. 'Hey! You brought my half-sister!'

'Do you want to hold her?' Gabe asked with a smile.

She hesitated, then nodded. 'Yes, please.'

He unhooked himself and gently transferred Lily into Sky's arms, though I noticed he kept a watchful eye, ready to jump in if necessary.

'She smells incredible.' Sky sniffed Lily's head. 'And she's so peaceful.'

'Only because she's been up all night,' I said. 'She'll start chuntering for her next feed any minute. She's not the little angel that sweet face would have you believe.'

As if on cue, Lily screwed up her nose, clenched her little fists and stretched, an inevitable prelude to the piercing feed-me-now wail that followed.

'And how are you getting on here, Sky?' Gabe asked when I'd got Lily plugged on to my breast.

'Oh . . .' She took a deep breath. 'Pretty good, I think. But they tell you not to rush things. It's a twelve-month minimum stay, with meetings at the start and end of every day. Sometimes in between, too. Anyone can call a meeting any time, and when they do, we all have to go. The idea is that the whole community becomes the doctor. So we make all the decisions together – what to eat, what to do, even who gets to come here.' She smiled shyly. 'I've introduced a WhatsApp group, actually. So we can post updates without having to get everyone out of bed. It seems to be going down OK.'

'That's great,' I said. 'We're looking forward to you getting out, of course, when the time's right. But it's good that you like it here.'

She nodded. 'Thanks for . . . making it happen.' She looked at Gabe, who only nodded back. No need to go over the details. But it was his quick thinking that saved her life. When he glanced out of the kitchen window and saw her pouring petrol over herself, he'd sprinted outside and wrestled the jerrycan and cigarette lighter off her. Somehow, we got her into the house and it all came out. How she was living on the streets, terrified the gang or the police were going to find her and she'd end up like her friend Jaylen. How she desperately wished she'd never acted the way she did.

'But whenever anything's any good, I end up wanting to destroy it,' she said tearfully. 'I'll do it again. I know I will. I want to be better, but I don't know how to change.'

That's when Gabe told her about the kid his friend Marcus had fostered, the one who ended up being sent to a therapeutic community after he'd set fire to his carers' house, and how he'd come out a different person.

'If you're really serious about wanting to change, it might be the only answer. But they won't do it except as a last resort. We'd have to arrange things so it looked like you'd done something similar.'

She looked at him. 'You'd do that for me? You'd burn down your house?'

'Well . . . Maybe the studio. I can replace everything in that. It's not like I'm going to be needing it any time soon, after all.'

She'd nodded. 'Thanks. And, Gabe . . . I'll really try to get better. I promise.'

'I know,' he said. 'And for what it's worth . . . in some ways, this has actually been good for us – for Susie and me, I mean. It's made us say things to each other we should have said years ago.'

That was six months ago – getting the reports together and fighting for a court order took most of that time, and swallowed up most of the remaining money from the Banksys as well. But we'd both agreed it was worth it, if it meant Sky actually getting some help.

Now, Sky reached across and stroked Lily's head as she suckled. 'I want to get out of here before she's too big.'

'You will,' I told her. 'And, however long it takes, however hard it is, you know we'll always be there for you, don't you?'

'Yes,' she said quietly, still stroking Lily's head, 'I know that now.'

So this, it turns out, is a story about second chances.

Kai never did go back to his TV show, and Danny had to sell his car collection when the royalties from WHT dried up. But Gabe surprised everyone by releasing a statement apologising for his past misconduct. The consensus was that he needn't have done – the PR storm was dying down by then. Only a very few people, including Ella and Fi, knew what he was really saying sorry about.

Sky, we're told, continues to make good progress. But the damage that's been ingrained over fifteen difficult years won't be undone overnight. We've been warned there are no guarantees, and that it could take years. But, already, we think we can see glimpses of a new maturity.

And I have a baby. There are some people who think that means we should never let Sky anywhere near us – as Stu and others have said to me, how can we ever be sure Lily will be safe when she's around? They clearly think I'm still blinkered when it comes to my older daughter. But I have Gabe to tell me if that happens again, and so far, we have every reason to think her therapy will be a success.

Not that it's even certain she'll want to live with us. For one thing, she's in touch with the Mulcahys again, and Jenny's been to visit. Sky knows they did their best to love her – though personally I'll never forgive them for changing her name. She has a boyfriend now too, one of the other residents, and there's talk of a group of them all applying to the same uni when they leave Studley Court. Who knows – it may be that she'll live in a mixture of places, and our house will just be one of the locations she calls home.

Recently, I've found myself thinking about the night she was conceived. At the time, I thought it was just a bad night – yet more bad sex in what, by then, was a bad relationship. Even afterwards, when I'd met some decent men and had a better idea of what respectful encounters looked like, I told myself that it was mostly my fault. I chose him, after all. And, as I said to Gabe, there was a superficial attraction, a transgressive thrill, in being with someone I knew everyone else disapproved of.

For his part, he always said I was slumming and that he was my bit of rough. And, since I believed him, who was I to object when the rough gradually got rougher? The most I could reasonably do, I told myself, was to insist he wore a condom, which he hated.

Until that time I realised the condom wasn't there.

'Where is it?' I said frantically, looking round.

'Burst. Don't worry, princess, I got out in plenty of time.'

Back then, it never even occurred to me he might be lying – a lie that, these days, the law would treat as sexual assault. But now, having encountered him again and seen him through clearer, more adult eyes, I'm certain of it.

How fitting that it's the fruit of that assault who delivered his comeuppance in the end.

And, speaking of Sky, now that I've accepted I can't be a mother to her, what am I going to be? Clearly, we share a kinship based on blood – an umbilical attachment that can never be undone. But there's no word to describe exactly what that means in a situation like ours, and perhaps that's as it should be. Because a word might define us, and curtail our expectations. This way, we'll decide for ourselves what we are, a journey we'll go on together; and who knows where that might take us, or what we might become.

AUTHOR'S NOTE

> *I am a passionate believer in the value of adoption in appropriate circumstances ... But I fear that, in making all those orders, I never gave much attention to the emotional repercussions of them. In particular I fear that I failed fully to appreciate that an adoption order is not just a necessary arrangement for the upbringing of some children ... The order is an act of surgery which cuts deep into the hearts and minds of at least four people and which will affect them, to a greater or lesser extent, every day of their lives.*
>
> Lord Wilson, Denning Society Lecture, 2014

Although birth certificates of adoptees in the UK are sealed until the adoptee turns eighteen, the Adoption Society estimates that one in four now make contact with their birth families before then, usually via social media. In particular, the practice of leaving Later Life letters with them – a statutory requirement in the UK since 2005 – has resulted in a generation who can track down their birth relatives quite easily. For many, this leads to ad hoc 'adoption reunions', and sometimes these can help to answer the adoptee's questions about their identity and past. But there are also potential pitfalls, particularly if biological parent and adoptee come to the reunion with different expectations.

In writing about an adoption reunion that initially goes wrong, I've used details gleaned from memoirs, first-hand testimonials and personal interviews. The story of Sky and Susie is, of course, by no means typical – the vast majority of adoptions are successful, as are most reunions – but I've tried to make it authentic, and a small minority of adoptive parents will recognise some of the attachment issues I've described.

The therapy Sky is subjected to is also not a product of my imagination – although now discredited, it was being advocated in the UK under the term 'holding therapy' as recently as 2010. The Wikipedia extracts I quote are excerpted from a 2006 report by the American Professional Society on the Abuse of Children (APSAC), widely seen as being a turning point in how coercive restraint therapy was viewed. These days, therapeutic communities are considered a better intervention, although cutbacks mean that – in the UK, at least – fewer and fewer exist.

My thanks to my editor, Stef Bierwerth, for her sensitive reading and suggestions; to the many adopters and adoptees who shared their experiences with me; to consultant child and adolescent psychiatrist Dr Emma Fergusson, who allowed me to pick her brains on everything from attachment issues to child-parent violence – any errors, misunderstandings or liberties are of course my own – and in particular to my agent, Caradoc King, whose own book *Problem Child* is a brilliantly written account of one adoptee's journey. This book is dedicated to him: living proof that these stories can indeed have happy endings.

Read on for an exclusive extract from
JP Delaney's addictive new thriller,

THE MOVE

For a moment, she thought nothing was happening, that the scaffolding wasn't going to give, but the savage wind was helping her and she felt movement underfoot. She wrapped her arms round the metal corner bar and got her feet against the wall, putting her back into it, trying to ignore the huge clots of icy snow pelting her face, and with a sudden wrench she felt the scaffolding peel away from the house, ripped off by the wind, the metal poles flying like matchsticks, the wooden planks collapsing under her feet. She saw his look of incredulity and shock, and then they were both falling, in a blur of wood and metal, a cascade of spars and planks and debris, and she mentally braced herself for the impact that was about to come—

ONE

As it turned out, the house was lovely. No, Kate thought, more than lovely: it was spectacularly, breathtakingly perfect. She hadn't expected that, to be honest. The agent's particulars – such a quaint word for what was, these days, little more than a two-page printout and a listing on Rightmove – had been almost impossible to make sense of, even with the help of the floor plan. Rooms appeared to open into other rooms almost at random; there were two staircases; the kitchen windows looked out into the sitting room; upright oak beams were stranded in the middle of floors, like the ghosts of long-removed walls. But when they got there and actually saw it, it all made sense. Trade Cottage, it turned out, had originally been not one house but three, a small terrace of knapped flint built as accommodation for the retainers of a nearby estate. The estate had long since shrunk to the other side of the woods that bordered Trade Cottage's garden, though its traces still lay all around: the farm next to the house was very much a working one, its fields dotted with sheep and dung, but the rusted iron fences and guards around the trees hinted at a past grandeur as parkland. Even as they made their way up the dilapidated drive, Kate had been imagining the Mitford sisters hunting their ponies across it.

The agent, Damon, had got there before them, his spotless blue Tesla parked a discreet distance from the house so as not to detract from the wow factor of its façade – the big bay window at one end, the ancient oak porch at the other; the former topped by a wisteria, pendulous with blossom, the latter by the carved crest of the estate and a delicate climbing rose. As Matt parked their Kia alongside the Tesla, Tilly said wonderingly from the back seat, 'Is this really it?', and even Will looked up from the game he was playing on Matt's phone and muttered, 'Cool.'

They got out and walked slowly towards the front door. The outbuildings, about which the particulars had been a bit vague – possibly exhausted by the effort of breathlessly describing the house's interior: *As you ascend the second staircase towards the sumptuous main bedroom, dazzling views past wildflower-strewn woods await . . .* – looked to be substantial structures in their own right. Kate glimpsed a small barn, some stables, and an open-fronted thatched shed containing a sit-down mower and a battered old Land Rover. That was good; converting one or two outbuildings into Airbnbs was the only way they could possibly make this work, even with the bonanza from Matt's earn-out and the sale of their house in Dulwich.

Damon must have seen them arrive – the door opened a moment before they could knock. 'Come in, come in,' he said, stepping back and beaming with almost proprietorial pride as they took in the utterly beautiful entrance hall – not large, but lined with manorial oak panelling. Kate tried to guess its age, but couldn't.

'The story is, a sea captain related to the Pelham family retired here in the 1840s – he was the one who had it converted into a single dwelling,' Damon was explaining. 'So, some parts are late Georgian, some Victorian – although there's a bit in the middle that may be the remnants of an older building still. Tudor, quite possibly. The seller can tell you more – she's done loads of research on the place. Anyway, it's hardly a cottage, I know, but I guess when your frame of reference is Pelham House . . .'

'And the name?' Matt asked. 'Where did that come from?'

'Ah, yes – Trade Cottage, on Smugglers Lane,' Damon said with relish. 'Short for "Free-Trade Cottage" originally, I understand. In the eighteenth century, the government slapped tariffs on imports of brandy and rum to pay for the Napoleonic Wars. Apparently, this was one of the main smuggling routes up from the coast, and the sea captain wasn't above taking a few barrels off his old naval contacts and selling them on. There's even a secret cellar under the dining room.'

'Hear that, Will? A secret cellar,' Kate said encouragingly, hoping their son wasn't being put off by all this talk of Tudors and Georgians. But, when she turned to look, she saw he was hanging on Damon's every word.

'Come on through.' Damon opened another door – also oak, and also impossible to date; the latch, she saw, had been hand-hammered in a forge. 'It's a bit of a warren, but that's part of its charm. We'll say hello to the vendors, then I'm generally just letting people wander.'

So there had been other viewings already, Kate noted. It had only come on the market that week – they'd got an alert from the selling platform. Well, the interest wasn't surprising, given how unique it was. But no actual offers yet, or Damon would have told them.

A small passage – oddly misshapen, as if tunnelled round obstacles – led into a lovely light-filled sitting room. This was the room that had perplexing windows opening into it, but, she now saw, that was because it was actually an oak-framed structure that had been added to the rear of the house at a later date. The spaces between the beams were mostly glass; the view was of the large, pretty garden, but also beyond that, to rolling fields of grazing sheep. She was trying not to fall in love with the place – she'd had her hopes dashed so many times when they were looking in Dulwich, four years ago – but, at the thought of having her first coffee of the day in this room, overlooking that valley, her heart melted.

'Hello! Welcome!' a voice boomed. A tall, white-haired man was coming round a sofa towards them. He was using canes to support himself – even so, Kate noticed, both knees were buckling slightly – but was clearly determined to greet them properly. He had to fiddle with the sticks to get a hand free. When Kate took it, he clasped his other hand firmly over hers as well – as much for support, she thought, as out of hospitality: she could feel a slight tremor in his fingers. He had clearly once been handsome, possibly dazzlingly so; even now, a lock of white hair flopped fetchingly over one of his blue eyes as he pumped her hand vigorously.

'Oh, Paul, there's no need . . .' A slight woman jumped up from an armchair – that was the thing Kate noticed straight away, how she almost sprang from the chair, the agile movement of someone far younger than her neatly-coiffed grey hair suggested her to be. 'Hello.'

'Nonsense! Guests!' the man – Paul, presumably – said

cheerfully. He turned back to Kate. 'Normally I'd have a glass of champagne in your hand as soon as you walked through that door, but I suppose it's a bit early for that.'

Kate wondered if he meant a bit early in the day or a bit early in the process. Probably the latter, she decided. She knew some sellers liked to stick around for viewings, to answer questions or simply to keep an eye on things, but she'd never been called a guest before.

'Rosemary,' the woman said, indicating herself. 'And Paul. Please, make yourselves at home. Would you like a scone while you look round? I baked them this morning.' She turned to the agent. 'Damon?'

'I don't mind if I do,' Damon said happily. 'Particularly if there's some of that raspberry jam . . . ?'

'Masses!' Rosemary turned to Kate. 'Do you make jam? I'm afraid you'd have to, living here. The fruit cage is far too large – we built it forty years ago, when we were younger and more sprightly – and we always get a glut.'

'Well,' Kate said apologetically, 'we live in London at the moment, so . . .'

'Oh, of course.' Rosemary turned to Will and Tilly. 'And what are *your* names? Any takers for a scone and raspberry jam while you go and choose your bedrooms?'

'It might be a bit soon for—' Kate interjected, but the children were already telling Rosemary their names, and she was pointing them in the direction of 'the back staircase, the one that leads all the way up to the attic, and then why don't you see if you can find the room with a pony in it.'

Kate watched them beetling off, already appearing somehow

energised by the house, or perhaps the country air, or perhaps just Paul and Rosemary's effervescent welcome. As for choosing bedrooms – she worried about getting their hopes up, of course she did. They'd debated whether to even bring the children on a whole day of traipsing round viewings, but there was the problem of what to do with them if they didn't – and, besides, she wanted them to want this move too. Leaving London would be a wrench for Tilly and Will, despite the fact they were both, in their different ways, struggling where they were. It would be better if they were committed to it, even if it did take a while to find the right property.

Although, she thought dizzily, perhaps they already had.

As promised, Damon let them wander, while Paul and Rosemary stayed downstairs in the sitting room – Paul levering himself back into a chair with some difficulty, Kate noticed. She was surprised they were so relaxed about letting people just roam around their house. When she and Matt put Liphook Crescent on the market, the estate agent had been under strict instructions not to let viewers out of his sight. But Paul and Rosemary, it seemed, were more trusting.

The listing had called it 'a family home of character and charm', and for once that had been no exaggeration. From the children's heights proudly recorded in black felt-tip on a wall – each one signed and dated, all the way back to the 1980s; from the look of it, 'Jamie' was older than 'Tessa' by about eighteen months, the same age gap as there was between Will and Tilly – to the framed hand-drawn map of the house and garden in the loo, the sense of a childhood lived here to the full was palpable.

The map's features were labelled in neat, childish handwriting: *Paul's Pool*, *Christmas-Tree Thicket*, *Jamie's Citadel*, *The Silver Brook*. It was signed *Tessa 1986*. The same feel was there in the enormous boot room – bigger even than the dining room – crammed with the detritus of a dozen outdoor pastimes: fishing rods, croquet mallets held together with electrical tape, ancient tennis racquets, shooting sticks, a plastic ball-thrower with a chewed tennis ball jammed into it, all stuffed into two huge old chimney pots, along with half a dozen walking sticks and a shepherd's crook. The tennis ball, she guessed, was for the grey-snouted black Lab which thumped its thick tail lethargically at her from its bed by the back door.

The kitchen, by way of contrast, was almost comically ugly: small and functional, with two fluorescent strip lights overhead, the countertops made of pale Formica. The only redeeming feature was the cream-coloured Aga, and even that had Dalmatian-like patches where the enamel had flaked off, revealing the black iron beneath. It was oil-powered, the listing had said – surely, therefore, the least climate-friendly cooking device on the planet, but one she instinctively yearned to keep. Could Agas be re-enamelled? Or, indeed, converted to electric? She made a mental note to google it on the way home. And of course it wouldn't stay here, in this room; it was the dining room that cried out to be made into a spacious kitchen-diner, while this poky little space would become a utility room . . . She was good at this, she knew, reconfiguring every place they'd ever lived in, from their first flat in grotty Camberwell to the four-bed semi they were selling now. And it was great that Trade Cottage hadn't been touched in decades. Matt, ever practical, might have objected if there'd been some expensive designer kitchen she wanted to rip out, but, as it was, she'd have free rein, their stretched finances permitting.

'Mummy! Mummy, we're going outside.' That was Tilly, still fizzing with excitement, dashing in and immediately out again. Behind her Kate glimpsed Will, also heading for the back door. It was great to see them so upbeat – Will, in particular, was capable of announcing he was bored and slouching back to the car after a few surly glances, but there was absolutely no sign of that here.

'Take Daddy,' she called after them, unsure what dangers might lurk in the garden – one of the photographs had shown a pond, complete with a small island for ducks and a rowing boat for getting to it – but Matt was ahead of her.

'Let's go right to the end and see what's in the field,' she heard him say as he followed them out, and she could tell from his voice that he, too, was excited.

She continued her tour alone. Upstairs, it was very much a house of two halves, with no interconnecting door or passageway between the children's bedrooms, up one staircase, and the main bedroom, up another. Checking out the latter, she couldn't help noticing that one of the nightstands was strewn with pill bottles. Paul's, presumably.

She went to the window to look at the view, which turned out to be even lovelier up here than it was from downstairs. At the end of the garden, beyond a belt of woods, farmland stretched for mile after mile. Off to her right, admittedly, was a huge green cliff of leylandii, but that was OK: it was far enough away not to overshadow the house, and, in any case, it gave them privacy from the property next door. On the other side, to her left, the woods had a faint shimmer of blue in them. *Wildflower-strewn*, indeed.

It was musty in the bedroom, and she longed to throw the window open, to lean out and gulp down that clean country air. But that would have felt discourteous to Paul and Rosemary, whose private space this was. When we own it, we can sleep with the windows open, she thought, and was surprised to note that it already felt like a foregone conclusion.

The bathrooms were as ancient as the kitchen – avocado-green baths that doubled as showers; vinyl shower curtains; sinks with spluttering taps that sported drooping moustaches of discoloration and limescale. It was as if the whole house had been stopped in time, a slumbering giant. But, again, that was all to the good: they could live with it perfectly happily while they renovated.

She realised she hadn't yet found the room with the big bay window she'd seen as they approached. Going back downstairs, she followed her sense of direction down a passage, the floor tiled in a black-and-white geometric pattern, the walls hung with painted oars. One, she saw, commemorated a victory for *Brasenose College 1st Torpid 1961*, whatever that was; among the crew's names was *No. 3 Paul Finch*. On the opposite wall, a similar oar recorded that, in 1994, Jamie Finch had rowed stroke for Balliol.

She walked into a room that turned out not to be the one she was looking for, a smaller second sitting room. There was a television, a comfortable mishmash of chairs around a small marble fireplace. And a huge, dappled rocking horse, with scarlet nostrils and real leather tack. Its sides were worn where little feet had kicked it into a gallop.

Going back into the corridor, she got her bearings again and went on. What had looked at first glance like an alcove, a counterpart to one opposite containing a floor-standing oriental vase, was, she now saw, a door, and the room she was looking for lay beyond it. She stepped inside.

The particulars – and the more she explored Trade Cottage's quirky, sprawling interior, the more appropriate that word seemed – had called this 'the study'. She'd scoffed inwardly at that – estate agents' 'studies', she'd generally found, were box rooms at best, cramped work-from-home cubbyholes at worst. But this was neither. Even 'study' undersold what was almost a small library, the walls on two sides lined with oak shelves. In the middle sat a big pedestal desk, with a wheeled leather chair facing the window. 'Captain's chairs', they were called, she vaguely remembered. So perhaps this was where the sea captain himself had sat in his retirement, and the desk was where he'd spread his maps.

She realised that the bay window, too, had a nautical feel – it jutted out at each side, like the windows that projected over a man-of-war's stern. Yes, this had definitely been his favourite room, she decided, looking around, just as it would be hers. In such a room, with its view over the quiet front garden and drive, she might even be able to carve out a few hours a day to realise her long-held dream of writing something, once the children were settled. *I for this, and this for me* – she'd forgotten where she'd read those words, but it was exactly what she felt now: as if Trade Cottage was somehow choosing her, just as much as she was choosing it.

As she went to the window, she couldn't help glancing down at the sheets of writing paper neatly laid out on the desk. They were thank-you letters, she saw, written with a fountain pen, the signature a shaky but regal *R*. She bent closer to see who or what was being thanked, then jumped back as the door opened and Rosemary herself came in, holding a plate of scones.

'I see you've found Captain Pelham's cabin,' she said, with a smile. 'I always think it's the nicest room in the house.' She gestured at a small portrait Kate hadn't noticed before, hanging beside the door. It showed a short, thickset man in naval uniform. 'I like to imagine that his spirit still watches over the place, though Paul thinks that's sentimental nonsense.'

'The whole house is lovely,' Kate said truthfully. 'But, yes – there's something about this room, in particular.' She hesitated. 'It must be so hard to leave. Where are you going, if you don't mind my asking?'

Rosemary waved the question away. 'It's a wrench, of course it is, but it's time to move on. This house should have children running round it.' She nodded outside, to where Will had discovered a rope hanging from the elm tree that bordered the pond. 'Yours seem to have taken quite a shine to it already.'

'Do you have grandchildren?' It wasn't as intrusive a question as it might have been; all around them were framed photographs, including several of a tall, bearded man – Jamie, presumably – with a blonde woman and two dark-haired children.

Rosemary picked up the nearest one, her eyes softening as she looked at it. 'Yes. Hamish and Flora. But Jamie's something big at the IMF, so he's based in Washington. They come over every year, and of course we Zoom, but . . .' Her voice trailed off. 'The children have American accents now, which feels strange. And Tess never wanted children. She lives in Wales, on a sort of commune.'

There were many more pictures of Jamie and his family, Kate noticed, than of Tessa. And a whole shelf of him as a young man – Jamie in cricket whites, Jamie with a surfboard, Jamie brandishing a football trophy – all flanking a single picture of Tessa in her matriculation garb.

'Jamie's a bit cross we're selling, actually,' Rosemary went on. 'But it's him who keeps telling us we have to have a wet room. And Paul will need a wheelchair soon. His Dalek wheels, he calls them – he's already been measured up. Really, a wheelchair in this house would be impossible.'

Kate nodded sympathetically. Trade Cottage was a house of many levels, with a step up or down into almost every room, and both staircases were narrow and steep.

'And the fact is, I'm not getting any younger.' Rosemary sighed. 'I think I'm doing pretty well for eighty-three – ' Here Kate nodded again; Rosemary had so much energy, Kate had assumed she was early seventies at most – 'But my bones are creaky now and I'm getting forgetful. So we're downsizing, to a lovely little bungalow.' She looked around wistfully. 'But I have been excessively fond of my cottage.'

'"There is always so much elegance, so much comfort about them",' Kate agreed.

Rosemary shot her a glance, clearly pleased Kate had picked up the reference. 'Oh, are you a Janeite, too? She's my guilty pleasure. I take to my bed and reread *Sense and Sensibility* whenever I feel under the weather.'

'I'm like that with *Love in a Cold Climate*,' Kate confessed. 'And some of Dodie Smith. But I like Austen, too.'

Outside, Will was swinging on the rope, out over the duck pond and back in a wide looping spiral, lifting his knees high to avoid getting his feet wet. A part of Kate wanted to run out and stop him – the rope, if it had been there since Jamie and Tessa's day, must be forty years old at least, and the sludge-brown water was presumably full of duck poo – but something held her back. Rosemary was watching Will with an indulgent smile on her face, and the moment felt, somehow, like a kind of test.

When she didn't move, Rosemary's eyes came back to scrutinise her face, a strangely searching look.

'I do hope you buy it,' she said quietly. 'I mean, I'm sure you're looking at lots of other nice places too, but perhaps ... Damon says, for the money we're asking, most people want something grander. We had someone yesterday who said the first thing he'd do is rename it Monkwood Manor. Can you imagine? Just throw away two hundred years of history, to make himself look posh. Like those awful people who buy themselves a title, or rename pubs so they sound like wine bars. But Damon thinks the right person might walk through the door and fall in love with it – just like we did, forty-odd years ago.'

You were meant to play it cool, Kate knew. Matt always said it was a bad negotiating tactic to appear too keen at a viewing. But something about Rosemary – the fact Kate genuinely liked her, for one thing – made her say, 'Well, I *do* love it. And I can tell that the children adore it. I'll have to talk to Matt, of course, and we'll need to do our sums. But I can see us being very happy here.'

Rosemary beamed, and was about to say something else when a noise in the corridor signalled the approach of the others – Tilly and Will bursting in first, followed after an interval by Matt and Paul. Matt was loitering discreetly by Paul's side, Kate saw, ready to catch him if his canes slipped. The children wanted to tell her excitedly about the lambs they'd seen in the field, and Paul and

Matt were discussing irises – 'They're called Purple Knights,' Paul was saying, 'and they like a bit of grit every autumn –' and Matt was making a point of getting out his phone and noting that down, and she could tell from his body language that he liked Paul, and liked Trade Cottage, too. If Rosemary and Paul hadn't been moving, Kate could almost imagine them all becoming friends.

'Well, darling,' Rosemary remarked, 'I don't know about you, but I'm very much hoping the house has found its rightful heirs.'

She was smiling, but was that the glint of a tear in her eye? It was hard to be sure, and, of course, older eyes like hers were more prone to watering.

'Not heirs, darling. We're not dead yet!' Paul said cheerfully. 'A new chapter, that's all.' He put his arms round her, but with the sticks in his hands he was clumsy; one swung round and hit her lightly on the back. 'How exciting!'

'Yes, of course,' Rosemary said, and Kate saw her discreetly blink the tear away. 'How very, very exciting.'

Discover more from the million-copy bestselling author,

JP DELANEY

To sign up to JP's newsletter
for book updates, upcoming events and
exclusive news, scan the QR code here:

RAISING READERS
Books Build Bright Futures

Dear Reader,

We'd love your attention for one more page to tell you about the crisis in children's reading, and what we can all do.

Studies have shown that reading for fun is the **single biggest predictor of a child's future life chances** – more than family circumstance, parents' educational background or income. It improves academic results, mental health, wealth, communication skills, ambition and happiness.[1]

The number of children reading for fun is in rapid decline. Young people have a lot of competition for their time. In 2024, 1 in 10 children and young people in the UK aged 5 to 18 did not own a single book at home.[2]

Hachette works extensively with schools, libraries and literacy charities, but here are some ways we can all raise more readers:

- Reading to children for just 10 minutes a day makes a difference
- Don't give up if children aren't regular readers – there will be books for them!
- Visit bookshops and libraries to get recommendations
- Encourage them to listen to audiobooks
- Support school libraries
- Give books as gifts

There's a lot more information about how to encourage children to read on our website: **www.RaisingReaders.co.uk**

Thank you for reading.

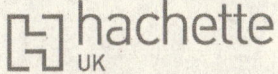

---

[1] National Literacy Trust, Book Ownership in 2024, November 2024
https://nlt.cdn.ngo/media/documents/Book_ownership_in_2024

[2] OECD. 2021. 21st-century readers: developing literacy skills in a digital world. Paris, France: OECD Publishing.
https://www.oecd.org/en/publications/21st-century-readers_a83d84cb-en.html